MILLENNIUM FEVER

Ann's voice had dropped again; it was deep and thick with desire. Nikki's eyes were closed, the receiver clamped so close to her ear that she felt Ann was next to her, talking to her while she stroked, fondled, caressed, nibbled.

'I want to lick you slowly, so slowly that you want more and more, you can't get enough of me licking you. It's so gentle that you are moving against me, wanting me to lick you harder, chew on you, drink from you. You want more of me inside you; you want to come; you're climbing; you're going crazy. What are you doing now?'

'Stroking myself.'

MILLENNIUM FEVER

JULIA WOOD

First published in 1999 by
Sapphire
an imprint of Virgin Publishing Ltd
Thames Wharf Studios
Rainville Road, London W6 9HT

ISBN 0 352 33368 5

Cover photograph by Trevor Watson

Typeset by SetSystems Ltd, Saffron Walden, Essex
Printed and bound in Great Britain by Mackays of Chatham PLC

To SW for the original inspiration.

To JJ for the belief in me.

To my darling Sarah, for turning the same corner as me. We are as one, we simply are.

ONE

The day had started badly and fallen away to fuck. What was particularly irksome was that it was only 11 a.m.

'Goddamned creatives, you give them a goddamned deadline and they ignore it,' Nikki fumed, drawing furiously on her cigarette, gulping down a mouthful of tepid machine coffee and grimacing.

Her PA said nothing but noted the drumming fingers on the desktop and how Nikki had pushed her glasses forward and was massaging the bridge of her nose. Always a danger sign.

'I'll get you a fresh coffee,' said Marion, and quietly left the office.

Nikki groaned. Yet another fucking day in paradise. A husband who had decided five minutes before she left that she should attend his banking dinner that night and 'wear her best frock'. Another evening loomed of boring trivial conversation, a fixed girly smile and having to have the lamb because Steve was too stingy to pay for a nicely turned piece of rare sirloin. Bastard.

Into work, expecting a professionally turned-out set of visuals to accompany the direct-mail campaign strategy she had prepared for the pitch at 2 p.m., and the creative director with his stupid bald crown and five-inch ponytail and George Michael stubble had blithely announced that 'his people' had had difficulty interpreting her brief.

'Your people. Your fucking collection of trendy pissing illiterates, you mean,' she muttered. 'Why couldn't you tell me ten days ago that you couldn't interpret the brief. Fucking state-of-the-art design technology, looks like the bridge of the Starship *Enterprise* in the studio, and your guys are still using fucking crayons to fill in between the lines. Probably can't even write your own goddamned names without –'

Her fevered mumblings were interrupted by Marion's cautious approach to the desk with fresh coffee in one hand and a fax in the other.

'What now?' she growled.

'I've read it first . . .' Marion trailed off.

That invariably meant bad news. Marion had been her faithful, loyal PA for ten years and was one of the very few people who could not only judge her moods and likely reactions but could also read her appalling handwriting. She should have been a doctor. It probably paid more than this forsaken, backwater, tinpot, tuppeny, two-bit pretentious agency.

She scowled and snatched the fax. Nikki scanned it and laid it on the desk. The pitch had been cancelled, the prospective client had had a board meeting and, due to a 'corporate change of direction', the decision had been made to suspend marketing activity for the current quarter. As a footnote, the client was making it clear that no pitch fees would be payable as it was against company policy. Probably read that phrase in *Marketing Week*, the son of a bitch, Nikki thought.

'Well, on the bright side at least we don't have to worry about the visuals not being ready,' Marion ventured.

'Yeah, let's look on the bright side, shall we? A week of my time down the pan, I've got Alistair breathing down my neck for new-business development and this would have been a honey to get. I've got that advertising campaign schedule to draw up, I'm still waiting for that newsletter copy from that freelance that Gillian recommended, MTS are bitching about their latest invoice again, and all I've got to look forward to is dinner at the Grand with yet another of Steve's potential big corporate accounts.'

'Lamb again?'

'There's got to be more to it than this, working your bloody tits off in the back of beyond for clients who think they're the bee's knees. They're big fish in little ponds, throwing their weight around and putting you through the hoops, frustrated goddamned designers and copywriters every single last one of them, sticking their bloody oar in and it's all bollocks.'

Marion sat down. It was going to be a long tirade, one she had heard many times before. It was moving into the 'I'm worth more than this. I should be in London.'

'I'm worth more than this, Marion. A London agency would snap me up tomorrow. But no, Nikki is married to Mr Goddamned Can't-leave-his-mother-on-her-own even though he only sees her every other pissing Christmas because I force him to. Who remembers the birthdays and anniversaries of all his family and friends? Is that why men get married, so their shirts are ironed, their pants are clean and their Auntie Ethel gets a birthday card on time every year? Is it?'

Marion stayed silent but smiled, waiting for the predictable next turn.

'What I need is a bloody good orgasm, get all this tension released, grab some bloody pillows or bite my arm, thrash around and get all sweaty, make stupid noises and daft faces and get into impossible positions until I get hip lock or cramp. That's what I need. What do I get? Every third or fourth fucking Saturday, after his game of golf or fucking rugby, *Match of the Day* and five pints, I get old beery-breath pawing at me and grunting. Missionary position, Man from Atlantis, thrusting valiantly away for two minutes and wallop that's yer lot missus, "Was it good for you? I'm still Steve the Main Man Jones", and straight to sleep.'

Marion knew the mood was shifting. Nikki's constant verbal onslaughts against her husband were always an indicator that her sense of humour was coming back. In a way she felt sorry for Steve: Nikki was a handful to work with, let alone live with. But having met him – and he was a bore – she felt sorrier for Nikki.

Nikki was so dynamic and lively, life and soul of the party; she worked so hard and was genuinely talented, Marion thought. Marion believed implicitly that Nikki could have made it in London without the emotional baggage that was her husband. She also believed that Nikki would be so much happier and contented if she had found the right man in the first place. There must have been something about Steve originally to snare such a creature.

They'd been married now nearly twenty years but, for all ten of the years Marion had worked for her, Nikki had bitched about him. He was dismissive about her career, her achievements. Marion, who had two teenage children, also knew that Nikki would have loved to have had children but didn't have them because Steve didn't want her to get fat and end up with stretch marks. She should have left him years ago, gone to London or stayed here and got herself a decent, strong and honest bloke who really appreciated her rather than took advantage of her.

As far as Marion could judge, Nikki's main reason for staying with the pompous lout was the cheap mortgage on the large house they had. Steve's 23-year career with the bank had ensured favourable interest rates and, now he had reached the dizzy heights of Assistant Manager, Business Banking Centre, their home was more secure than ever. And, if Nikki was fair, low-interest finance – and her mother's wisely invested inheritance – had also helped secure her that black Saab Turbo parked outside. It was the love of her life.

'I'm going to pop over to the photographer's, see how that shoot is doing,' Nikki suddenly announced, interrupting Marion's musing.

Marion knew the drive would do her good. Nikki was an excellent if aggressive driver and a clearing out of the cobwebs with a burst in the Saab would help calm her down for the rest of the day. Marion checked her watch. It was still only 11.15.

'I'll see you in about two hours then.' She smiled. 'And in the meantime I'll ring that freelance about the copy delivery.'

Ten minutes later Nikki was settled in the air-conditioned cockpit of the Saab, a loud and gusty track blasting out on the

4

CD, roaring out of the car park, the turbo kicking in and pushing her back into the leather seat.

'God, I love this car!' she laughed out loud.

The Swedish Beast had been one of her main pleasures in life the last few months. Still smelling of fresh leather and walnut, she purred into life, raring to race, ready to go, nearly a half-ton of performance machine holding the road like shit to a blanket. The almost silent engine with that whistle of the turbo kicking in, the superb engineering coupled with the sheer luxury of the cockpit securely wrapped around her made her feel invincible, safe. And horny.

The car was always guaranteed to change her mood. It settled her into an arrogant, can-do-anything frame of mind. It lifted her spirits, blew away the blackness – the power of being able to control such a machine with a tickle of the accelerator, a stroke of the brake pedal. When she was in charge of the Beast nobody could take her on.

It was also at moments like this, when the adrenalin surged as she hit the bend at 60 with a slight touch of the brake, and accelerating out of it, watching the turbo needle flicker, that Nikki would start fantasising, and reminiscing, again.

Marriage to the Man from Atlantis had few advantages but they were big ones. The house. The mortgage. The Swedish Beast. Her wages primarily were her own, to spend on herself. So it was cut and colour every four weeks to maintain the Sharon Stone look (and hide the grey hairs that had started to creep in); nice designer numbers, particularly for work; a great – if somewhat middle-of-the-road and seriously untrendy – CD collection for the car; the statutory one holiday without him each year, because that was all Steve would allow; the girly lunches and jaunts; and the other thing.

Ah yes, the other thing.

Nikki fought the impulse for a fraction of a second and instead rammed the gearstick down to fourth and booted her: the Saab flew past the articulated truck with the familiar jolt in the pit of her back. Safely well past him, she pulled back in, smoothly changing gear and noting with satisfaction the flashed headlights of appreciation and thumbs-up from the truck driver.

'Horny bastard,' she muttered, 'in your dreams, big boy.'

I'm a horny bastard too, she thought. It's been a while. At least four weeks. The feel of warm, supple, smooth flesh against her, the nuzzling of a finely arched neck, the curve of a hip under her fingertips, the hardening of the nipple against her tongue, the delicious combination of a light perfume and musk of arousal, the soft sighs and moans in her ear. She wanted to bury her face deep, stretch her tongue. She wanted another woman. Again. The familiar pulsating throb of her clitoris, the trickling wetness, had started, the ache in the bottom of her stomach, that almost physical pain of yearning. She shifted slightly in the seat; she could feel herself beginning to ooze with the wickedly delicious thoughts buzzing round her head, the memories filtering through. She did need an orgasm, and badly. She needed to look into another woman's eyes and gauge the promise there. She needed that first tentative touch that leads to a feather-light stroke, a gentle brush of the lips, a moving together of bodies for an exploratory kiss which gets heavier and stronger while hands begin to move around bodies.

She screeched to a halt in the lay-by, absent-mindedly patting the dashboard to apologise for the rough treatment. The glove box sprang open and she rummaged under the handbook, the atlas, the emergency first-aid kit and scooped up the mobile. She plugged it into the cigarette lighter to charge up, switched it on and glared at the LCD.

'Shit. No messages.'

She scrolled the memory, dialled the number. Answerphone response.

'Hi, it's Sue,' said Nikki to the airwaves, 'calling in to see how you are and how your diary is fixed. I'd like to see you soon. Call me.'

She threw the phone on the passenger seat. Bad move. Must always cover tracks. Always tell lies closest to the truth. Always make sure the alibi knows they are an alibi. Hide incriminating evidence.

She returned the phone to the back of the glove box, checked her mirrors and pulled out.

Marion was away from her desk when Nikki returned after lunch. The shoot had been mediocre but adequate for the purposes. How creative do you need to be with a collection of cleaning chemicals for Chrissakes? How can clients get such a fucking hard-on over such boring shit? How was she expected to commission sparkling body text and tag lines for dishwasher rinse aid?

Nikki shuffled through the message sheets and Post-It notes left on her desk.

Sparkling copy. Hah. Marion had contacted the freelance who was coming in that afternoon at 3 p.m. She had also compiled a list of the journals most likely to be suitable for advertising, so Nikki spread her papers over her desk, booted up her laptop and, chewing on a paperclip, started to put her ad schedule together.

She was deeply absorbed as Marion entered.

'Your three o'clock is here. Do you want more coffee?'

'She'll have to wait. I've got to the vinegar strokes of this schedule. Give her a drink and a magazine to read and I'll be straight out,' said Nikki without looking up from the screen.

Then all hell broke loose. The power went off in the building, her screen went black and the laptop groaned and died. So did her schedule. Two hours' work gone, irretrievable because once again she had forgotten to save on a regular basis. She hadn't saved the document at all, let alone anything that could be salvaged. Nikki Jones had just laboured for two hours for fuck all. The power came back on and the screen stayed obstinately blank. Disbelieving, she booted the book up again. Nothing, just a blank file with a bleeping cursor waiting for input. She went to the file menu, scrolled down to find a file. Shit, shit, fuck, bollocks, goddamned Taiwanese piece of crap, how could it find a file if she hadn't saved it in the first place? Why did she always forget the basic rule: save as you go? Why didn't people still use fucking secretaries and typewriters? Why did she do this job for a living?

Why was she married? Why was she born?

'Marion!' she screamed.

Marion moaned. It must be something to do with the computer. She glanced across at the freelance, who had been startled by the yell. They shared a look of bemusement followed by fear as Nikki burst out of the office.

'I lost it. I lost the lot. Get Phil out of the studio to come and look at that piece of shit before I throw it out of the window. He's supposed to be a fucking wizard – let him get it back for me. Please let him get it back for me,' shouted Nikki.

Oh God, thought Marion, she didn't do the save as you go again. Nikki had clearly forgotten the tirade of abuse she had heaped on Phil and his team that morning. Admittedly she had had some justification in doing so, but creatives were notoriously temperamental. If Phil was sulking it was extremely unlikely he would even deign to come down the two flights of stairs from the studio. He wouldn't piss on Nikki if she was on fire right now. Marion sighed.

'I'll get you a coffee, go and sit down with a cigarette, and then I'll see if I can get Phil down here,' she said quietly.

Nikki stood shaking, clenching her fists to regain control. She would have to redo the whole thing again, probably having to stay late, which would piss Steve off and she would have Frosty the Snowman opposite her all night.

As Marion rose from her desk, Nikki became aware of the woman sitting by her. That must be the freelance, she thought. Why is she sitting there looking like a rabbit caught in headlights?

'You'd better come in my office,' said Nikki, and stomped through.

The woman approached the desk cautiously.

'You did say you didn't want the copy until Tuesday,' she started, 'and although I'd made a start when your PA called, I obviously haven't had time to finish it.'

'Tuesday? Tuesday? The client meeting is on Monday. Why would I tell you Tuesday? Don't people like you keep diaries, time managers, calendars, watches? I have deadlines to meet, I give creatives deadlines and briefs which could be understood by a five-year-old and I give them plenty of time to apply their highly paid creative minds and talent to the job in hand. This is a newsletter for a CCTV company, it can't be that difficult, you had the bulk of the content handed to you on a plate. All you had to do was jiggle it around and put it into English and I gave you at least a week. This is the first time we've used you, isn't it? You were recommended to me by a friend of mine. She said you were reliable. This is hardly an auspicious start, is it?'

Marion had appeared in the background and Nikki was refusing to acknowledge the strange gestures she was making.

'Could I just —' said the freelance.

'This is not good — one simple bloody job I could have done myself, tossed off in half an hour, you've taken a bloody week and it's still not finished, and no doubt you'll bang in an inflated invoice that you'll want paying by return.'

'Would you just —'

'And look at this copy you've done already. The first paragraph of the main story doesn't even make bloody sense, so what I have got is neither use nor ornament. How am I supposed to present a half-finished piece of crap to my client on Monday?'

Marion couldn't stand it any longer. Her facial gestures, her frantic slash of the finger across the throat to signify that Nikki should shut up had been ignored. Nikki was on a roll, but Marion cleared her throat and plunged in.

'Nikki, your meeting is a week on Monday and the copy wasn't due till Tuesday, to allow for rewrites, and it's all on that action report in the live folder in your tray,' she blurted in a rush.

'Well, even so, I don't like what you've done to date,' said Nikki lamely to the freelance, who by this point was stepping from foot to foot in anger.

'Can I just —'

'You've got till Friday to have another crack at this because, if it's still no good, I've got a chance to either brief it to someone else or do it myself,' said Nikki, 'and I'm sorry I got the dates wrong. But I'm just not happy with your style, so try again.'

She handed the copy back; their eyes met in a mutual challenge and locked. Without breaking the contact, the freelance folded the paper and shoved it in her shoulder bag.

'Thank you —' the sarcasm was barely veiled '— I've taken your constructive criticism and suggestions on board and I'll endeavour to incorporate them in the revamp.'

Their eyes were still locked in mutual hostility.

Marion coughed.

'Shall I show you out?' she said to the back of the freelancer's head. The girl turned, the look of contempt clear on her face, and walked out.

Nikki debated about blasting Marion out on her return but wisely decided against it. It wasn't often that Marion spoke out like that; in fact Nikki could only recall a handful of occasions when her PA had turned on her, and every time she had been absolutely right to do so. Nikki had been wrong and she had compounded it by all that bluster about the copy being crap. She hadn't even read it properly. For all she knew it could have been perfect. That poor bitch had taken the full vent of her temper tantrum when it wasn't her fault. She had come highly recommended by her best friend, Gillian. In fact Gillian had pestered Nikki for months to use her. The girl was apparently the daughter of one of her old school chums, Nikki vaguely recalled.

She had always trusted Gillian's judgement, and Gillian had been full of praise for the girl. But Nikki was now the girl's client and paid her invoices so the freelance would just have to put up with it. She made a mental note to be really nice to the girl on Friday as a way of apologising.

Marion, equally wisely, left Nikki alone for the next hour while she and Phil pored over the screen. Phil, having had his monstrous ego massaged subtly by Marion for ten minutes, and knowing that this would deserve a huge favour in return, had with a great show of grudging reluctance offered to help. But there was no rescue: the file had been lost for good in cyberspace.

Packing her laptop up – the screen now had a Post-It note taped to the top of the screen saying SAVE AS YOU GO – Nikki sighed heavily. Her eyes felt gritty, she was so tired. Even the prospect of her throaty Saab had a muted appeal. She knew she was going home to two hours of reformulating the ad schedule while Steve fussed and bothered around her and whinged about being late for dinner. Fuck it, quick retouch of the make-up, clean the teeth, more wax in her hair and throw on a dressy trouser suit with high heels and she was ready. She grinned evilly – the four-inch heels tonight just to really piss Steve off. The same height in bare feet, the couple looked like Little and Large when they went out, as Nikki towered over her husband with his rotund beer belly and saggy trousers which draped over the top of his trousers.

What had she ever seen in that dolt? At what point did the last vestige of respect fly out of the window? Why didn't the moron go and have an affair with his secretary, announce a mid-life crisis and fuck off to sail the high seas in search of himself? Because, she told herself, he's a bone-idle bastard and that's too much hard work.

Risk for Steve Jones was opening the mail in the morning and avoiding a paper cut. She smiled as she remembered that odious, hateful mother of his nagging her in that first year of marriage – 'Don't you lay his clothes out for him of a morning?' Steve was a thorough Mummy's boy in those early years. He complained endlessly about her pathetic attempts at cooking. Now Nikki was a fully paid-up founder member of the Don't Do Oven cookery school, and for the last fifteen years had relied on the freezer, microwave and top burners to prepare the few meals they had together at home. She was lousy at ironing shirts, always putting in double tramtracks on the sleeves. Nothing she did ever matched up to how his mother used to do it. No doubt the sex was better with his mother, too.

Now the poisonous old coot was in a home with Alzheimer's, an affliction Nikki was convinced was a gift from God in her case. She could no longer remember who Nikki was, let alone berate her for real or imagined sins against her precious Stevie. She made another mental note to remind Steve to go and visit.

The leather in the car was cool against her back. She adjusted the seat electrically to ease the pressure on her aching lower spine. She ferreted in the glove box – still no return messages. No illicit sex on the horizon for her, then.

Tired, grumpy and with that aching clit still giving her constant reminders that she was horny, she pulled out of the car park –

straight in front of a BMW which braked so violently the whole car rocked on both axles. She put a weary hand up in acknowledgement of her mistake, but the driver was already out of the car, his face puce and twisted with anger, his fists clenched and spoiling for a fight.

She kept her windows shut, activated the central locking and waited for the right opportunity to swing the Saab round the sharply angled BMW and take off. He banged his hand hard against her windscreen and spittle flew from his mouth as he roared expletive after expletive at her.

'Oh, for fuck's sake,' she breathed, and shook her head. Then he made the biggest mistake of all – he booted the side of her car. In a flash her belt was undone, the door was opened with a violent shove into him, knocking him off balance, and he fell on his back. In a fluid movement she was out of the car and sticking the boot in to his flabby paunch and kidneys. Desperate to ward off the kicks, he curled into a ball and she drew her foot back to plant one on the back of his neck.

'I wouldn't do that if I were you,' said a calm, quiet voice behind her. It was one of her creatives, on his bicycle with wrap-round Stallone polar sunglasses and speed helmet. 'Just get in your car and drive off. Leave him be. I think he knows he was in the wrong place at the wrong time to be pissing you off.'

She gulped, quickly surveyed the dent in the door, got in the car and drove off, watching in her mirror as the creative dropped his bike and helped the bastard up. She started to shake; she could feel sweat between and underneath her breasts. What the fuck was wrong with her: she would have willingly kicked his brains out. And for what, a dent? Christ, what a fucking day. She needed a drink.

Steve poured her a Jack Daniel's on ice, without speaking. He had myriad faults, but judging her mood at the end of the day was a talent he shared with Marion. It was actually one of the few positive traits he had that was of any assistance in their marriage.

Her hand shook so badly that the ice clinked violently against the glass. Steve waited, knowing his wife was badly shaken up by something.

12

'Goddammned bastard kicked my fucking door in,' she wheezed as the JD seared the back of her throat. 'He kicked my fucking door in and that was after I had apologised to him. He kicked my fucking door in so I went to kick his fucking head in and Gary got off his bike to help, and the pitch was cancelled, and my computer crashed, and I yelled abuse at that poor girl, and I really don't fucking feel like eating lamb tonight.'

The torrent was delivered in one breath; most of it he missed but he gathered it had been a bad day. He sighed dramatically with impatience as she threw the rest of the liquor down her throat.

'I really think you should make that your last drink tonight. The last thing I need tonight is you being half-cut before you even turn up.' He logged her frosty glare. 'Look, I'm sorry you've had a lousy day, but if we're going to make that dinner we had really better get a move on. I can't afford to turn up late. These people have virtually promised me their account, and I know they are looking for development loans to buy that town-centre retail-park site, and I can do them a cracking deal. So go and wipe your face, put your glad rags on and let's close them. All you have to do tomorrow is put the car in for an estimate. I'm sure the damage isn't that bad. It's only a piece of metal on wheels, after all,' droned Steve, who had unfortunately missed the danger signal of Nikki running her hand around the back of her neck, because he was pouring a generous Scotch for himself.

With the back of his head presented to her, looking so vulnerable, Nikki was toiling to control her urge to hit him with the bottle of JD.

'I'm not going,' she said coldly. 'I'll be lousy company. I have work to do anyway.'

'You can't let me down now: you know I'm crap at social trivia. I can't just bluster in and get straight down to business. What the hell do I say to them, to keep them occupied until the liqueurs, coffee and cigars? This is just too much. I don't ask you for much, do I? You have a rotten day and I'm the one who loses out. This is an absolute disaster. Probably the most important deal of my life, and what happens? My own wife can't even put herself out for a few measly hours. Well, I'll ring Sophie and see if she wants to come then. She'll drop anything for a chance to help me grab an account like this. You know Sophie, don't you? That busty blonde junior in my department. You know, the one with the legs up to her ears.'

'Drop anything? Ask the little slut to drop her knickers, then. That'll give all of you corporate suited bastards something to talk about. And I hope she likes lamb,' said Nikki spitefully, and stomped off to run herself a bath.

Steve shrugged, swallowed his Scotch in such a large gulp that his eyes watered, and started to cough and splutter.

'Ah, go choke to death, you bastard,' Nikki muttered as she got to the top step, half her clothes already discarded. 'No, Steve, you twat, I didn't have a nice day. No, I'm not having a nice life. I should be in London, that's where I should be . . .'

Her muttering trailed away as she slammed the bathroom door behind her.

'Am I to gather I should ring Sophie, then?' Steve shouted up the stairs when he had composed his heaving chest and had begun to breathe normally again.

TWO

Georgie threw her bag on to the back seat, papers scattering. She stood by her open door, breathing heavily to try to regain calm.

'Bitch. Stuck-up bloody power-shoulders bitch,' she spat through clenched teeth. 'Just because her fucking computer failed and she probably didn't get laid last night I get it in the neck. Bloody high-heels-wearing trollop couldn't have read the copy in that time. She couldn't have. I break my neck to deliver something early and what happens? Bitch queen from hell decides to take it out on me. The hell with her, I don't need her bloody newsletter.'

She ground her teeth. Georgie Rivers did need the bloody newsletter. Her road tax had run out six weeks before and she was irritated at having to park her car carefully. British Telecom were kicking up a stink because she had missed the second instalment of her phone bill. She was in arrears with her rent – again. She had been delighted to receive the call out of the blue offering the job. Her Auntie Gillian – she called her that even though they weren't officially related – had said she would put her name forward to all her contacts when Georgie first moved to this godforsaken town. She'd thought Auntie Gillian had forgotten her promise: she was renowned for her scattiness.

'I need a beer,' she sighed, climbed into the car and drove off to pick up a slab of Stella.

At home, she stared disconsolately at the screen. CCTV customer installation stories did not excite her, but the job was worth about £600. If she cleared this one out of the way quickly, she could spend the rest of the week banging away on the phone drumming up some more business.

Georgie always had the news agency to fall back on. Keith was constantly in need of a body at the Crown Court, coroner's court or some bloody industrial tribunal. It was lousy pay, long hours, but it kept her shorthand speed up, and now and again Scoop Rivers came up with the goods for Keith to get a nice fat bonus from the nationals.

She sighed. She had long given up on the so-called glamour of journalism. Although she had managed to occasionally scoop rival reporters on business news, she hadn't got that ruthless edge for the really big stories involving human tragedies. More often than not she had had to leave incidents with tears in her eyes: she always felt too sorry for the victims or their families. Georgie Rivers knew she would never have made it on any national tabloid. She would have been laughed off it. And if she had made it, and buckled down, she knew she wouldn't have liked the person she would have turned into. So national by-lines had never even been an unattainable ambition for her. She had stayed in the safe world of local papers until the day she got sacked.

'Hah, if you think you're a tough cookie,' she said aloud, thinking about Nikki Jones. Against the chief reporters and news editors who had browbeaten Georgie over the years, Nikki was chickenshit. But Georgie had deserved the sack: it had been just one cock-up too many.

She had been sent to a crime scene, a murder – big news locally – in favour of the usual crime correspondent, who could not be found. Despairing, the news editor – who had a nervous twitch of the eye which for some reason doubled in frequency every time Georgie was around – looked ostentatiously around the vast newsroom. It was empty apart from Georgie, who was banging away as usual on a 'women's' feature.

Her head bent over the trusty Olympia, she had failed to notice his shoulders slump, the shake of his head, and the deep sigh.

'Georgie! Get your arse out to Willen Hill. There's been a murder!' he yelled, brandishing his crib sheet at her and fixing a madly twitching gimlet eye on her. She raced out of her seat, snatched the paper from his hand and ran out of the door.

Willen Hill was a rough estate, with pre-war terraced council houses separated by dim alleyways, gardens full of discarded old bicycles and car parts. Dirty, snot-nosed kids running around causing damage and havoc, and slatternly, blousy girls old before their time with reddened skin and cheap perms which had gone wrong and turned their hair frizzy.

It was also always a good source of human-interest stories of some description: wife beatings, sudden deaths, drunken semi-riots between feuding teenage gangs. Georgie knew the score – unemployed hubby, who had probably finally lost it with his slovenly wife or one of a number of children, snapped and fuelled by cheap cider had committed the dire deed.

Thoughts buzzing about her by-line on the front page, she abandoned the car with door swinging to race down the path and through the almost black alleyway. It was only at the end of the little tunnel as she blundered through into the light, temporarily dazzled, and fell over something soft that she realised she had stumbled on to the murder scene. Literally.

'Oh, Jesus,' muttered the DS as Georgie had burst through and disturbed the pretty vital evidence of the body lying where it had fallen.

'Oh, fuck,' muttered Georgie as an assortment of uniformed and plain-clothes coppers had turned in absolute silence, disgust and contempt and stared at her.

'That's why you're writing about CCTV customers for a living now.' Georgie smiled as she brought herself back to the present day and the blank screen waiting for her sparkling prose.

The door flew open and Kim burst in, laden with carrier bags no doubt full of toiletries. Kim had a thing about toiletries. Georgie had never had so many groaning bathroom shelves, bottles of hair potions, bath gels, fifteen varieties of perfumed and unperfumed soaps, three different kinds of toothpaste and four flavours of mouthwash. Toiletries spilt out everywhere. They had invaded the bedroom, neatly stacked on the windowsills, bedside tables, under the bed. Wherever Georgie went she fell over bloody toiletries. And now the silly bitch had bought some more. And the bags – Georgie eyed them uneasily – looked also to have a collection of medicines in them.

'I am having the worst period of my life,' announced Kim.

So am I, thought Georgie, and it's been since you moved in. What was it about these women? If they didn't bring emotional baggage with them they brought fucking toiletries. If it wasn't toiletries it was pets – usually scabby, mangy dogs or cats from some flea-ridden rescue sanctuary. Why didn't lesbians ever invest in pedigree animals? If it wasn't pets it was a collection of framed photos of all the ex's. If they weren't alcoholics, they were manic depressives, each and every one of them with a propensity for forgetting to take their happy tablets. Why couldn't she just find a stable bird with a great sense of humour who enjoyed shagging without all the emotional bollocks and pressure for commitment that came with it? Why did she roll over and just let them all move in? The old joke, 'What does a lesbian bring on her second date? A removal van', sprang into her head.

Putting her powerbook into sleep mode, Georgie knew that was it for the day. Kim had a disconcerting habit of standing over her shoulder when she worked and, unforgivably, would point out spelling errors. Didn't the damn fool realise that broke her train of thought and concentration, and that everything would be corrected and laid out properly AFTERWARDS? If Kim used a computer there would probably be Tippex on the screen, Georgie thought viciously. She resigned herself to an evening of whinge-ing. Just three months old, this relationship, and already every-thing the girl did annoyed her. Just looking at Kim irritated her. Listening to Kim breathe irked her. Fabulous arse, but time to move on, Georgie Girl, she thought. But she couldn't do it while Kim had her period. She was likely to get either the flat or her face shattered.

Kim wasn't big, but she had a propensity for explosive bouts of temper. In three months Georgie had had to replace two telephone handsets and there was still a Kellogg's Cornflakes packet over the crack in the window. And taking the carving knife off her had been a bit hairy, even for Georgie.

Georgie could hold her own in most situations, particularly with a bottle of Bud in her hand, but anyone pulling her hair made her sick. Taking the knife off Kim had seemed instinctive and natural but it was only afterwards, as she threw up in the sink, that she had realised how nasty it could have turned.

Lovely, lovely arse, Georgie mused, but definitely time to ship her out. Time to start looking again for fresh meat. She swore to herself that this time she would not move anyone in, that she would relish her own space for a change. The longest she had lived alone was seven months and most of that had disappeared in a blur of Jack Daniel's, Budweisers, too many cigarettes and not enough food. Georgie hated being alone. Crashing loneliness, coupled with her low self-esteem, was a lethal combination with the booze. Rather than be alone, she would move someone in after a matter of days – sometimes overnight. An initial meeting in a club, back to her place for a session, and five weeks later the bird is still there, taking up wardrobe space and watching fucking soap operas every night. But, think on the bright side, Georgie, there's always someone new out there. She had never had difficulty pulling. Her cheeky grin and laughing eyes and witty one-liners never failed her. Admittedly, some of her conquests had obviously got more attractive in proportion to the amount of Stella, Bud or JD consumed, but she hadn't had too much of a lousy track record in terms of good-looking girlies.

And they were girlies, more often than not younger. But the women, full-blooded experienced lesbians, she had captured were more than keen to teach the little YTS some extra tricks on a regular basis. She preferred them too, as they were less willing to move in lock, stock and barrel after the first fuck. They usually had their own places, quite often with a partner already ensconced.

Yep, Georgie decided there and then, time to move on and find an older woman with great tits, I think.

Meanwhile, Kim had embarked on yet another monologue about her perceived illnesses, scrubbing at her hands in the kitchen while she droned on, her voice fortunately drowned by the running water. Georgie's reverie was broken as Kim's voice grew louder – why was it so piercing? – as the girl came into the lounge.

'. . . then, while I'm trying to deal with the customer, I started to flood . . .'

'Yeah, yeah, I'm not really in a mood to hear stuff like that. Fancy a pizza tonight?' said Georgie, reaching for the menu by the phone.

Later, five cans of Stella later, Georgie was beginning to mellow towards Kim as they curled up on the settee.

'You really do have a great arse,' she mumbled into Kim's neck, stroking her back and feeling that familiar, treacherous, Stella-driven throb of her clit.

'Enough of that. My stomach hurts,' said Kim briskly, bounding off the settee to grab the remote for the TV. '*EastEnders* is on.'

Georgie groaned and rolled on to her back, absently watching Kim's arse cheeks in the tight Levi's as she bent to retrieve the remote. I'll miss those, she thought.

'I'm going out,' she announced.

'Where?'

'Just out. I won't be long. Don't wait up for me, will you?'

Kim's face set. Oops, thought Georgie, wrong move: telephones are going to start flying in a minute.

'What have I done this time? You know, I don't seem to be able to do anything right for you these days. You're always on at me, having a go. You don't love me any more, do you?' Kim whined.

Weighing up the chances of a carving knife reappearing against the lesser sin of flying telephones, Georgie took a deep breath.

'No.'

'You never loved me, did you?'

'No.'

'That's a bit harsh, isn't it? A bit brutal, a bit fucking blunt and straight to the point?'

'Yes.'

'You're going out to find yourself a fresher model, aren't you? Aren't you? That's where you're going, isn't it?'

'Yes.'

'I mean nothing to you, do I? What was I, just a passing diversion? I thought we had something special between us. I thought we had a commitment.'

'I never said anything about commitment. In fact, I have never said I loved you either. I never promised you anything. You and I got horribly drunk at that party, you came back with me, we shagged and before I know it there's fucking shower-gel mountains piling up and I'm suddenly privy to every single godforsaken ailment you've ever had, in glorious Technicolor.

'I listen to your whingeing and your whining, I have to wait half an hour every morning before I can use my toilet because you're busy piling on gallons of whatever and manically scrubbing your hands. I never have clean towels, I'm always having to clean the bathroom after you. Just what do you do in there for half an hour at a time? How much fucking hair mousse can one woman use? My bathroom looks like Boots. I can't get to any of my own stuff, you leave clothes all over the place, the fucking television is always blaring some miserable bloody soap opera and I've never liked your taste in music – it's always songs to slash your bloody wrists to.'

Georgie took in some air and was about to launch into another tirade when Kim put up her hands in supplication.

'OK, OK, perhaps I have some weird habits and tastes. I'll do whatever you want. Just let me stay. I love you – let's try and work this out.'

'There's nothing to work out. It's over, it's finished. I'll get some boxes from Safeway and pack your stuff for you tomorrow. Come and pick it up after work,' said Georgie icily.

'You're a cold fish,' said Kim, 'you'll never find happiness, bouncing from one to another. I knew what you were like but I thought I was the one who could make the difference. I was obviously wrong.'

'Obviously.'

Kim sighed dramatically and threw herself on to the settee.

'Can I stay here for a while?' she said mournfully. 'I've got to make arrangements for somewhere else to go, you know. It won't be easy.'

'Yes,' said Georgie, shrugging into her leather jacket, knowing that Kim would scurry straight off home that night to Mummy, who had always thought this gay thing was just a passing phase and that Kim would settle down and meet a nice boy one day.

Kim seems to be taking it quite well, she thought, firmly closing the door. The crash of the plant pot against the back of the door behind her told her otherwise.

She steeled herself to return to a vandalised flat later, zipped up her jacket and headed out for the gay bar.

Within the crowd – many of them familiar faces who nodded as she walked in – was Phillipa, an average-looking, slim girl who for some reason kept dashing off to the loo on a regular basis.

Clearly she was snorting something, because as the evening wore on her energy, stamina and sexual hunting tactics began to show marked levels of increased activity. Georgie noted her antics with some amusement – Phillipa was well known for it. The bottles of Bud were sliding down Georgie's throat very agreeably and Phillipa was moving from looking average into looking like a safe bet for the night, particularly when she finally sidled up to Georgie, squeezed her arse, said she had always fancied her, and asked if she wanted some fun.

At Phillipa's flat, Georgie was assaulted within seconds of setting foot inside the door. She had never been undressed so quickly in her life. Throwing her flat on the carpet, and still fully dressed, Phillipa sank to her knees and buried her face between Georgie's legs.

Still somewhat shocked at the speed of the event, she was also crucially aware that Phillipa still had a lighted fag in her hand and there was a real danger of getting a badly singed minge. On the pretext – shouted with a strangulated cry – of needing a pee, Georgie scrambled away. Returning after a suitable interval she was relieved to see Phillipa was fagless and sprawled on the settee.

Thinking foolishly that the girl had passed out and that she could probably slink off, Georgie quietly made for the crumpled heap of clothes by the front door.

A noise behind her alerted Georgie to the reality of Phillipa not only still wide awake, but full of energy and without doubt horny as hell. She grinned, undid her trousers and stepped out of them to reveal stockings, suspenders, no knickers, and a wonderfully trimmed bush. She undid her shirt to reveal a half-cup bra. Georgie's breath caught in her throat as she raked hungry eyes over one of the most beautiful bodies she had ever seen – not many had matched it .

This time Phillipa contained herself enough to slow the proceedings down. Pushing Georgie firmly down on the settee, she kissed her neck and straddled her. Georgie began to kiss her slowly and then became aware of Phillipa's hand between her own legs, gathering some of her copious juice and spreading it over Georgie's nipples. Despite her earlier misgivings about the wisdom of taking on the probably awesome challenge of Phillipa in full flight, Georgie could not help responding. She began to relax and enjoy as Phillipa bent her head and sucked Georgie's come off, massaging both breasts hard. Again Phillipa gathered her moistness and rubbed it into Georgie's breasts, her tongue probing her mouth until Georgie began to move her hips and thrust up towards her. Georgie wanted to stroke, feel and caress, but as she moved her hands Phillipa pinned her down.

Georgie was beginning to moan and writhe with wanting as Phillipa pushed open her legs with her thigh, licked her fingers and immediately found Georgie's clitoris. Moving her finger slowly in a circle, she then flicked the clitoris from underneath, slid her finger down and buried it deep inside the other woman. Still inside her, she quickly moved down Georgie's body with quick darting movements of her tongue; her other hand pushed back the hood of her clit and she began to lick the open, exposed and rapidly swelling flesh, increasing the pressure, pulling back then pushing hard again, gently nipping it with the edge of her teeth, moving in circles and then from side to side. Now, encouraged by the gushing wetness of Georgie's cunt, she slipped another finger inside, moving in and out to the same rhythm as her tongue, French kissing the clit while the pressure mounted. Phillipa was moaning softly with desire at the taste and feel of aroused woman and, as Georgie looked down, she opened her eyes and raised her face slightly and smiled. Georgie could see her own wetness glistening on Phillipa's lips and her chin.

Phillipa moved upward again, still with her fingers inside, still moving to that maddening rhythm, increasing the pace, and began to kiss Georgie. The taste and the smell of her own cunt, sweet and musky, filled Georgie's senses. Phillipa's hand was beating hard and fast against her cunt as her fingers went even deeper, and she finger-fucked her until her head began to swim, her stomach knotted.

Georgie could feel her vaginal muscles contracting around Phillipa's fingers as if to not let them go, and then she realised she was coming because the deep growl started at the back of her throat. Her breath began to shorten as she gasped into Phillipa's mouth and still she would not stop kissing her. Georgie's back arched, as she began to pump her hips furiously against the hand, searching for release as the waves began to build and then she was awash, lost, delirious, not wanting to let go of Phillipa, grabbing the girl's hair, raking her back with her fingers, finding her arse and digging her nails in hard as she finally reached the top and exploded, not just shuddering but jerking as her whole body gave in to the feeling.

Georgie's legs shook; her breasts heaved with the exertion of lungs grabbing for precious air; her mouth was dry; her throat constricted and she groaned as Phillipa slowly withdrew her fingers.

'Wow!'

That was what Georgie intended to say, but she didn't get as far as the first letter before Phillipa was at her again. Fuelled by drugs and alcohol, Phillipa was a sex automaton, an emotionless, technically honed machine in high gear.

Georgie began to have serious misgivings again about this woman. It was apparent that the stuff she had been snorting, coupled with the copious amounts of booze, had given her a superhuman and probably endless level of stamina and horniness. Despite the fact that Georgie desperately wanted to fall asleep or pass out, whichever came first, because her head was now spinning and her cunt had gone numb, she pushed Phillipa backward.

It occurred to Georgie that if she shagged her, and she came, Phillipa might just pass out herself. Georgie also suspected that whatever she did would be OK: Phillipa was beyond the stage of finesse and technique.

How wrong could she be?

She licked Phillipa until her jaw locked; she ran out of saliva; her top lip stuck to her teeth; her tongue went numb. She finger-fucked her until she thought her hands were going to fall off – alternating them to overcome cramps didn't make much differ-ence. Georgie dry-humped Phillipa until she thought she was going to be stuck forever with her back arched and that she had suffered terminal damage to painfully locked elbows. But Phillipa carried on pounding and hammering away, inexhaustible, insatiable.

Georgie got to the stage of seriously considering giving Phillipa a right hook to knock her out because still she wanted more and Georgie just wanted to sleep.

A mumbled offer – in between frenetic tonsil-hockey bouts – of a third bottle of Bud to add to the quantity of alcohol she had already consumed that long, exhausting night finally gave her a break.

Halfway down her bottle, guzzling like it was Coca-Cola, Phillipa asked Georgie if she had ever had beer licked off her cunt.

Already anxious about the effect the noise of this marathon lick-a-thon was having on the neighbours, and crucially aware of the sting of carpet burn affecting her arse, Georgie somewhat irrationally panicked about the effect any spillages would have.

'Babe, I've got to go,' she said gently, unwinding herself from the tangle of arms and legs. With relief, she noticed that Phillipa's eyes were closed and a faint dribble of Bud had escaped from the corner of her mouth.

She dressed warily, keeping an eye open for either another assault or the possibility of Phillipa choking on her own vomit. With a pang of conscience, she rolled the unconscious girl on to her side, packed settee cushions against her back and tiptoed out, leaving her in the recovery position for the likely eventuality of illness.

My God, I've been Phillipa'd, she thought, adjusting the seam of her jeans as she lurched out of the door and did a pinball machine down the corridor, bouncing off each wall in turn.

It was the perfect end to a perfect day, she thought savagely. I'll probably get cystitis or thrush in the morning. My God, it is morning: it's dawn. And I've got a flat to repair and a newsletter to finish.

'Where the hell am I anyway?' she said aloud as she walked out of the block of flats into a bright new day.

THREE

Nikki smiled to herself in the car. She had just caught herself leching at a lithe and leggy German or Scandinavian back-packer with minuscule shorts riding up the cheeks of her tight arse bouncing across the pelican crossing in front of her.

God, Nikki loved summer. She loved to fantasise, emboldened by the acres of bare flesh that usually began to appear in mid-May.

Just as her sister Lynda and her mate Gillian constantly enter-tained delicious thoughts on a regular basis about police outriders and fire officers in waders and helmets, Nikki could grow wistful about policewomen and jail cells; nurses in stockings and their in-bed manner; female firefighters flinging her over their shoulders; blonde and busty paramedics giving her the kiss of life for hours on end.

Summer could turn Nikki, usually, from the original road rager of winter into the most amenable and courteous driver on the road. She and her Saab would sit quietly purring together at crossings while unfettered nims bounced in skimpy tops, and long, tanned legs in strappy high-heeled sandals strode out in the summer sunshine.

She would always, without fail, let attractive female drivers (blondes in black BMWs in particular) out of a junction in front of her so that she could watch the driver in her wing mirror. And Nikki always smiled.

The beauty of it all for Nikki was that she could do all this glorious lechery in complete safety, because virtually all the rest of the world around her at the time was totally unaware of what was going on. If she were a man she would have been arrested for loitering, for stalking, for basic harassment.

None of these women undergoing Nikki's scrutiny – probably 98 per cent of them were straight – would have any idea that the tall, blonde, blue-eyed professional woman standing next to her or sitting behind the wheel of a powerful performance vehicle had completely wet and dripping knickers and a clitoris the size of a football.

God, I love summer so much, she thought as she gestured a woman out of the junction ahead of her and received a cheeky wave of thanks.

Marion raised an eyebrow in surprise at Nikki's cheerful mood as she entered the office. Perhaps Steve had come up with the goods, she thought, or, at the very least, bought Nikki a steak.

'Morning, Marion, here's the disc with the schedule on it. Can you toss it upstairs to the studio for a bit of tarting around on layout, then get me five copies? Then I want you to ring the Saab garage and book her in for an estimate. Had a bit of a *contretemps* with a fat old wanker last night on the way home. I also need an update on the BMRB figures for evaluation on that product brand-development project. And I need to have a progress report on the finished artwork for the MTS ads. But, before anything, I need caffeine and nicotine . . .' Nikki's voice trailed off as she sailed into her office.

Hmm, thought Marion, looking at her watch, I'll give it half an hour.

In fact, Nikki's mood lasted most of the morning, wavering only slightly when the boys from the studio appeared with a mounted cartoon showing a heavily caricatured Nikki beating three kinds of shit out of a defenceless BMW driver. Feigning good-natured acceptance, she scowled as she tucked the cartoon into her filing cabinet.

'Don't forget you're having lunch with Gillian,' called Marion, knowing full well that that would be Nikki's afternoon written off and Marion would have to cover for her in the event of her boss, Alistair, wanting to know her whereabouts.

Nikki's good humour returned in a flash. She had forgotten about lunch – an appointment supposedly to discuss complementary PR activity to a marketing job she had on at the moment. She and Gillian, who ran her own small PR operation, would talk about work for about ten minutes and then about sex and booze for the next 240. Their lunches had decreased over the years to around once a month, twice if work was slack.

Gillian hated Steve with a passion. She had never liked him, even from those early days when he had first appeared – oozed more like it – on to her horizon as Nikki's marketing career was taking off. He had compounded her dislike for him by describing her to a mutal friend as a man-eater. Nikki knew there would be at least 45 of those 240 minutes devoted to a diatribe of abuse about her husband from her closest and dearest friend. She was looking forward to it.

Nikki raced on with her work, determined to clear her list of tasks in time to ensure a free afternoon.

At the restaurant, Gillian had already ordered their pre-lunch drinks.

'Darling, sweetie!' they cried in unison, with loud, smacking, air kisses, enjoying the startled looks of other business diners.

Gillian settled comfortably – Nikki knew it was going to be a long, long lunch. She also knew that she was going to have to cab it home and send Steve back for the Saab. So she settled in comfortably, too.

'How's work?' said Gillian.

'Crap,' said Nikki. 'You?'

'Crap. How's your love life?'

'Shit. And you?'

'Shit. Well, I say that,' said Gillian, warming to her theme, 'but the agency has come up with an interesting opportunity.'

Nikki groaned inwardly. Gillian's tortured love life had always been the subject of much intense discussion. They couldn't talk about Nikki's – to all intents and purposes Nikki was a faithful married woman – unless it was to swap incredibly malicious and deliciously funny remarks about Steve's prowess as a sexual animal.

Nikki had never been able to tell Gillian about her other life. She respected their relationship too much for that, couldn't allow her friend to carry the burden of such a massive secret. She had a suspicion that Gillian would be shocked, would not understand. She was also more than slightly ashamed of her furtive other life.

'And precisely what have they come up with this time? Their track record of providing you with the ideal mate has so far been appalling,' said Nikki.

The two women began to giggle.

'I know, I know,' Gillian coughed as the wine went down the wrong way. 'Cheshire gent requires classy filly to share his life with. Do you remember? You know me, always late for everything and I went dashing in to the Savoy like the Wild Woman of Wonga, all hot and sweaty with my hair sticking up, and there he is, arms rigid, holding his crisp copy of *The Times* a regulation two feet away from his *pince nez*.'

Nikki began to choke herself on her wine. She had heard this story several times and it still cracked her up.

'Tell me, young woman, what school did you go to? Do your people have land? And then when I asked him what he expected from a relationship . . .'

In unison the two women chorused: 'Some bedroom activity of a horizontal nature!'

Tears rolling down their faces, they could hardly speak to order their lunch. Nikki's laughter was tinged with a touch of sadness. Gillian deserved a decent guy, though admittedly he would have to be somewhat unusual. Gillian was a wonderful, kind-hearted and sensitive soul but she was eccentric. Years of living alone had established a set way of life that just did not allow for a full-time male partner intruding on her space.

As much as Gillian would have loved a man in her life, he would not be allowed to get in the way of, for example, her sudden impulses to take off on unusual jaunts. The husky sledding in Greenland sprang to Nikki's mind. The result had been a short-lived liaison with The Great Dane: a huge bear of a man who would have looked at home trapping grizzly bears, he was the world's noisiest snorer and had a propensity for chatting up Gillian's friends on his infrequent trips to the UK. Nikki had disliked him on sight.

Gillian's taste in men was wide and varied. She was not at the stage, yet, of going after anything with a pulse in trousers, but she had had a number of ill-starred relationships. A phase of 'aestheticism' had resulted in her throwing caution to the winds, attending a residential creative-writing course and ending up wistfully dreaming of Robert. Robert, it turned out to her chagrin, was homosexual. Then Gillian's penchant for 'delicious young things' had led to furtive liaisons with a 24-year-old fitness instructor in the sauna at the course hotel. And Nikki had a sneaking suspicion that Gillian had never forgiven her for the fiasco with the pretty young Dutch boy she had met on a hiking holiday in Turkey. Madly in love with the boy – whom Nikki had to admit was exceptionally pretty, judging by photos of him – Gillian had proposed that she and Nikki visit him in Holland and he could provide an equally pretty friend for Nikki to amuse herself with. Unbeknown to Nikki, Gillian fired off photos of her which did include a drunken snap of Nikki in a Donald Duck hat. Gillian had never heard from the boy since.

'Perhaps I should give up on this lark,' said Gillian with a mouthful of salmon, 'it doesn't seem to get me anywhere. Nothing seems to work out; nothing seems to count.'

The two eyed each other across the table and began to giggle again.

'The don't-count theory!' said Nikki.

'Can't remember his name, doesn't count.'

'Can't remember your own name, doesn't count.'

'Didn't come, doesn't count.'

'He couldn't come, doesn't count.'

'I was pissed, doesn't count.'

'I was sober, doesn't count.'

'He had a small dick, doesn't count.'

'Wouldn't perform oral sex, doesn't count.'

'Penetration was not achieved, doesn't count.'

'I was unconscious, doesn't count.'

'Didn't pay for the meal, doesn't count.'

'Can't remember where, doesn't count.'

'Can't remember a fucking thing, doesn't count.'

'The batteries were flat, doesn't count.'

By this point both women were wiping their eyes with napkins, diners around them were agape, the waiter was dashing off to regale the kitchen staff with stories of the two horny older women at table 36, and Gillian's mobile phone had accepted three answerphone messages.

'Talking of doesn't count, how's that miserable-bastard husband of yours?' said Gillian.

Somewhere in her own distant past Gillian had been married. In all the years Nikki had known her, Gillian had only ever referred to him as That Rodent. She had left him behind in New Zealand, where they had emigrated when Gillian was twenty and freshly married. A twelve-week return journey to the UK by boat had resulted in Gillian working her way through most of the complement of officers – tropical whites, long white socks and tanned knees were still a particular fetish with her.

'I managed to escape one of his awful dinners last night because my computer crashed and I had to work,' said Nikki, motioning the eager waiter for another bottle of wine. 'In fact yesterday was fucking awful. Do you know some twat kicked my door in because I had pulled out in front of him. I did apologise but he decided to attack me. Yesterday was not good.'

Nikki had adroitly avoided mentioning her counter-attack on the man. She was still ashamed of her loss of control.

'Why is it that we both have more bad days than good? I seem to have a succession of Shitty Job days. You know, the ones where you've put things off for so long that you have to eventually do these things,' said Gillian, as Nikki nodded furiously. 'Then it just seems you're busting a gut for people who don't appreciate you anyway. I mean, do some of these people get out of bed in the morning feeling like fuck and think, Oh, that's all right,

Gillian works for me. I'll kick her arse today and that'll make me feel better? So I end up running round like a blue-arsed fly, usually saving their jobs because they've cocked something up.'

Both women were fully paid-up members of the Life Begins at Lunch Ladies' Society, and its associated organisation, Work Smarter, Not Harder.

'I'm beginning to think we should start the Couldn't Give a Shit Club,' mused Nikki. 'Everything just seems to be such hard bloody work. Even simple things. I just feel so restless all the time, you know, the 'there's got to be more to life than this' scenario. I know Marion gets fed up of me saying it, but it's true. I mean, for Chrissakes, we're eighteen months away from the end of the twentieth century. I'm a year away from the big forty . . .'

'Passed that years ago, sweetie, and it's not pleasant,' said Gillian, pouring more wine, 'been there, seen it, wish I'd bloody done it.'

'I talk to so many people who feel the same – dead-end job, dead-end marriage or relationship. There's something in the air. I think there's going to be a revolt of the masses or something and we'll all suddenly take off on December 31st 1999 and do what we have always wanted to do: start the year 2000 with a bang.'

'So, what would you do? Dump that boring bastard Steve and bugger off to a desert island?'

Nikki smiled sadly, twirling her wine round in the glass and watching the condensation trickle down the outside of it. If only it was that easy.

'I'm sorry, I've touched a nerve.' Gillian reached across and squeezed Nikki's hand.

'No, no, it's just that I seem consumed by this need to *do*, and this fear of doing it. I've always wanted to run my own agency. I know I'm good enough. I know I'm too old to make a fresh start in London. I'm probably fifteen years past it by now with all those flashy suits and designer glasses and convertible BMWs. Young graduates with all the fucking theory in their skulls and flashy jargon. I'd burn out within a fortnight. There's loads of equity in the house, the car's paid for, it's just taking that step of saying: Take half of it, it's yours, you deserve it, step out and do it.

'I know what I have to do is just take the clients, open a little office somewhere, rent a cottage, drive a Peugeot . . . maybe not that. But I could do it, Gillian, I know I could. And then I'd find the perfect partner, someone who understood me and my emotional needs. Someone who was there for me at the end of the day to hold me and cuddle me and say it will be all right, let's take it on together. Someone who believed in me, had faith, appreciated me.

'You know, Gillian, I feel like a box of Persil. I sometimes feel I was put on this fucking planet to wash Steve's shirts and that's it, my role in his life.'

'What you need is a wife,' Gillian tossed out carelessly.

Nikki couldn't help herself, sitting bolt upright on the chair. 'What do you mean by that?' she demanded.

Surprised by the vehemence of Nikki's reaction, Gillian didn't know what to say. Suddenly realising, with a sinking feeling in the pit of her stomach, that she had over-reacted, Nikki tried to soften the mood, brush over it.

'I'm sorry, I'm on edge all the time. I know what you mean, someone who will look after me and care for me like a wife is supposed to do. I don't suppose Steve has much of a bargain in me either. Do you remember that time when he was playing amateur football and had those "lucky" underpants?'

Gillian, still somewhat unnerved by Nikki's mood swing, put an obligatory smile on her face.

'I forgot to wash them the night before a match, remember? So he gave me some stick and I handwashed them and put them under the grill to dry and nearly set the house on fire?'

The mood was now fixed. An uneasy tension had settled on both women and they sat in silence. Nikki wrestled with her conscience – Gillian had not deserved it. Faithful, loyal Gillian, one of the very few people Nikki trusted without question. They would lay their lives down for each other. Gillian had always been there for Nikki over the years, never been judgmental, had not even tried to talk her out of marrying that pig of a husband.

Gillian had never even once said 'I told you so', despite some monumental personal and professional cock-ups in her life. Nikki was right 90 per cent of the time; the other 10 per cent normally constituted massively expensive or hugely emotional mistakes and still Gillian had always stood by her, often helping to extricate her. Surely Gillian would support her this time if she unburdened herself? Nikki took a deep breath.

'Gilly, I think we need another bottle of wine. There's something I need to tell you,' she said to the top of Gillian's slumped head. She signalled again to the waiter, who appeared with a fresh bottle and then hovered. A steely glare swiftly dispatched him.

'Gilly, how long have you known me?'

'About a century, I think, since we met at that conference that time. And you were all stroppy with me because you thought I was treading on your toes and I was after your client.'

'Why do you think in all that time that I married and then put up with Steve? Why do you think that even on our girly holidays and long weekends I've never put out to other men? Why do you think I've never had that middle-age crisis affair you've been pestering me to have for the last five years?'

Gillian was bewildered by the venom in Nikki's voice: she thought it was directed at her. But then she looked at Nikki's face – her eyes were far away, looking into the middle distance, her hand gripping the wine glass tightly. Gillian kept silent.

'Gilly, since I was at school I've been attracted to other girls. It was more than just teenage crushes, I knew it was. I fought it and fought it, good Northern girl, get married, have kids, two cars, en-suite bathroom. For the last few years I've been giving in to those feelings, those needs.'

Gillian stared speechlessly at her.

On a roll, Nikki blurted: 'I've been meeting women on the quiet, all those years, Gilly. Steve was just a cover, a useful cover with access to cheap finance and mortgages. So long as he can service me in his usual, clumsy fashion once a month and I can be draped over his arm like some little trophy wife, he is OK. I don't know, and I don't care, if he is happy, I just know he is OK. Good old, boring, dependable Steve. I don't interfere with his golf, his squash. The man could be having affairs left, right and centre for all I care. He gives me convention. I can indulge my little sordid secret without anyone suspecting. I've never told a soul about this, Gilly, not a soul and now it's beginning to tear me apart . . .' She trailed off as tears began to well.

'How do you meet these women?' said Gillian quietly.

'Escort agencies. Expensive discretion and emotionless detachment assured. I have a dedicated mobile phone which I hide in the car, and I talk to them, sometimes for hours. Then we will meet in a safe place, have a drink and more chat. Sometimes we stay in hotels; sometimes we do it in the car; sometimes I go to their place. Sometimes I feel dirty and ashamed afterwards; sometimes I just feel carefree and fulfilled. If I feel dirty I leave it alone for a while, sometimes weeks, months. It always depends how well I can control myself. I throw myself into my work, I take the car out for a drive, but there are days – and nights – when it just overwhelms me.

'I have to be with a woman, sometimes any woman, and not just on a physical, self-gratification, paying-for-quickie-sex-with-a-stranger basis any more. I know in my heart what I am, what I have always been when I am with one. I want a relationship, a caring and sharing, equal partnership, not just a succession of pretty, although instantly forgettable, faces and bodies. I can pretend all sorts of things. I can hide behind that facade of respectability. I torment myself with scenarios about what would happen if I was caught. Would I lose my job, would it be a nasty divorce, what would my family think?'

'Well,' Gillian started cautiously, 'if you had your own company you wouldn't lose your job. You could do what you liked. Divorce Steve now, get the cash, start up, and steal your clients. Take Marion with you, and to hell with it. There's no stigma any more in being gay, Nikki. It doesn't need to take over your whole life, does it? If you do come out and manage to meet someone for a real relationship, you won't need to feel ashamed, furtive or dirty. You can still be discreet where it matters or where it could cause you problems. Christ, it's not as if you look like a lesbian.'

Nikki smiled inwardly. Gillian probably wouldn't recognise a lesbian if she fell over two naked women shagging.

Gillian was warming to the theme: 'What you said came as a bolt out of the blue, Nikki, but it doesn't make a scrap of difference to me. I just want to see you happy. Would this . . . this being a lesbian, out and proud I think they say . . . make you happy?'

'Oh, yes.' The words came out in a rush of relief. 'It's what I need, where I want to be, Gilly. I don't know how I'm going to meet this woman of my dreams but I just can't stand this any longer.'

'So do it, sweetheart, and whatever I can do to help you achieve it, I will.'

They squeezed hands again as silent tears trickled down Nikki's face.

'In fact . . .' Gillian was again cautious, 'I only know one other lesbian. Perhaps you could talk to her: it may help.'

'Who's that?'

'My goddaughter. Lovely girl, bit flighty, but she's always been up front about being a lesbian. She's the daughter of a girl I went to university with. Bless her, Genevieve wasn't the most talented or the brightest girl. She just dreamt of being married and having children and settling down like her mum had done.

'So she got her degree and immediately married, got pregnant on the honeymoon and that was it. She's got four children and I think at least three grandchildren and is perfectly happy with her lot in life. I'm sure I've told you about her before.'

Nikki smiled. She and Gillian joked that they both had pre-senile dementia: there were times when Gillian phoned to tell her something she had previously recounted; there were times when Gillian was convinced she had told Nikki something and she hadn't. Gillian was the sort of person to leave an identical message on Nikki's email, with Marion, on Nikki's home answerphone, her office hand-held mobile and the mobile fixed in the car.

'I'm sure, bearing in mind what I've just told you, that I would have remembered the fact that your goddaughter was a lesbian if you had told me,' she remarked drily.

'Well, whatever –' Gillian was brisk '– I've not seen her for ages. She moved here from up North about five years ago, something about being sacked from her last job and wanting to fly the nest. Well, I don't know about flying the nest. She had lived away from home for some time but I think the upset over her job made Genevieve despair.'

'How did Genevieve feel about her daughter being gay?'

'I think, bearing in mind some of the escapades that went on, it was just the latest in a long line of revelations. Genevieve is pretty unshockable. For someone who basically went from uni straight into being a housewife she has a great deal of street cred. She takes most things in her stride. Anyway, with three sons I suspect that a gay daughter probably fitted in quite nicely.'

'Yes, I'd like to meet her.' Nikki seemed absent-minded.

Gillian was about to inform Nikki that the two had probably already met through business, as she had put Georgie's name forward as a possible copywriter, but was distracted by the waiter replenishing their glasses. The thought immediately left her head.

'Well, sweetheart, I can feel a party coming on. I'll get the sitting room finished and we'll have an unveiling do,' Gillian announced.

'Sorry, darling, I don't think I can wait that long,' Nikki remarked amiably.

Gillian had never really needed any excuse for a party. Celebrations for a milestone birthday – no one was exactly sure which milestone had been reached as she was fiercely guarded about her age – last year had lasted most of the previous twelve months. Gillian was also constantly remodelling her house, as small as it was, to the despair of the myriad tradesmen locally. A third of the way into any project she would change her mind, imagination fired by a glossy spread in a magazine and usually at the stage a plumber or electrician was required, necessitating a whole rescheduling of diaries for the builder, carpenter or decorator. She had never cottoned on to the fact that most of her frantic messages to the companies involved were ignored. Her sitting room had been the last project and still wasn't finished. Intended to be a seduction palace for a planned succession of

38

delicious young boys, it was missing the vital ingredient of a chaise longue for Gillian to drape herself over. Consequently the 'unveiling' party had now been on the cards for more than two years.

'Do you know that damned upholsterer is avoiding my calls?' Gillian remarked with indignation. 'I think I'll just organise one of my little themed soirées. Barbecue with salad and copious amounts of wine, perhaps fancy dress. I'll get a few people together and then it won't seem so obvious. I've never had a pair of luscious lesbians in my house before.'

'I only want to talk to the girl: I'm not expecting you to fix me a date,' said Nikki with horror.

'Leave it to me, sweetheart,' said Gillian, and Nikki couldn't help the slight flare of panic flutter in her heart. It was going to get out of hand. She just knew it.

Later that night, as she lay in bed next to Steve, she mulled it over. Maybe it was a good idea, to at least be able to talk and express her feelings. Her attachments over the years had been emotionless couplings; just professional jobs for the other women. There had been no room, or requirement, for in-depth conversations about sexuality. She had recognised that look in the eyes of some of the professionals. She was perceived as just a bored, rich housewife having a dabble. The look had annoyed her but, as she handed over the cash with not a little shame, she did not have to explain herself. Doing so would leave her open, vulnerable, exposed, her safe way of life threatened.

Nikki looked over at the snoring hump in the bed. Why did he always take all the goddamned quilt? She sighed heavily, grabbed the corner of the quilt and turned over violently, pulling hard on it as she did so. Cool air on Steve's podgy arse made him whimper in his sleep.

Friday dawned to overcast skies and drizzle. The Saab hated rain. She had a disconcerting twitch to the tail-end in rain. Nikki drove to the office carefully, and Marion noted straight away that Nikki could turn either way on a whim. Thank God it was Friday,

Marion thought. She adored her boss, shared every emotion with her, protected her, defended her, even worried about her when she was at home with her own family. Marion never switched off. She was Nikki's right hand who knew everything about every job and project, solid, reliable, thoroughly dependable. Nikki would be lost at sea without her. Marion knew it and so put up with a huge amount when the moods were vile. Marion never complained but kept an endless stream of coffee on the go, fielding colleagues and phone calls that would make Nikki spiral down even further.

It had been Marion to the rescue – as usual and with great discretion – the day that Nikki had really lost it last summer. An appointment in the morning with a print rep had turned into a boozy lunch, and Nikki had forgotten her mobile. By the time Marion tracked her down to her favourite wine bar, Nikki was so drunk she had actually forgotten who she was.

A taxi was dispatched with the money – Nikki had forgotten her purse as well – to get Nikki home to sleep it off before Steve arrived home. She had feigned a virus illness to excuse her desperate need to sleep the Bollinger and Tia Maria off.

Marion had never mentioned the incident to another soul, but had quietly said to Nikki on the following Monday morning, 'Please don't do that again. I was worried sick. You sometimes drink too much for your own good, you know. You need to get a hold of it, pull it together.'

Nikki had felt like Marion's eighteen-year-old son at that point, as she stood and took her bollocking. But Marion had been absolutely right – as usual. Only three people in the world could talk to Nikki Jones like that: Marion, Gillian and her sister. Her mother, if she was still alive, would have been much more brutal. Eight years on and Nikki still missed her mother every day of her life. There were times when, despite being 39, Nikki just wanted her mum to come and sort the crap out for her like she used to.

Despite being the same age as Marion, Nikki had always felt like her surrogate daughter. It was to Marion she always turned for that same sort of support, and she had behaved herself ever since last summer.

'When's that freelance due in?' asked Nikki, remembering her promise to herself to be nice.

'About now,' said Marion as the knock came on the office door.

The freelance approached and looked nervous. She also looked horribly hungover, as she thrust the copy at Nikki.

'I would like to apologise for the other day. I was a bit harsh on you,' Nikki said disarmingly. 'I shouldn't have yelled you out like that. Are you OK?'

The freelance had sunk gratefully and wearily into the chair and looked about ready to pass out.

'Sorry,' she mumbled, 'I've got a bit of a virus coming on, I think.'

Nikki nodded. The girl clearly had a hangover, but it was a common excuse that Nikki had used on a regular basis, too. She started to skim through the copy. It was good, exactly what was needed. Nikki had a pang of guilt again as she realised that the copy had probably been OK the other day, too. The girl's head had slumped and there was a faint aroma of stale beer drifting across the desk.

'Would you like some coffee?' Nikki asked gently. 'Black? Lots of sugar? Three gallons' worth?'

The freelance looked up and grinned at her as she realised she had been caught out.

My God, Nikki thought, she has lovely teeth. I'm sure she has nice eyes when they're not bloodshot, and I'm damned sure she hasn't washed her hair this morning. Probably couldn't stand the pressure of the water on her head. She's very pretty. Her whole face lights up when she smiles. I bet she's broken a few hearts in her time.

'This is good. Have you got it on disc?' Nikki took the proffered disc. 'Draw up an invoice and I'll push it through for payment as quickly as possible. Look, if you're up to it, I've got another little job for you. Won't take long to brief you. I can let you have a fixed fee of £350 for it. What do you think?'

Georgie fought to keep an impassive face. That would get her landlord off her back. Looks like she's forgiven me. That recommendation from Auntie Gillian is going to pay off for me. This is a huge, respected agency with some seriously classy clients. Perhaps she'll pass my name on to some others if I do another good job for her. She's not so stern and fierce-looking when she's in a good mood. Looks better without her glasses.

'When do you need it?' Georgie said. She went to shake Nikki's hand as a goodbye, then gave the woman a full-wattage smile that reached her bleary eyes.

Nikki stopped her jaw from dropping as the freelance took her hand and shook it.

Actually, Nikki thought, she's more than pretty. Now, if she was working as an escort girl I'd be more than happy to pay double the going rate. Stop it, you horny mare, she's obviously straight as a die.

FOUR

Georgie awoke with a long groan. The phone was ringing, her head was spinning and her mouth felt like the bottom of a parrot's cage.

'My God, someone's swapped tongues with me in the night . . .' she mumbled, her hand grabbing for the phone to stop the incessant ring.

On hearing the voice on the other end she suppressed another groan. Why was Auntie Gillian so shrill? And so fucking cheerful?

'Morning, darling. Well, it's getting close to afternoon. How are you? What are you up to these days? Why don't you ever ring your Auntie Gillian?'

Probably because you ask too many fucking questions when I have a hangover, Georgie thought ungraciously. Is it really nearly afternoon?

'Sorry, Auntie, I'm not quite with it yet,' said Georgie, sitting up and then wishing she hadn't.

'Georgina, do you by any chance have a hangover?'

'I've had a hangover most of my adult life, Auntie Gillian.'

'Hmm. Can't really tell you off, can I? It would be like the pot calling the kettle black. You know I like growing old disgracefully. Talking of which, I've rung you to ask if you would like to come to a little gathering I'm having soon.'

'Are you going to end up snogging some youth on the settee as usual?'

'I do hope so. Do you know any?'

'Auntie, you're on the verge of seducing paperboys these days. You know I don't mix in the sort of circles where gorgeous male models are available. Well, not heterosexual ones anyway.' Gillian went quiet. Georgie knew something was coming.

'Look, I don't know if you can help or not,' Gillian started cautiously, 'but there is a very dear friend of mine who announced something rather surprising the other day. She's married – I'm sure I've mentioned her to you before – but apparently she has always felt like a lesbian and she has been doing whatever it is you lesbians do on a regular basis for some years now. She's at a bit of a crossroads, you know, the Got to Do Something for the Millennium thing, and as you're the only lesbian I know I thought you might help her by having a chat about that sort of thing.' The final sentence came out in a flurry and Georgie was hard pressed to keep up.

'That sort of thing, Auntie?'

'You know, how she goes about it.'

'It?'

'Georgina, you're not making this easy. She wants to pack up her marriage. Good thing too because he's an absolute prick. Do you know he had the audacity to make a pass at me once? I just thought that, if you two got together and had a chat about life as a lesbian, then she might be a bit clearer on where she goes from here.'

'Auntie, you make it sound as if I'm a world expert on female homosexuality. I'm not. I just go out and do it . . .'

She was interrupted as Gillian got flustered and embarrassed.

'Quite, quite. Whatever it is that people like you get up to, I think it might just help her resolve some issues in her mind. She's getting herself in a bit of a state about the whole thing, but I know her. This is what she wants to do. I think she would appreciate an understanding friend. I can only help her so far, you know.'

Georgie's heart sank. Now she was expected to be some sort of gay agony aunt to some married bi-curious tart who wanted to have a dabble to see if she liked it or not. And if it was one of Gillian's friends she would have to tread carefully. God, she hated married women, more trouble than they were worth. She became brusque.

'All right, Auntie Gillian, I'll try and help if I can. But I've come across women like this before, you know, and it usually ends in tears. Either they declare undying love and want to turn their backs on their family and you end up with an enraged husband on your doorstep, or they ask you if their husband can join in.'

The final sentence was too much for Gillian to bear as visual imagery flashed across her brain. Having once narrowly avoided such a scenario after a drunken binge, she was not keen to even remember the incident.

'A week on Saturday then,' Gillian said, equally brusque. 'Bring a bottle. There'll be snacks, a bit of music, usual thing, late finish. You can crash down on the floor if needs be.'

Georgie was well aware that she would be smashed that night. When wasn't she?

Christ, holding the hand of a married woman – what was she getting into? She would have a quick chat and hit the JD: that would put her off. It had been a while since she had seen Auntie Gillian. It would be nice to see the game old bird again. Georgie had a pang of guilt as she fumbled the receiver down. She realised she hadn't spoken to her mother in over a week. She knew those two were old friends from college days and some of the stories her mother had recounted about Gillian were outrageous. She might be eccentric – she would definitely grow into a dotty old woman – but Auntie Gillian was great fun. Perhaps the evening wouldn't be so bad after all.

But a married woman? One of Gillian's dearest friends?

Georgie sank back into the pillows. She had only once made the mistake of stepping over her own imposed boundary and taking on a married woman, and it was one with a child. It had all ended rather swiftly, if messily. But the girl was a nursing sister and Georgie had a big thing about uniforms. She had a private fantasy – so far not indulged – of a policewoman with handcuffs and a large truncheon.

Georgie settled back into the pillows as her head slowly stopped banging. It had only been two years ago, her fling. It had been a diversion for a few weeks, and at a time when she had a lucrative magazine contract with plenty of spare dosh.

It had been a particularly raunchy, and massively expensive, weekend spent in a hotel complete with a Jacuzzi you could swim in, endless champagne, a massive bed with seductive lighting, mirrors and a draped ceiling. It was the most expensive shag of Georgie's life to date.

Jackie had been pretty in a plump sort of way and she did have enormous breasts. Perhaps breast-feeding had its merits. But they were so big they were insensitive. Childbirth had resulted in an unfortunate positioning of certain internal stitches which frequently led to her discomfort, and her stretchmarks gave her a complex.

Despite this, Georgie could still remember Jackie with not a little fondness.

She was most fond of that second afternoon at the hotel, when Jackie had dressed up in her uniform complete with stockings. Georgie had had no idea she had brought it with her. Jackie had suggested an afternoon nap and Georgie dutifully trotted off to bed, thinking genuinely that she could sleep off the several bottles of beer she had tanked at lunchtime.

Instead she was nudged awake to discover Jackie bending over her, with a look of concern and a pert little white cotton hat perched on top of her hair.

Fuzzily, Georgie recognised a nurse and honestly thought, A: I've had a heart attack/stroke and am in hospital and I promise I'll never overindulge again, rapidly followed by B: I've died and gone to heaven.

Jackie told her to lie still and do as she was told if she knew what was good for her. So Georgie did. Well, she tried, but as Jackie slowly pulled back the duvet and ran her tongue from the tip of one nipple, down Georgie's side, across her stomach and to the top of her clit she couldn't help her hips moving.

Her own body, Georgie had always felt, was one of the most sensual natural wonders of the civilised world. Nothing special to look at, but every single nerve ending seemed attached to her clit. Apart from ears and feet, any naked woman, doing anything, could provoke a reaction, with erogenous zones in the most unlikely and uncharted territories. Georgie's top lip was a mirror of her clit, with both of them swelling and twitching at the same time.

For women with experience, it was always a dead giveaway when having a reasonably impartial or exploratory conversation with her. All they had to do to gauge response was to look at Georgie's top lip to know if she was secretly entertaining naughty thoughts. If Georgie dribbled her drink, she was close to orgasm. And Georgie didn't waste alcohol freely.

So, anyway, there she was that day, with Jackie, with a cold and damp October afternoon outside and a raging heat indoors, cocooned in the drapes of the bed, while a fully qualified and authentic nursing sister administered to her every need. Jackie had nuzzled her for a long time while Georgie silently screamed for her to lick her properly, to get inside her, to lower herself on that waiting tongue.

Jackie ran her fingers – no nails because she was a nurse – down the backs of Georgie's thighs as her legs involuntarily raised, then suddenly she plunged inside her, massaging the clit with her thumb; then her mouth was on Georgie's, her other hand spreading her wide.

She moved to straddle Georgie, still inside her with at least three fingers, moving tantalisingly slowly then giving her a quick burst against the G-spot as she just as slowly unzipped her uniform to waist level.

Those fabulous breasts strained against the material and Georgie would have happily watched them alone if Jackie had not hoicked up her skirt on either side. Exposed were those breasts, creamy white thighs against lacy black hold-ups, and an overall package of a horny nurse with fingers deep inside her.

Georgie could hardly stand it. Then to her surprise Jackie withdrew and spun round, legs either side of Georgie's head, and just hovered, then quickly sank her head down. Georgie reached up and pushed the uniform back to see the black lace thong. By now Jackie was so aroused that she had swollen heavily round both sides of the thin material. Georgie hooked it to one side, grabbed Jackie's thighs and pulled her down towards her hungry mouth. She was so swollen that Georgie couldn't fit all of her in her mouth. She was so wet that she was slippery, sliding away from Georgie's tongue.

Both were pulling each other as wide apart as possible, darting tongues in, then burying them deep, flicking clits, sucking on lips and tugging with teeth. French kissing and chewing on clits, spreading apart with both hands and then closing to take the whole cunt at once. Running tongues up and down the whole length of the cunt, down or up to the arseholes and teasing gently, a mirror of each other, both to the same rhythm.

Georgie could reach, with long arms, to not only spread Jackie's cunt apart but also to stretch her arsehole, and tease it with a finger lubricated by her flood of juices. Georgie cautiously and slowly entered it with the tip of a finger. Jackie jiggled her hips and, from way down and reverberating against Georgie's cunt, came a deep moan.

With her tongue firmly clamped on her clit, Georgie raised her slightly and slipped two fingers inside her vagina, moving all her fingers to the same rhythm. The finger in her arse getting deeper and easier and wetter as she opened up, her hips started to move frantically.

Jackie was desperately trying to concentrate on what she was doing but Georgie knew from her breathing that she was close. Georgie quickened the rhythm, got deeper and deeper inside both her holes, harder and harder, chewing on her clit and increasing the pressure, moving her head quicker and quicker to the same rhythm, moving from side to side as well as up and down. Jackie raised her head to take an intake of breath and Georgie, relentless, knew she was gritting her teeth against her orgasm but she couldn't stop it. She started to buck wildly against Georgie, who held on hard and carried on fucking her hard, faster and faster, riding it out with her, slowing as she started to come down from the peak, as she gasped great lungfuls of air. The bucking became a jerking and then a series of shudders. She sank on to Georgie's face, her thighs trembling with an occasional jerk, and there was an enormous, heavy and long sigh.

Georgie had been so busy with what she was doing that she had put her own orgasm on hold but she could feel that she was gushing, as wide open and ready as she had ever been, and that it wouldn't take long to finish her off.

So Jackie did, hard and fast with four fingers deep inside. The second that she had stopped trembling she was off Georgie and kneeling between her legs, forcing her to bend her knees and bring her legs back, so she could reach Georgie's G-spot.

Georgie started to climb, breath short and ragged. Jackie quickly withdrew her hand, then pressed her fingers inside Georgie's cunt and up her arse, ramming hard. She found Georgie's mouth with hers, deep tonguing, nipping the tongue with the edges of her teeth, pushing her head further into the pillow with her own as Georgie started to arch, legs over Jackie's shoulders, beginning to jerk against those uniformed breasts as she continued to climb.

Georgie didn't want to stop climbing. The feeling kept rising. With a handful of Jackie's hair entwined round her fingers, she began to pull as she neared the top. Jackie's cap fell off, her hair began to tumble, and still Georgie was going up and up. She thought she would explode; that she couldn't take any more pleasure than she already was. Still Jackie was hammering hard, and she was now moaning with desire, and Georgie was vaguely aware that Jackie was going to come herself. She wanted to try to plateau until she caught up, so that they could come together, and then she thought, Fuck it, and sure enough it happened. Together and without missing a beat, both plunging against each other and riding the rhythm together and shouting out together and Jackie's sweat dripping on her face and making their bodies stick together, they slipped and slid while they bucked and rolled and leapt off the top of the mountain as one.

Georgie was now slipping off her own mountain. The memory of that glorious, sex-laden weekend had taken her over, completely absorbed her. She lay alone in her bed with eyes closed,

49

hangover, work and most of the western hemisphere forgotten. As her own fingers burrowed deep inside herself and massaged her clit, her hips began to buck and she came, a heavy and loud gasp tearing from her at the moment of release.

She lay, shivering and breathing heavily, fingers still inside herself as she slowly began to come back down.

The phone rang.

Guilty at having wasted a whole morning, Georgie answered it, still with the vestiges of orgasm cloaking her.

'Georgie? Nikki. Nikki Jones at BFCP. How are you? Recovered from the other day yet?'

'I'm just fine, thank you.' Georgie's voice was still thick as she desperately tried to breathe normally.

'I'm going to be a pain, I'm afraid. The client's pulled the meeting forward. Is there any chance you can let me have the job this afternoon?'

Shit. Bollocks. 'What time?'

Five minutes later Georgie was in the shower; ten minutes later, her hair dripping, she was slouched over the computer, face screwed in concentration as she tried to get to grips with the bullet points for a digital presentation. Her fingers were obstinate, her brain cells stubborn. She had two hours to complete the job and Nikki Jones had promised a cheque would be waiting for her.

Damn, damn, why did she drink so much Bud last night? How come she came back alone? When was she going to get laid next? Why did wanking always make her horny for three days? Concentrate, concentrate.

Almost two hours later the final sheet appeared from the printer. While it had been printing she had rushed to save her bad-hair day and make herself look half-presentable. She still felt like shit, but she didn't look like shit. It would have to do.

Georgie attempted to breeze into Nikki's office, but one look at Nikki's thunderous face told her that perhaps silence was the best policy.

Nikki was on the phone. Marion appeared silently at Georgie's elbow with a cup of coffee and motioned her to sit down.

'No, I can't, I've got to work late. The pitch has resurfaced and we have to get it ready for the morning. No, Steve, I can't. You'll just have to take that busty, leggy blonde bitch again . . . Steve, I'm telling you there's no way I can get away before about eight . . . Steve . . .'

Nikki glared at the receiver. He had hung up in a fury of childish pique. She sat quietly, unaware that Georgie was watching her. Closely. Intrigued.

'Sorry, domestic dispute,' Nikki finally said when she had regained her calm. 'Look, I really appreciate you doing this at such short notice.'

Nikki reached into her tray and withdrew the cheque. Absently, she handed it over. Georgie went to take it and their fingers touched. The cheque hovered between them.

Nikki looked up. There was such a pained look of sadness on her face that Georgie suddenly had the ludicrous urge to dash round the desk and hug her. Instead, she took the cheque and held out the disc and hard copy. Nikki didn't move, so Georgie placed the stuff on her desk instead.

'I've done my best with it,' she faltered. 'I know you said it just needed a bit of tarting up but, to be honest, the basic material wasn't very good to start with and there were a few terms I didn't quite understand.'

'I'm sure it will be fine.' Nikki was still not quite with her, gazing beyond Georgie, probably beyond the room. She didn't even hear Georgie thank her for the money and say goodbye; didn't see her leave the room.

Nikki Jones was in a world of her own.

Steve had been out until very late the night before. Nikki had desperately hoped, as the hours ticked by, that he would come home with lipstick on his collar. She could confront him and throw him out. Instead, he fell out of a taxi that had four giggling grown-up men packed inside, staggered into the house and lurched up to bed without so much as a hello.

So much for him having a rampant affair, Nikki had thought, crushed with disappointment. Just when was Steve going to have his mid-life crisis and fuck off? Struggling with his hangover that morning he had tried to tell her about the Round Table dinner, but she had no interest in him.

Flat, she had driven to work. Checking her illicit mobile for messages, she discovered the offer of a date that night if she was free.

Hurriedly calling back, she fixed the date for 8 p.m. and bounced into the office, to be told by Marion that the pitch was back on and all three agencies were presenting the next day. She knew she was pushing it to have the work completed to leave enough time for the half-hour drive to the pub, where she had arranged to meet the girl. She would have to cancel. She left it until the afternoon to see how the design team had progressed with the visuals, but it was now obvious that it was going to be a very late evening.

Steve's pathetic whining just now about her letting him down was almost the final straw.

My first chance for sex in weeks and this happens, she thought bitterly, as her extension rang.

Marion put Gillian straight through, one of the few calls allowed that day.

'All arranged,' said Gillian brightly.

Why was she so shrill? Nikki was feeling particularly intolerant. 'What is?' she snapped.

'The little soirée, you know, chance for you to talk to my goddaughter. Week on Saturday, my place, bring a bottle.'

Nikki felt contrite.

'Sorry I snapped. Having a bad day. Sounds great, I'll be there,' she said.

Half an hour later her day deteriorated even further. She had not had time to check Georgie's copy: she had simply had Marion photocopy it for the client. The client was not impressed.

'This doesn't make sense,' he groused, 'and it's not in the right order. And there's at least two text sheets missing. I was expecting something a little bit more professional from you people. Isn't that what I'm paying this vast amount of money for?'

Nikki rubbed the bridge of her nose.

'With respect . . .' she began.

'Don't give that "with respect" stuff either. It usually means there's no respect whatsoever. I've used that line myself. I'm not impressed with the visual imagery, either. My logo doesn't come out as prominently as I instructed, and the charts you've drawn up are inaccurate.

'In short, what you've done is crap. I'm not paying you for it, and I think I'd be better off asking someone else to do it. You advertise all these fancy services that you charge the earth for. I'd have thought my job would have been quite straightforward.'

His face was set, his chubby jowls rippling slightly as he clamped his teeth together in a show of macho bullshit.

Nikki sighed. The job was only worth about £500 profit if they completed it to his satisfaction, and so far costs against the job were reasonable and could be absorbed on something else. She made a mental note to ask that freelance woman for a refund. She also made a mental note to kick ass in the design studio.

Her final mental note was to herself. She had not checked the job — it had been a last-minute rush, as usual to meet the client's whim — and she should have known better as project manager. If things can go wrong, they will go wrong and the buck stopped with her.

'I'm sorry you feel that way —' her voice was icy '— you are the client and we appear to have let you down badly. I know you are on a tight deadline for the presentation for your sales conference and it would take time to source another agency and brief them. How about we start from scratch and I'll knock twenty per cent off the quote?'

Nikki sat tight, watching the man scowl and mentally squirm as he worked out the final invoice in his head. She knew she had him against the ropes but he would still have to come out of this with his pathetic client dignity intact.

'Twenty-five per cent discount, but it had better be shit hot,' he finally said.

Impassive, she nodded, but inside she was boiling. That was the profit virtually down the tubes and it was going to be a ball-acher to sort out, but at least she had saved the agency's reputation.

When she came out of the meeting she asked Marion to call Georgie. Georgie's answerphone kicked in, to her annoyance. She left a curt message about the client rejecting the work and that she expected either a refund or a partial refund coupled with a proper rework. An internal call to the studio confirmed that the pitch visuals would not be completed much before 7 p.m.

By now it was 5.30 and she knew she would have to cancel her date for sure.

Georgie, meanwhile, had heard the phone ring, had listened to Nikki's message. At the first sound of Nikki's voice she had almost weakened her resolve to stay away from the whole world for at least 24 hours. Then, as the message progressed, she heaved a sigh of relief. There was no way that she wanted to speak to an angry agency trollop, particularly when she had worked her tits off to an earlier deadline, and with a hangover and a throbbing clit.

Out loud, and with a pensive salute to the phone with her bottle of Bud, Georgie shouted as Nikki rang off: 'Bollocks. I don't need your sort of shit. I don't need you. Go to hell.'

FIVE

Nikki was happy. Seriously happy. Her pitch had gone well, Steve had behaved himself the previous night and not given her any hassle and her date had been rearranged for that night. The Saab was flying, eating up the miles on the motorway with no discernible effort as she hurtled to her appointment. Keeping her wits about her she frequently checked mirrors and slip roads for the boys in blue. Bastards. She had once lost her licence for speeding, resulting in three months of feeling like her legs had been chopped off. Having to rely on lifts. Nikki was one of the world's worst, grumpiest, critical passengers. Steve hated driving her anywhere: they inevitably argued about his driving prowess – or lack of it. She hated not being in control. Flying was a necessary evil to Nikki. Long-haul flights consisted of Nikki getting half-pissed in the bar beforehand, totally smashed on the plane, sleeping it off to sober up and starting all over again. It was the only way to assuage her fear that her life was in someone else's hands. She had been fortunate not to be manacled to her seat by the crew – but then 90 per cent of the time she was a harmless, happy drunk.

Flying back once from an exhibition in Chicago, Nikki had started talking to the girl next to her, who fortunately had a similar philosophy on how to pass the flight and was just as drunk and bored. The red-eye flight was halfway through when Nikki, emboldened by Tia Maria and aware that almost everyone else was asleep, made her pass. The other girl, equally brave, took the pass graciously.

Five minutes later they were squeezed into the toilet cubicle, giggling like schoolgirls and frantically shushing each other to be quiet. Both were too pissed to make a serious attempt at full sex and the cubicle was too tight for comfort. Nikki, having spotted the girl's large breasts, had failed to recognise until she stood up that the girl was equally large everywhere else. As contorted as she got, Nikki just couldn't manage to manoeuvre herself into a position that would be either comfortable or satisfying to either party.

By this point, hot and sweaty, Nikki suggested that they snog instead, particularly as the combined effects of 38,000 feet, standing up and the realisation that the Tia Maria was possibly about to regurgitate became obvious.

The girl couldn't snog. If there was one thing that frustrated the hell out of Nikki it was a lousy snog. In her opinion, a lousy snog usually meant lousy sex.

Tumbling out of the cubicle, they came face to face with a stewardess who had become only too well aware that something was going on and was annoyed at having had her break disrupted. The two sat down, red-faced with embarrassment, swapped business cards and passed out.

It had been, so far, Nikki's only opportunity to join the Mile High Club and she had failed miserably. She had also made herself very ill with the booze. A copious amount of coffee at the airport had failed to have any effect. Lurching off the courtesy bus she had found her car and fallen asleep.

She had never called the girl. Equally, the girl had never called her.

Nikki spotted the patrol car some way ahead and slowed down gently to a reasonable cruising speed. She set the cruise control and coasted for ten miles.

It always seemed to be the way, she mused. She had always made the running, paid for sex or not. The illicit – if somewhat routine now – thrill of the sex, without any emotional involvement, was begining to pale. She realised with a jolt that in fact she seemed to have missed out on an awful lot sexually and emotionally.

Perhaps that will change tonight, she thought to herself. Paula seemed reasonably competent, if a little coolly detached. Goddamnit, as Nikki was paying her, then perhaps she should be bolder with her requests. She was quite a regular with Paula and the girl had made a reasonable amount of money out of her so far. She often had the disconcerting feeling that Paula was a technical performer, the whole act seemed so perfunctory and emotionless. But then, she was nothing more than a hooker, however kindly you wanted to look at it. And Nikki was no more than just one of Paula's paying johns. Or did they have another name for female clients?

The thought occupied a portion of her brain for the rest of the afternoon as she mechanically went through her new business presentation and drove home. Steve was out, a scrawled note on the worktop.

Nikki ran a hot, deep, perfumed bath, lit some candles and just soaked with her glass of Chardonnay. She made a special effort tonight: full make-up, faded denim shirt and Levi's because she knew Paula had admired them before. If there was one feature she knew turned men and women on, it was her rear. In skin-tight Levi's it was particularly horny. Her eyes were also a feature, hugely expressive, and as Nikki was one of the world's biggest flirts she used them to full advantage.

By now, she was so happy and so horny she was almost whistling.

Paula was waiting for her at the pub, with another girl, Diane. She was blunt and businesslike.

'Diane's new to this. I thought it about time you had a change of scenery,' Paula started before Nikki could even sit down. 'Diane, this is Sue. Sue is one of my regular customers so treat her nicely, won't you?'

With a wink, Paula drained her Coke and disappeared. Nikki was not disappointed by the sudden change of events. Diane was more than shaggable. But extremely nervous. Nikki was crucially aware of her thoughts that afternoon. It looked as though she would, once again, have to dominate proceedings.

'When she says I'm new, I'm really new. I mean, I haven't done this before . . .'

Oh, Christ. A complete novice.

'Well, I've had sex with women before. I just haven't done this escort lark before,' Diane added.

Well, perhaps not a complete novice. But she can't be more than twenty.

'What normally happens,' Nikki started gently, 'is that we have a couple of drinks and a bit of a chat and then we go upstairs. I have a room booked.'

The two drinks turned into four as Diane was clearly getting more nervous as the evening wore on. Nikki had almost resigned herself to pouring the girl into a taxi and going home alone when the girl found her second wind.

'Shall we go upstairs, then?'

The room was clean and functional, nothing more. Nikki had never had a problem with the gay-friendly landlord. Once or twice he had made a risqué comment and she had a sneaking suspicion that video cameras were installed behind the mirror. There were probably pirate copies of home porno movies featuring her floating all around the country, but Nikki was beyond caring.

Slightly taller than Diane, Nikki bent and kissed her neck from behind with the lightest of touches, gently stroking hair out of the way. She lightly ran her tongue up and down Diane's neck and behind her ear, fingers almost imperceptibly stroking the insides of her forearms. Then she cupped both of Diane's breasts in her hands and squeezed gently, moving them round in a slow, circular motion. Diane arched her neck and Nikki applied more pressure with her tongue, then flicked it around her ear. She stroked the top of her back just inside the T-shirt then turned her round.

The kiss started slowly, with hardly any pressure, those wonderfully soft and sensuous lips pressed against each other. The tip of Diane's tongue grazed Nikki's teeth; her tongue flicked across

Nikki's top lip and she slowly kissed each corner of her mouth. Then Diane's tongue parted Nikki's lips again and she embraced her tightly, wrapping her arms round Nikki as if never to let go, stroking Nikki's back, squeezing her arse, moving her hips against her.

She pushed Nikki away slightly and took her hand. Her eyes never left Nikki's as she led her to the bed and, as Nikki sat, her eyes followed her down. Nikki leant back and watched as Diane lifted her T-shirt over her head and released a pair of quite magnificent breasts. Irrationally, Nikki wondered if Diane would be disappointed by hers.

Still with their eyes locked, Diane shimmied out of her combats and lay down beside her. Nikki couldn't tear her eyes away: Diane's brown eyes were like a magnet.

Like a cat, Nikki moved quickly until she was astride Diane, her back arched, her legs stretched, her arms either side of the girl, bending her head to kiss her. Their breasts brushing against each other.

Nikki began to suckle, wrapping Diane's long hair around her fingers. She increased the pressure of her lips, teasing and sucking with only the barest hint of a nip of her teeth on a nipple.

While her lips concentrated on one breast, she moved her hand to the other, stroking and caressing across the top of the nipple and then taking the whole breast in her hand, squeezing tight, pulling hard on the nipple until Diane gasped with the mixed feelings of pleasure and pain. Then she reversed and sucked on the other breast while coaxing the other nipple erect with her fingers.

'Undress for me,' Diane said quietly.

Nikki stood and was about to peel off her clothes when Diane lay back against the pillow, parted her legs and put her hand down below. She smiled lazily and Nikki realised she had a lop-sided smile, revealing large white teeth, and then her tongue tip appeared as her hand began a rhythmic motion and her hips moved with it. Nikki looked deep into her eyes, which were now smoky with desire and heavy lidded.

Then Nikki was next to her, naked, and she rolled over on to her side, propped herself on her elbow, slid her thigh over Diane's and began to kiss her.

Stroking Diane's breast, the kiss grew deeper and her tongue more urgent. Her hand began to stroke Diane's side and move downward, and Nikki realised her hips were moving, too, in the same rhythm. Her back was arching and she was yearning for something, anything, to release the pressure that was building up in the pit of her stomach. Still kissing and probing with her tongue, Nikki moved her hand to the inside of Diane's thigh and softly stroked her, lightly scraping her nails along the outside, and then brushing her cunt as if by accident.

Then quickly she moved, still with her mouth on Diane's, so she was on top of her, one thigh between Diane's, breasts against breasts. She was breathing heavily now as she manoeuvred herself into position. Her hip bone pressed against Diane's clitoris. The top of her thigh was against a wet cunt as she began to move against the girl, so that Diane could feel the wetness of Nikki's cunt against her thigh as Nikki rubbed against her. Nikki's breasts flattened against Diane's; her mouth became more insistent as her hips moved faster and deeper; her arms stiffened as her back arched and her low moan reverberated in Diane's mouth, and then she raised her head, her eyes closed and she shuddered against her. Nikki let the feeling take her over, completely unaware that the girl underneath her had been taken by surprise.

She rolled over on to her back, arm draped over her eyes.

'That was good, thank you,' Nikki said.

Diane raised an eyebrow. Nikki still hadn't moved. She waited expectantly for the next round. It didn't appear. Diane realised with a sinking heart that Nikki's breathing had slowed and she had fallen asleep. She looked at her watch. Nikki had paid her for three hours and, taking into account the extra drinks, Nikki still had a half-hour credit. Diane was now in a quandary. Should she wake the woman for the extra half-hour or let her sleep? When Nikki whimpered and turned on her side, curling up into a ball, Diane had her answer. She dressed silently and left.

Nikki awoke with a start about two hours later, cold and shivering, and very much alone. She checked the time and began concocting her story for Steve. A furious rally-style drive, cutting across country to avoid the main routes and the police breathalyser kits, got her home in record time. She needn't have worried – Steve arrived home twenty minutes later, by which point his wife was fast asleep.

At the office the next day Nikki was bright and cheerful. Marion had a message for her.

'Georgie Rivers called. She has apologised for the copy she submitted and is happy to consider a rewrite and knock fifty pounds off. Shall I tell her that's OK?'

'Yeah, yeah, whatever. Ring her back and tell her I want it on my desk by 4 p.m. Make the little bugger work for her money,' said Nikki, taking a slug of coffee and disappearing into her room.

Marion rang Georgie back, leaving the instructions on the answerphone. At the other end Georgie sighed as she listened. She booted her computer up and got to work.

For once in a long time she was hangover-free on a Friday morning. She had wisely stopped after three bottles of beer, had something to eat and gone to bed early. She knew she hadn't made the best of Nikki's job and was determined to do it properly this time. Losing track of time, she was thoroughly engrossed in the work when the phone rang again. The answerphone kicked in.

'Hi, look, it's Nikki Jones. I hope you haven't started the rewrite yet. I've had a look at the copy myself. It didn't actually need that much work doing on it, all things considered. Keep £300 of the £350 and we'll call it quits . . .'

Georgie snatched up the receiver.

'Yes, I have started the rewrite. In fact I've spent all morning on it,' she snarled at Nikki.

Nikki was cool.

'I am sure, knowing the client as I do, that I'm in a better position to judge whether the work I have done with your original copy is more suitable or not.'

'I got instructions from your PA at five past nine and got

61

straight on it. Are you seriously telling me that I have just wasted four hours of my time and I'm down fifty quid as well?'

Nikki was icy now. She had always loathed snotty suppliers.

'If you'd done the job right in the first place instead of attempting to do it with a hangover – which seems to be a frequent occurrence from what I've noticed already – then you wouldn't be in this position and I wouldn't have looked such an idiot in front of my client.'

Georgie was almost speechless with rage.

'You gave me a matter of hours to do that job and the stuff you gave me was crap in the first place. If you hadn't been so busy sorting out your personal problems when I brought it in, you would have heard me tell you that I had difficulty understanding some of the terminology and that I had done the best of a bad job.'

Nikki hated suppliers answering back. Marion, in the next office, had already heard her raise her voice and, magically, if silently, appeared with coffee.

'As I recall –' Nikki's glasses were flung across the desk as she stood '– I was good enough to have a cheque waiting for you to take into account the deadline being pulled forward. And I did hear what you said when you came in. I never let my personal life interfere with my work and I resent some drunken freelance insinuating that I am unprofessional.'

'Drunk? Drunk? Are you calling me a drunk?'

'Every time I have seen you you've had a hangover. Pretty clear to me, so it's probably just as well that I won't be using you again, if this is your attitude.'

'I'm not the one with the attitude problem. You think because you sit in some fancy office you can push people like me around.'

Both women's voices had amplified. Nikki was gripping her coffee cup tight. Georgie pounded her fist on her desk. Both phones slammed down simultaneously.

'Drunk?' Georgie screamed at her computer.

'Unprofessional?' Nikki shouted at Marion.

'I'm sure she didn't quite mean that,' said Marion soothingly. She didn't want Nikki to spoil the rest of her day, and everyone else's, with a tantrum. It was Friday, after all. She pitied Steve: his weekend would probably be ruined if Nikki festered on this one.

Nikki sat down heavily, her coffee spilt on to her pad.

'Goddamned cheek of the woman. She does a lousy job, I get my arse kicked, I rescue the work and what happens? She gives me a mouthful of abuse. Get accounts to issue her an invoice for that fifty pounds for wasting my time.'

'Why don't you just leave it alone? You did tell her you wouldn't use her again,' suggested Marion carefully.

Nikki rubbed her forehead. Marion was right. The agency was one of the biggest in the town and Georgie would never get work out of it again. Plus, Nikki knew enough people in the industry to ensure, if she wanted, that Georgie bloody Rivers would be hard pressed to get work from the other big agencies locally. It had been a chickenshit job to start with and now Nikki wanted it out of the way. Was it worth boosting her blood pressure? She shouldn't have made that remark about Georgie's hangovers. God knows she'd had enough in her own time. And on work time. It was unfair to have judged like that.

Nikki scowled. But then she shouldn't have been called unprofessional. OK, Georgie didn't actually say that. And it was true, as far as Nikki recalled, that the phone call with Steve at the time Georgie had walked in had pissed her off. It wasn't fair to take it out on the girl when, after all, what had been uppermost in Nikki's mind had been having to cancel her date, and Steve being such an arsehole. As usual.

Nikki's scowl grew deeper. As she turned it over in her mind she realised that she had gone over the top. Again. It was happening far too often. Nikki had always been volatile. She had been a temperamental baby, even. But the past few weeks had highlighted just how her mood swings were getting more frequent, and more negative. What was wrong with her? Perhaps she was going through the menopause. Perhaps, instead, it was the loveless, lousy marriage, the furtive tumblings with the hookers, the pressure of her job with precious little praise or thanks, the relentless grind of long days at work with no relief in the evenings or weekends. Nikki suddenly realised she had hardly anything to look forward to; no goals in her own mind to try to aim for. Enormous decisions loomed large in her mind; awesome steps she would have to take to pull herself out of this dull rut.

'You've got to do something, Jones, before life passes you by.'

Marion realised, with Nikki talking to herself, that her boss was now buggered for the afternoon. Marion knew it wasn't the row on the phone that had unbalanced her: that Nikki was wrestling with much larger concerns – real or imagined. As far as Marion could see, it had been six of one and half a dozen of the other with the freelance. They both seemed such similar, sparky characters that both would now dig their heels in with stubborn pride.

On the odd occasions she had met or spoken to Georgie, Marion sensed that Nikki had met her equal. All Nikki had over Georgie was her power to grant work. Now Nikki would hold back out of misplaced spite. Georgie would probably be too proud to weaken and ask for more work.

Georgie was indeed feeling proud and stubborn. She had railed at her computer for more than ten minutes, pacing restlessly, eyes darting to the phone as she resisted the urge to pick it up and tell that trollop exactly what she thought. She was also desperately hoping the phone would ring with the Bitch Queen on the other end issuing a grovelling apology. Fat chance. The cow was probably scoffing some expensive lunch somewhere on someone else's fancy credit card, getting herself ready for the weekend. Hubby was probably whisking her off somewhere in a posh car where they would indulge in champagne and Jacuzzis, lobster and steak. I've probably been completely forgotten by now. I'm nothing more than an irritating pimple on her arse.

By now Georgie was also scowling. She rubbed the bridge of her nose, fuelled by frustration and fatigue. There was no more work on the immediate horizon and she had already issued cheques equal to, or probably above, the amount received from the agency. At least she now had her car taxed and the landlord was leaving her alone. Until next month.

Why can't I find someone like Nikki Jones, she thought. Someone with dosh, designer clothes. I bet she has a flash car and a *Homes and Gardens* cover house. Someone with flashing blue eyes and dimples. As temperamental as she is, at least she has a personality. She's strong, too. I suppose you have to be in the position she's in. I've only seen her smile once or twice. She's probably under enormous pressure to deliver the goods. Her face changes completely when she smiles: she doesn't look so intimidating and fearsome. I wonder how old she is? I know she's married, judging from the rings on her finger. Nice hands, long fingers.

'What the hell are you doing, Rivers?' she said aloud and broke her reverie. My God, she was on the verge of entertaining a bloody fantasy about the woman. Goddamned heterosexual, power-shoulders-wearing, married bloody agency suit trollop in high heels.

Completely out of the blue an image flashed in her head of Nikki Jones wearing nothing but high heels and stockings. When they had stood together Nikki had been a clear four inches above her.

Jesus Christ, now you're getting carried away. Just because she's tall doesn't mean she has long, lovely, supple legs and a tight arse. Christ, what if she does? She must have. I'll bet she's a real bloody handful. I pity the poor fucker she's married to. I bet she makes his life hell. But screwing that is probably worth it. What am I thinking about?

Georgie's temper had subsided. She was actually smiling to herself. Things must be bad if she had to resort to fantasies about a straight woman who had just chewed her out.

Christ, there I go again, thought Georgie as an image of Nikki's head between her legs, mouth chewing and sucking, suddenly popped up out of nowhere. Georgie almost scurried into the kitchen, not knowing whether to drink the chilled beer or pour it over her head. She decided to drink it. As the Bud slipped down her throat she became almost wistful. Perhaps she should swallow her pride and apologise. She needed, desperately, to keep in with the agency. She swallowed more Bud instead, draining the bottle quickly and reaching for another.

'Hah, drunk, eh?' she said aloud, gulping the Bud so quickly that she burped.

'I'm no more a drunk than anyone else,' she told the wilting plant on the windowsill, emphasising each word with a point of the bottle. 'At least I'm not as bad as my father.'

Georgie's dad had always been a drunk. When he dies, she thought, we'd better bury him. If we cremate him the bastard will burn for three days like a goddamned Jubilee beacon. He had ruined every Christmas as far back as she could remember, and he was the sort of drinker who could not wait for home-made beer to ferment. Drinking yeast and water after a week had laid him up in bed for a week afterwards. Georgie's father was the sort of drunk who would drink Bistro Chef because it had one per cent alcohol content. Georgie firmly believed she did not have a drinking problem; that she drank socially; that she drank because she was under pressure, or because she had something to celebrate, or to feel sorry about. Georgie would blame the sickness on a dodgy sausage or kebab rather than admit the vomit could have been the result of eight pints of strong cider. She would claim her legs had given way because the fresh air had hit her without warning. It was never the drink. Never.

'Cheeky bitch. Anyone would think I sat on a park bench with a PET bottle of cider getting wrecked at half-past eight in the morning. Now that's a drunk.' The plantpot was beginning to blur as Georgie drained the second bottle. She hadn't eaten since last night. The third and fourth bottles were also drained in quick succession and Georgie had one last lucid thought before she fell asleep on the settee.

Must get some more Budweiser for tonight.

SIX

The day of Gillian's party loomed closer. As usual, her 'little soirée' had mushroomed and more than fifty people were now expected to descend on her country-lodge house. The weather, luckily, was fine that Saturday morning as she stumbled out of bed. Everyone could congregate on the patio: the house was far too small – and decor still unfinished – to cope with those numbers indoors. She had about four hours' worth of cleaning the conservatory and clearing a passageway through to it from her small lounge. Then there was the Safeway Shuffle for the nibbles and little party packs, boxes of wine, and a couple of hours to do something with her hair. She needed at least half an hour free for the customary indecision about what to wear. As she gazed at the clear, blue, cloudless sky she regretted that she had not decided on a barbecue. There were men coming to the party. Men always loved barbecuing meat. It must be some primeval thing with them, all pyromaniacs under the surface, she mused. It meant they could wear plastic pinnies, slug beer, burn the sausages and go back to their Boy Scout days while she and her friends could concentrate on drinking. Barbecues were fun. She debated about changing her mind on the food, then realised she hadn't cleaned the barbecue since last time.

Haven't got time for that, she decided, and went back to the original plan.

Georgie was in no quandary about what to wear. She was in a quandary about how to lift her head off the pillow, though. She was sort of conscious that there was another person in the bed. Moving her head proved painful, so she racked her brain. As hard as she tried she could only remember up to the point when she ordered a drink at the bar of the club. Must have been 2 a.m., last orders, because it was a real crush. She remembered a gay guy in leather chaps being pushed against her back and a vague, fuzzy recollection of a little blonde standing next to her, also frantically waving a fiver at the barman. The memory of the Jack Daniel's double slipping down her throat prompted another recollection which involved snogging the cheeky little blonde.

'Morning, mate!' said the cheeky little blonde cheerfully, propping herself up on her elbows.

Georgie opened one eye. Yes, it was true: she was not alone. The blonde must have been all of nineteen, Georgie thought with despair. She screwed her eyes in concentration, but memories of leaving the club, getting home or anything else eluded her.

'Did we . . .?'

'Yeah, mate.'

'Was I awake?'

'Yeah, mate, you was a fucking animal. Brilliant. Cool.'

Georgie despaired even more. The thought that she could have been an absolutely tireless, magnificent shag and couldn't even remember it depressed the hell out of her.

'Look, I don't mean to seem rude, but . . .'

'Sharon. Me name's Sharon, mate. I'm a motor mechanic. You was out of it at the end, though. I thought you was going to puke. You kept going on about me tits and me bum and then you passed out on me. I'm not surprised you don't remember nothing. I put the waste bin by the bed in case you threw up.'

A dreadful thought occurred to Georgie. She had once been so pissed that she had actually passed out while finger-fucking a bird, and still had her fingers inside the girl when she went. The girl had not been impressed.

'Sorry,' she mumbled. The room was still blurry round the edges and she still hadn't had the courage to look Sharon in the face. Sharon, meanwhile, bounded out of bed and stretched.

'Fancy a cup of tea, mate?'

For some reason, Sharon's skills in the kitchen did not include the ability to stay silent. Crockery clattered, teaspoons got dropped in the sink and she even had the knack of being able to slam the fridge door. Every noise – Georgie could swear that Sharon could even make the kettle boil loudly – resonated around her aching head, the pain solidly fixed between her eyes.

Sharon clearly believed that life as a motor mechanic was merely a stepping stone to a preferable career as a nurse. She fussed and bustled around Georgie, propping her up on loudly fluffed-up pillows, straightening the quilt, until Georgie cracked.

'Enough! I'm struggling here. I don't need a nursemaid!'

Sharon's stricken face – and very cute it was too, Georgie noticed – was enough to make Georgie think again.

'Sorry, mate, I'm just trying to be helpful. Do you want me to bugger off?' Sharon said.

Georgie debated briefly about the wisdom of begging the girl to stay, sleeping off her hangover and then leaping on her for some afternoon delight.

'Look, I tell you what. I've got the biggest bastard hangover in Christendom, and a monster headache. I feel sick and I think I'm going to have to put my fingers down my throat. I've got to sleep and then I've got to get ready for my Auntie Gillian's party, where I'll probably get so pissed I'll be in this same state tomorrow morning. But if you want to, we can go out tomorrow night, or stay in and watch a video or something?'

'So you do want me to bugger off, then?'

'Yes. But leave your phone number and I'll ring you later. Promise.'

'Cool.'

By the time Sharon had showered, dressed and left, Georgie was asleep.

Meanwhile, Nikki had been up for hours. It had started with Steve falling into the bedroom in the dark, drunk. Why did men always make such a racket? Why did they always try to be quiet with such spectacular failure? Nikki had awoken as he fell over the ottoman. Christ, it had been in the same place for five years now. Why could he never remember where it was? Then he had attempted to take his trousers off. One-legged, he had hopped around for about four minutes before resting his head against the wall to give himself stability. All his change, and his keys, had fallen out in an irritating jangle.

Giggling by now, he had actually ripped his shirt in an attempt to get it off as he had forgotten to take his tie off first.

Sighing, Nikki had sat up and put on the lamp.

'Oh, you awake, then?' he had beamed at her. She was aware of a sickly-sweet smell emanating from him, slightly masking the aroma of bitter and whisky chasers. He went to sit on the end of the bed, missed and sat down hard on the floor.

'How was the rugby-club dinner?' she had inquired sweetly, now acutely aware of the strange odour.

'Shtrippersh were good,' he'd mumbled.

She had rolled her eyes. That usually meant that a couple of local tarts had arrived, stripped, thrust their breasts at the drunks and then offered to put on an extra-special show if the lads filled a pint pot with money. Sometimes the girls did absolutely nothing special, just repeated their usual gyrations. Sometimes they put on a mock lesbian show. Sometimes they grabbed a guy from the audience and tried to have sex with him.

'Steve, what's that smell?' Nikki had said.

'Baby oil,' he'd said, and collapsed in a fit of giggles.

'Did you end up on stage, then?'

Steve, thinking he was in the shit, spluttered as he tried to formulate an answer.

'It's OK, Steve, the state you're in I have absolutely no doubt you were unable to perform.'

'Well, they took my shirt and tie off,' he'd said defensively.

'Steve, you're covered in baby oil. What did they leave *on*?'

'My watch,' he'd said proudly, 'and they tied a pink ribbon round my willy.'

Nikki peered over his shoulder. There was no evidence of a pink ribbon. God alone knew where it had gone.

'Go and have a shower, Steve. You smell disgusting,' she had said, rolled over and gone back to sleep.

The alarm had gone off early, she assumed for another Saturday-morning round of golf. The bed was empty beside her. She knew exactly where he was. Twenty years of marriage had hardened her to the knowledge that when he was seriously out of it he had two party tricks. One was to piss in the wardrobe. The other was to fall asleep in the mercifully empty bath.

That was exactly where she'd found him. She was relieved. The last time she had been caught out with the wardrobe trick. She had awoken to hear liquid bouncing off a pair of her finest leather boots. That particular party piece more than irked her. They had lived in the same house now for nearly ten years and the fitted wardrobes were in when they moved in and the shower room had never moved. He may have been excused the ottoman, but how he could confuse the wardrobe with a toilet she had no idea. And why did he always pick her wardrobe rather than his own?

It reminded her of the honeymoon. Greece. Straight to the hotel from the airport, quick change into beach gear and straight down to catch the afternoon sun. Still not unpacked, they had quickly showered and thrown on shorts and T-shirts before hitting the local tavernas.

Ouzo, retsina and metaxa had combined with stuffed vine leaves, moussaka and some sickly-sweet pastry in Steve's stomach. He had been so pissed he had simply sat bolt upright in bed, leant over and vomited on the quarry-tile floor.

Except Nikki's open suitcase had been alongside the bed.

The only time she had been skiing – an extremely expensive way of falling over on her arse on a regular basis, as far as she could see – she and Steve had awoken one morning following the *après piste*. That time she had been the one in the bath and he was comatose on the rug beside the bed.

Steve had immediately mastered the art of staying upright on two pieces of wood. Nikki never did. In fact she had never mastered any pastime that involved skis, skates, rollerblades or any other attachment to her feet.

Nikki had a hopeless sense of balance. How she stayed upright on high heels, particularly when pissed, was a constant source of amazement to her. The tallest girl in her school, at the height of the craze for platform shoes, she was regularly in the school sick bay having a twisted ankle treated. She was surprised she hadn't developed a fear of heights with the bloody things. At fourteen she thought she looked great in them. In actuality, she was tall and gangly with thin legs, and the shoes gave her the appearance of having two club feet. But at least her height got her into nightclubs.

She and Janine would get on the bus with no make-up on, to get half-fare, and disappear into a public toilet to put their faces on. The key was to drink Coke or orange juice until a lad asked them if they wanted a drink, then it was straight on to Bacardis and vodkas.

Nikki's father, being a teetotaller except at Christmas, was always suspicious of her behaviour when she rolled home. At the age of fifteen she had developed the knack of taking a deep breath before speaking and enunciating very precisely, plus masking her breath with a mouthful of Polo mints on the way home.

She and Janine had invariably ended up French kissing a couple of spotty youths in a bid to get a lift home. Janine had been the school knockout, a girl who had actually completed a training course at the Lucie Clayton School for Models, which was, in those far-off 70s, the ultimate in glamour and chic for mere mortals like Nicola Todd.

Janine knew nothing of Nikki's painful love and devotion for her because, like 96 per cent of the girls at the grammar school they attended, she was heavily into boys and dreamt nightly of marrying Donny Osmond. The fact that Nikki did a more than passable imitation of Donny, complete with an imitation purple felt hat purchased from the market, miming the words of that anguish-ridden *Puppy Love* hit, held her in good stead. The closest she ever got to Janine on a physical level was to comfort her in her arms in between holding her head down the loo after she and Nikki had demolished the full bottle of cherry brandy lurking in the drinks cabinet from Christmas.

The other four per cent of the pupils were either practising closet queens or, like Nikki, were too young to actually know what to do about it should the opportunity arise for a snog, grope and fondle. The day that Nikki climbed on to Christine Kent's shoulders to peer over the top of the toilet door after suspicion arose that two girls were in there together, she had her young fantasies plunged into a somewhat more realistic and sordid context.

While Nikki had harboured soft-focus, dewy-eyed, romantic visions of herself and Janine, her one and only true love, skipping off into the sunset hand in hand, the harsh image of the two sixth-formers against the toilet wall came as an initial shock.

Admittedly it was only a fleeting glimpse, and Nikki had no idea of how to relate what she was seeing to her eager and nosy friends.

All these years on Nikki could still remember how that shock was rapidly overcome by a rather warm, moist feeling between her legs and, as her clitoris was firmly clamped against the back of Christine Kent's head at the time, the pleasure was almost indefinable.

What followed in even more rapid succession was the abject fear of realising that the snogging girls had spotted her, and the sudden realisation that it is nigh on impossible to run away while squatting on someone's shoulders. Both Nikki and Christine were rather badly beaten that day.

Still, here I am now, nearly forty, she thought savagely, and I'm stuck with a man who gets a pink ribbon wrapped round his willy; who believes the clitoris is a climbing plant to decorate your outside wall; who spends his nights at the golf club, rugby club, Rotary Club, Round Table or some other goddamned do-gooding charity; who thinks a wife should be no more than a hanging bauble on a Christmas tree to show off to his buddies. The man cannot even wield a drill without the wall looking like it's been machine-gunned.

A sudden wave of fondness overtook her, a complete surprise. He wasn't all that bad, was he? He didn't beat her, didn't gamble, did his drinking with his mates, wasn't suffocating with his demands for conjugal rights and he did leave her very much to her own devices. He accepted her lack of culinary, ironing, sewing and gardening skills. He paid for tradesmen to sort out the house without so much as a murmur. He didn't really hassle her, just made pathetic whining noises now and again and tried to make her jealous with his jibes about busty blondes in his department.

Loveless it might be, but her marriage was more comfortable than most others she had come across. She and Steve had an understanding: boundaries were clearly drawn. She would probably miss certain elements of the chubby bastard if she upped and went.

Not if. When.

Fortified by thoughts of a hugely successful megabucks agency with her own name plastered across the stationery and a horny little devil to come home to, Nikki began to run her bath, after turfing Steve out of it.

Lying up to her neck in richly perfumed suds she began to daydream. Gillian described her goddaughter as a bit of a handful. I wonder if she's a horny little devil? I wonder what she looks like? It would be ironic if she turned out to be the woman of my dreams. What would Gillian say? I know it's only supposed to be a chat, but what if our eyes meet and I plunge straight away? If she plunges? My whole future could change tonight.

The excitement, and butterflies, were still there as she drove to the party. She knew never to arrive on time, primarily because Gillian was never ready on time to meet guests. Anyone who knew Gillian built in a 'faffing about' factor of at least an hour. She always, always had something else to finish, another two or three phone calls to make, or had forgotten something and had to dash back for it. Gillian had lists of lists to try to organise herself but usually failed miserably, usually because she invariably didn't allocate enough time for each chore.

Despite arriving at least eighty minutes after the allotted start time, Nikki was one of the first to arrive. Gillian was already in a flap, worrying whether all the people would come. She was also slightly tipsy as she hadn't allocated time to eat during the day and had sunk a half-bottle of chilled wine already. Nikki made herself comfortable with a gin and tonic and was soon absorbed in a conversation with a stranger. The stranger turned out to have a dog with zero personality. It was so bad that she and her husband were constantly leaving the mutt behind at friends' houses, pubs, garden centres and parks. As a result it had developed serious separation anxiety. Nikki was almost crying with laughter.

The party was filling out nicely. Gillian was by now quite unsteady on her feet and was wolfing down most of the nibbles and snacks in a belated attempt to soak up the alcohol.

Georgie was also unsteady on her feet when she arrived, almost falling out of the taxi outside. She had somewhat foolishly decided the instant cure for her hangover would be a hair of the dog. In fact it turned out to be an almost full coat of hair as the Jack Daniel's bottle had looked extremely inviting and comforting. Despite her front, Georgie was shy, and was always nervous of encountering a group of total strangers in a social environment.

Emboldened by the Jack Daniel's, she took a deep breath and swore to keep on Coke or fruit juice all night.

'Darling,' slurred Auntie Gillian, thrusting a glass of wine into her hand, 'I thought you'd forgotten us!'

Georgie was led to a group of unprepossessing people while desperately trying to remember all the names that Auntie Gillian was booming at her. She could usually only remember names if people were helpfully wearing name tags.

'This is my goddaughter, Georgina. She's a writer,' Gillian announced proudly, then disappeared.

Resigned to having to recount a round of stories about her days as a hack, Georgie took a step into the circle of people and began.

Nikki, meanwhile, had barely moved from her seat in more than three hours and was beginning to regret that she had not eaten before arriving. The gin and tonic top-ups had appeared with alarming frequency, thanks to the husband of her new friend, who had noted, with some alarm, Gillian's increasingly inebriated state. The husband had been instructed to take over the role of gracious host to ensure guests had drinks and nibbles, a role he undertook with generous gusto.

Nikki knew she would probably have a problem standing, let alone walking. The gin was feeling warm in her stomach. Standing people surrounded her; the small house was beginning to look even smaller with the crowd of people. She was actually beginning to feel claustrophobic and not a little warm. She was also feeling extremely pissed.

Georgie's third glass of wine was probably a major mistake. The room was beginning to close in on her and turn somewhat fuzzy. The group of people had turned out to be hugely entertaining and Georgie had hardly shifted position. Now, crucially aware that fresh air was needed, she began to make a cautious approach towards the conservatory and out on to the patio.

Nikki, too, had made her move, carefully rising to move away from the seat – just three steps towards the open French windows on to the patio and she could get some relief. She staggered slightly and hoped no one would notice.

The two women collided in the doorway as they attemped to rush out to the sanctuary of the mild night air. Automatically, both apologised and moved to let the other out. Standing there awkwardly, neither making the first move, both had to focus bleary eyes before realising who the other was.

Their argument started before either had put a foot on the patio.

'Call me a drunk, eh? You're hardly in a position to call me names like that!' Georgie was first in.

'At least this is a social environment, not a work one!' Nikki retorted, struggling with the sentence.

'I've never been drunk when working. Hungover, I'll admit, but never drunk.' Georgie's voice was beginning to rise.

'I've never been unprofessional . . .'

'I never called you unprofessional. I just said you were preoccupied with your personal problems . . .'

'I never let my personal problems take over my work and I resent you implying that they do . . .'

'And I seriously resent you calling me an alcoholic . . .'

'I never called you an alcoholic. I just said you had turned up with a hangover every time at my office . . .'

'Twice. I'll have you know there are plenty of days I don't get a hangover . . .'

'And there are plenty of times I don't have personal problems interfering in my day. You can't escape the fact that you did a poor job and I had to rescue it, and I don't expect suppliers to come to me every time with a hangover.'

Gillian had been alerted to the dispute on the patio. Breezing through her guests like a galleon in full sail she burst on to the patio, beaming beatifically.

'Girls, girls, let's not spoil it, shall we? Come and have another drink, do. Let's just calm it down.'

Glaring at each other, Nikki and Georgie allowed themselves to be led, somewhat unsteadily, back into the fray.

Gillian sensibly decided that it was not the right time to introduce the two officially. They were obviously not in the right frame of mind to have a cosy chat about that lesbian thing. She separated them by thrusting Georgie at one group of people, Nikki at another. Still hostile, drinking wine without tasting it, and exchanging mutual glares, the two women remained separated for the next hour.

Nikki and Georgie by that point were too pissed to remember that the gathering had been arranged with a specific intention in mind. Neither had spoken to the other since the showdown on the phone the previous week. Marion had been right: pride had overtaken both of them. Now, fuelled by alcohol, the spite had surfaced to double the supposed slights each had inflicted on the other.

The fact that Nikki's client had now approved the job without any complaint, and that she had nearly decided to perhaps apologise to the freelance, was completely forgotten now. The original dispute had now lodged at the forefront of her brain.

Georgie had no recollection of a mild fantasy about Nikki Jones: her outrage had consumed her.

Gillian kept a careful eye on the pair of them. She didn't want it to escalate, whatever dispute they had had – something about work she realised – and she was disappointed that her little plan was not going to come together. They looked about ready to kill each other, let alone become best gay buddies.

Nikki realised she had to leave, but there was no way she could drive. She also knew she would have a stonking hangover in the morning. Georgie, too, was coming to the rapid conclusion that if she didn't lie down soon she would fall over.

A final, mutual look steeped in hostility was shared between the two of them as Nikki took advantage of an offered lift home and departed.

Georgie sank on to a settee and closed her eyes gratefully. Well, that's blown any chances of ever getting back into Nikki Jones's good books, she thought. She'll probably get me blacklisted at every other agency around, as well. Why couldn't I have just left it alone instead of getting on my high horse? I'm not surprised Nikki reacted the way she did. The pair of us had had too much to drink to try to soothe the troubled waters which, let's face it, had been blown out of proportion in the first place.

Ah, for fuck's sake, why did I get drunk before I arrived? The demon drink has done it again, made my mouth loose at a time when I could ill afford it. Anyway, where's that married bint Auntie Gillian wanted me to talk to? Can't talk; can't think. The hell with it.

Georgie slept through everyone departing and Gillian's half-hearted attempt to clear up. Gillian threw a quilt over her and left her snoring.

SEVEN

Nikki was in a foul mood. The Sunday morning had been clear and warm, and the combined effects of the heat of the day and a hangover had produced a surfeit of sweat and an uneasy nausea. She had been dropped off the night before and had struggled for ten minutes to put her key in the door. Steve, having settled in for an evening of canned lager and football, had eventually given in to his irritation and opened the door for her. She had fallen into the hallway, stumbled up the stairs and walked straight into the ottoman in the bedroom. Now she knew why Steve had always struggled with the bloody thing when he was drunk. Convinced that the ottoman came to life in the dark, she had drifted off to sleep and into a slightly alarming dream about furniture.

She vaguely remembered having an argument. Shit, another bloody 'sorry' card. Sometimes she thought it would be better, and more economic, to buy the bloody things in bulk. She hoped Gillian wasn't too pissed off with her. After all, the whole thing had been arranged with her in mind. She had lost friends before through drunken excesses and Gillian was too dear to her at this stage in her life. Once she was upright, she would struggle to a phone. Her contrition was interrupted. She suddenly realised her husband was speaking to her, and probably had been speaking for some time.

'Sorry?'

'I was saying, Nikki –' Steve's patience was overexaggerated '– that I would have thought you could have been less obviously drunk last night. You're nearly forty. Don't you think you should start acting your age a bit more often? Isn't it time you stopped drinking so much, so often? God knows what the neighbours thought. You were yelling all sorts of things at the door.'

'You should have opened the fucking thing, then, shouldn't you? You'd switched off the porch light. How was I supposed to find my fucking key in the dark? Night after night I have to put up with your drunken behaviour and you're even older than I am. How come it's fine for you to sink eight pints and whisky chasers, get stripped naked by a couple of old slappers in front of a fucking audience with the idea of shagging one or both of them, come home smothered in fucking baby oil and then fall all over the bloody bedroom. I suppose you're going to tell me it's a man thing, aren't you? I had a few gin and tonics too many, sensibly got a lift home and, all right, I struggled to get upstairs and into bed. At least I didn't throw my clothes off in public with the intention of letting some hairy-arsed strippagram give me a good seeing-to in front of my mates.'

'I knew you wouldn't let that one go. I knew you'd come back to it. It all just got out of hand, that's all. That's what rugby players do.'

'I don't give a rat's arse what rugby players do. All I know is that I'm expected to tolerate your alcohol-fuelled blokey behaviour and smile indulgently and say, "OK, Steve, do whatever you want to do. It's all right, you're a man. You're a rugby follower. It's what happens."'

Steve mustered his indignity again.

'I just don't think it's clever, big, pleasant or even civilised to see a woman, particularly someone your age, and someone in your position, get so drunk. What if my bosses get to hear about it? What happens if you start behaving like an idiot at one of my dinners? I'm convinced you're on the verge of being an alcoholic, you know.'

'Sod off, Steve, let me sleep.'

Steve's disgruntlement was not really fed by her being drunk. He had spent the evening on his own, chugging lager, watching a pirate porn video through a snowstorm of static, and had dredged up some horny fantasies about his sex life. He had determined to make love to his wife on her return, flinging her on the carpet like Odin the Warrior and taking her there and then with brute force. When she had appeared looking more than dishevelled and reeking of gin, his ardour had disappeared in a flash. Now he was just feeling petty and resentful.

He also knew that Nikki knew it too. He was also annoyed, and had been for a little time, that she had been with that Gillian woman. When she had first announced the party and made it abundantly clear that she was going alone, his first thought had been that he was not welcome because the two of them were plotting some manhunting expedition. He wouldn't put it past that Gillian to lead his wife astray. She had probably been begging Nikki to embark on an affair for years.

The holidays they had together, the long weekends away, nights out at the theatre, drunken parties and those girlie lunches. Long phone calls. What did women find to talk about for so long, anyway? Why did they feel the need to speak to each other virtually every day? From overhearing Nikki's end of the conversation it seemed they were talking Swahili to each other for all he could follow.

As he watched his wife sleep, Steve once again mused that he knew very little about female friendship. He sat down on the edge of the bed. Nikki didn't stir. What if she was having an affair? What would he do? How would he react?

She could have been out with another man for all he knew. She spent a lot of time working late. She had overnight stops in hotels on business. She went away to conferences, sometimes abroad. He had never understood what she did for a living. In the early days she would come home and prattle on about clients and what she did for them, tell him all about the people she worked with. Sometimes she would be in fits, laughing so hard she couldn't finish the yarn she had started.

It had been a long, long time since he had seen her laugh like that. He idly wondered if his wife actually had any fun any more. She seemed so preoccupied with work and it certainly didn't seem as if her job made her happy any more. The pressure that she had thrived on seemed to be pulling her down now. The evenings, now rare, that they spent together at home were always in silence. She never asked about his job, his friends and family, his hobbies. He never asked about hers. He had a flash of guilt that he was probably responsible for part of this complacent life they led. They were not even companions in marriage. Christ, for most of the time they were not even friends. They just got on with it. And when she did deign to drape his arm at a function, he knew she was making an effort to make conversation with his colleagues and clients.

Steve actually felt good when she was there, unless she was wearing heels, because she did have the ability to mix with people. To be fair to her, she never drank alcohol either, was always on driving duty because she knew the three drinks he allowed himself to calm his nerves would be enough to take him over the limit. He was naturally shy and uneasy with strangers. She would just pile in to a group of people and have them in the palm of her hand within seconds. And they would all know she was his wife, the beautiful willowy blonde with the sexy deep-blue eyes, quick mind and wit, and fabulous arse. Yeah, Steve Jones had it all, they would think.

Steve Jones knew in his heart that in reality all he had was a wife who very probably despised him and the routine and drudgery of the lifestyle that they had. He also knew that the love and passion had died years ago. What confused the hell out of him was why she didn't ask to get out of it. Why hadn't she come home after one of her Caribbean jaunts with The Maneater and announced that she had shagged the entire complement of a US frigate and she was leaving him? Steve could not have asked Nikki for a divorce. She would have to ask him. He would say no. He had worked hard to get where he was and fund the house, attain his superficial middle-class level of respectability and convention-ality. All that was missing was the 2.4 children. He was the one in his family who had made it, and he was buggered if he was going to end up in a rented flat somewhere while his wife enjoyed the marital home – or half the proceeds.

It was only five years into the marriage that the cracks had appeared. They had stopped snogging. When he had broached the subject with mates, they had all wisely agreed that was usually the first sign. Wives would carry on shagging out of duty, and the blow jobs would dry up, but once the snogging stopped it usually meant that the marriage was moving into the 'companionship' stage.

From no snogging, they all sagely concurred into their lagers, the next stage would be the arguing.

Steve and Nikki spent another five years arguing. They argued about the washing-up, Nikki's cooking, Steve's golf, Steve's mother. They argued in the car about map reading. They argued in restaurants about the menu or which wine to choose. They could come close to blows over the TV remote control. They even argued about whether to go to marriage guidance. In the end they agreed to go, but when Nikki found out the waiting list was three to six months she had lost her temper.

'If I've got to wait six months for counselling about my marriage then I may as well put him under the fucking patio now and have done with it,' she had yelled at the receptionist before slamming the phone down so hard the handset had cracked.

The arguing had dried up: there had been little left to bother each other about. Then Nikki had got her current job – well, the job she secured before her rapid promotion – and thrown herself into that. He had had a few years' respite before the pressures built up. She had alarming weight losses and gains, was constantly fatigued, sleeping most of the weekends away. He had persuaded her to go to a doctor, having panic attacks about her being pregnant. Not much chance of that: the sex was virtually non-existent, but he had still lain awake at night sweating about the thought of babies.

She had gone for exploratory surgery. While he had been panicking about his life being turned upside down by brats, Nikki had been having constant anxiety attacks about cancer. Her weight had plunged to a disconcerting level.

She had crashed into the house after her appointment with the hugely expensive consultant and her mood was a mixture of anger and relief.

'It's not cancer. It's Irritable Bowel Syndrome. It's caused by stress. Stress! I sit there while he asks me questions about my life and all the time I'm expecting him to put his rubber gloves on and shove a finger up my arse. He asks if I have chest pains, headaches.

'What the hell's that to do with my digestive system, I ask. Ah, he says, and draws me diagrams, then tells me it's Irritable Bowel Syndrome and that I should remove the focus of my stress from my life. I turn round to him and say, "No, doctor, I don't care how many fucking degrees and qualifications you've got, you're wrong. It's not Irritable Bowel Syndrome: it's Irritating Bastard Syndrome and I'm going to go home and bury my fucking husband in the rosebeds. Will that help?"'

Steve had made the mistake at that point of laughing out loud. He had been so relieved that she was not suffering pregnancy or a terminal disease that he had completely missed the usual warning signal of Nikki's explosive temper about to blow. The drink that he had poured her ended up cartwheeling across the room, and he could still hear crashing and banging as he had made his sharp exit.

Nikki's IBS had taken some time to come under control. The further withdrawal from each other as a couple had helped. She had taken time off work, buggered off to Hawaii for a couple of weeks with The Maneater. On her return they had both naturally slipped into a routine of simply living under the same roof, sharing a bed.

She had suggested separate bedrooms – they had enough room for Chrissakes – but he had refused. That would have been too close to a divorce in Steve's mind. The king-size divan, however, suddenly became larger to both of them. They never cuddled at night: they would both wake up in the morning with a yawning chasm between them. Now and again they came together for a perfunctory coupling, usually when Steve's bollocks became painfully full and she was extremely pissed. He thought he had mastered the art. When his biological need became too much to bear he would ply her with champagne and a joint. He had to judge it finely. A bottle and a glassful would be enough to entice her into bed; one glass too many and she would pass out.

If he was honest with himself, Nikki had never been an animal with him. His mates had spoken with awe of women who scratched and bit, who howled like wolves when they came, who would lick and suck hungrily. Women with trick pelvises who could fuck like bucking broncos. He would sit uncomfortably, his half-erect penis nudging the seam of his jeans, desperately wishing his wife could be like that. His mates all fancied Nikki and he would indulge them by telling them she was the biggest howler of the lot. In fact, on the odd occasions they did do it, she was probably thinking about shopping.

Now he thought about it, Steve realised that there was no way his wife was having an affair. She just wasn't interested in sex. Never really had been. She was probably relieved that it had ground to a halt. He could still feel a flare of desire now and again when he saw her naked, but it seemed too much of an effort these days and she would probably annihilate him verbally if he tried it on when they were both sober.

He left her sleeping. Time was moving on if he was going to get to the pub in time to order Sunday lunch.

The minute she heard the front door close, Nikki threw the sheet aside and sat up. Her head was pounding but the nausea seemed to have dissipated. She showered for a long time, threw on a tracksuit and made herself a pot of very strong coffee.

Gillian, as usual, did not have a hangover when she answered the phone.

'How do you do it?' Nikki groaned. 'I know damn well you would have been pissed.'

'Habit, darling, habit. At my age my body is used to the abuse.

Now, are you going to tell me what all that foolish fuss was about last night?'

'Listen, I really must apologise. I'd had too much to drink on an empty stomach, and for some reason that girl is like a red rag to a bull to me. We've had a couple of set-tos before. Once I was unreasonable with her and . . . well, actually, it was my fault both times if the truth be known. I've only used her on one or two jobs and each time she's come in with them I've been in a foul mood about something else and taken it out on her. She probably thinks I'm a complete bitch. She was drunk last night as well and she started on me first. I should have let it go, I suppose, but you know what I'm like on gin. I should have stuck to wine. I should have kept my mouth shut. I'm sorry if I spoilt your party.'

'You didn't spoil it, sweetheart. I think people were amused. It's not often you get to see a possible catfight, is it?'

'Yeah, well, next time, advertise it as a mud-wrestling competition, but don't invite that girl. I'll find someone else to have a fight with instead.'

'That girl, darling, is my goddaughter. And if you remember, it was me that recommended her to you for work.'

The silence was long.

It was Gillian who eventually broke it, as Nikki sat rubbing her forehead in acute embarrassment. The nausea had returned.

'In fact, she's still here. She passed out on the sofa and I've tidied up around her. And you have to come and get your car, don't you?'

'Gillian, there's no way I can face her. Does she know . . .?'

'No, she doesn't. I didn't think the moment was opportune last night and as she hasn't even stirred yet she is not aware that you're the person she was supposed to be chatting to. I suppose I ought to go and check that she hasn't died in the night from alcoholic poisoning. I think you should come over, at least to try and make friends. You did just say that you thought it was your fault before, all the silly misunderstandings you both had.'

'Saying it to you and saying it to her are two completely different things,' said Nikki defensively, and beginning to feel the start of an anxiety attack.

'Look, Georgie is a bit of a hothead but she does have moments of sobriety and sensibility. If the word "sorry" actually sticks in your throat I am sure she is capable of recognising that you regret what happened. It depends how important it is to you that you talk to her. I told you, she's the only lesbian I know, so this is the only time I can actually help you. Don't be so bloody proud and stubborn. It's probably going to take me a couple of hours to get her upright and responsive. Have some more coffee at your end, read your Sunday papers, and think about it.'

Gillian was being brusque again, and on the verge of shrillness. Nikki recognised the steely determination in her voice. Gillian was a woman with a mission and she wouldn't give up so easily.

'OK, OK, I'll ring you in a bit. Steve's buggered off to the pub so I'm going to have to call a cab anyway to get the car, and you know what it's like getting a taxi on a Sunday round here.'

She sat staring at the phone for ages before she called for a taxi. She hoped Gillian wouldn't say too much to Georgie before she arrived so that she could keep her options open. What if Georgie was sufficiently pissed off with her to use the situation to her own advantage? Nikki could not afford for such a possible loose cannon to be set off at this stage. If Georgie decided to be mean she could let certain people know what was going on, and there was no way that Nikki could even contemplate dealing with it right now. But then Georgie didn't seem mean and spiteful. Temperamental definitely, but Nikki was used to that in her business.

While Nikki wrestled with her thoughts, Gillian was struggling with Georgie. The wretched girl was refusing to come round. Each time Gillian thought she had her in a sitting position, Georgie would go limp again and slump against the cushions.

'Now come along, Georgina. If you're still pissed now then this is the best you're going to feel all day because you still have the hangover to go through. I've run you a nice hot bath, and I'll make you a cup of tea. No, I'll make you a gallon of strong coffee and a sandwich. Come along, you're making my house look untidy.'

Georgie stayed sitting, her head in her hands.

'Auntie Gillian, I feel dreadful. I feel like shit.'

'Well, get yourself into the bathroom and stick your fingers down your throat. That's a start.'

'I'm really sorry about last night, Auntie Gillian. I had too much to drink. I should have eaten something.'

'I've heard this already this morning from Nikki. The pair of you are as bad as each other. I don't know what possessed you both to start that little fracas last night but, if it's any consolation, Nikki feels as badly about it as you do. In fact, she's on her way over in a little while to pick her car up. I think you should both kiss and make up. Oh, dear.' Gillian was suddenly flustered.

Georgie missed it completely. Fighting the rising bile in her throat, she quickly stood up, swayed, put one foot in front of the other and then ran to the toilet. Auntie Gillian was right, she thought ten minutes later, being sick has helped. She sank gratefully into the bath that Gillian had waiting for her. Strong coffee, headache tablets and a sandwich also helped.

By the time Nikki arrived, Georgie was on the verge of feeling human again. They eyed each other warily. Nikki had turned it over in her mind many times and knew that she should really make the first move

'I don't know about you but I think last night was a major mistake. We should have sorted out our differences before, really. I didn't know you were going to be here and I was pissed.'

Georgie said nothing. Go on, bitch, she thought, apologise.

'I have probably been a little bit, well, shall we say that I should really have, er . . . We got off on the wrong foot to start with and I know that I should have, in my position, perhaps thought a little more carefully about . . . Well, you know, these things can get out of hand and what I really mean by that . . .'

Gillian by this point was silently screaming inside. 'What she's trying to say, Georgina, is that she's sorry.'

Georgie still said nothing.

'And, Georgie, I really think you should be saying sorry too.' Suddenly Gillian sounded just like Georgie's mum.

'If you two are just going to stand there while I do all the apologising on your behalf then we're not going to get anywhere, are we? And if you two are supposed to be talking to each other about things then I think that would be a good start, don't you?'

'What things?' said Georgie, sulking because Nikki had not actually apologised directly.

'Things. You know, lesbian things.' Gillian stopped, realising that Nikki's face had adopted a frozen look of horror.

'You mean she's that married woman you talked about?' said Georgie incredulously.

An uncomfortable, tension-ridden silence cloaked all three of them. Nikki realised that all her angst about Georgie could have been unnecessary if Gillian had kept her mouth shut. She obviously hadn't said anything to Georgie until just now. Nikki could have blustered through an apology, climbed in her car, driven off and Georgie need never have known.

Gillian knew she should have left it alone. There was still too much unfinished business between these two without compounding it.

Georgie was in a welter of confusion. Her mind was being assailed with images of Nikki in various stages of undress, Nikki spread open and waiting before her hungry eyes, Nikki's nipples erect and beckoning her tongue. Nikki wet and wanting. In a fraction of a second, Nikki Jones, the stern-faced agency suit with the mystery husband, had been replaced by Nikki Jones wanton, stripped bare, begging Georgie to taste her dripping, glistening cunt.

'Jesus,' Georgie breathed, and neither Nikki nor Gillian had any idea that the expression carried so much meaning.

'Coffee, anyone?' Gillian said brightly.

Georgie went to sit down, her legs suddenly weak. She moved at the same time as Nikki towards the settee. They sat down together. Georgie imagined she could feel the heat from Nikki's body, despite there being at least a foot of cushion between them. Nikki's body language was defensive, arms and legs crossed, shoulder turned away from Georgie. She stared at her knees. Georgie's mind was working overtime: feverish finger-fucking was all she could think about.

All Nikki could think about was the potential for blackmail.

How did Gillian possibly think she could talk to Georgie, a freelance whom she had bawled out at least three times and who, until last night, she had only ever seen in a work environment? How could she reveal her soul to this girl? She should never have said anything, at all, to Gillian. Gillian crashed about in the kitchen. It was obvious she was staying out of the way.

'So . . .' Georgie realised it had come out a little high-pitched. 'Do you want to talk to me about these feelings you've been having, or do you want to leave it alone and pretend it never happened?'

When Nikki turned to her in surprise, Georgie smiled.

'It's OK, you know. I'm not the sort of person who is going to rush off to your husband or your boss to tell them you're a dirty-minded pervert. Auntie Gillian means well, but if it makes you feel more comfortable I'll shut up now, and we'll both act as if nothing was ever said in the first place.'

I'll shut up, she thought, but it won't stop me tormenting myself for ever more with visions of you naked, wide open and underneath me. She sensed Nikki's tension lifting, at the same time as she realised Nikki had changed position, her legs uncross-ing, and moved to face her. Georgie waited with all the benign patience in the world.

'This is all very strange, you know,' Nikki began. 'I mentioned something to Gillian, took me an awful lot to do it, and before I know it she's doing her best to sort me out. You must know that Woman with a Mission thing of hers. I've never mixed in gay circles. I wouldn't know where to start. I just know that I have to deal with this. I was just feeling lost and alone, wondering where the hell to go, what to do next, if anything.'

'I've never had that conflict. It must be very difficult for you. How long have you been feeling like this?'

'As long as I can remember. Back at grammar school, I guess. It wasn't something that I could discuss with anyone then. I thought I would grow out of it. Then I met Steve. He was my first proper boyfriend, I suppose, the first one that I really let . . . well, you know.'

Georgie realised she was jealous. 'So you married him. Convention. Safety. Image. All of that stuff.'

Nikki nodded. Her head had slumped slightly and she was silent.

'You never felt right; felt that there was something missing, disjointed? Do you have children?'

'No. Steve can't stand kids. I suppose that was an understanding from the start, really. All things being equal it's probably just as well: children would probably have slowed my career down. I wouldn't have the job I have now if I had had babies. But, yes, there was always something not quite right. I would look at other women, not other men, every time I debated having an affair to give myself some bloody excitement in my life. I would think about kissing another woman, holding a woman in my arms, stroking soft skin, the arch of a woman's neck.'

Georgie was fighting to keep her face impassive.

'Then it began to take me over. I knew I had to do something about it, at least find out for myself if that was what I really wanted, or whether I wanted to do it because it was just so fucking controversial and different. I saw an advert in a sex magazine my husband had hidden under the bed one day – you know, one of these contact things.'

Georgie realised she did not really want to hear any more. She did not want to hear details about any women that Nikki had made love to. She could not bear the thought of some faceless, nameless woman awakening Nikki to the delicious pleasures she had craved. 'And so it went from there, then?'

'Yes. I knew that was what I wanted; what made me fulfilled and satisfied. Once I'd been there I couldn't bear my husband touching me, unless I was seriously pissed on champagne. I met women through adverts, through escort agencies. But it's still not enough: it's just a convenient way of getting sex. It's not getting me a relationship, someone to share my life with, someone to come home to. That's what I was telling Gillian. How do I move on from where I am now to meeting someone who wants more, who would love and cherish me the way that I would love them? If I was going to take the step of turning my life inside out to devote myself to being gay, and all the risks and gambles that go with it, I want someone to be there with me and for me when I do it.'

'"When", rather than "if"?'

'Oh, Georgie, I can't keep this front up for much longer. It's a need to be and it's consuming me. I know there is a woman put on this earth for me.'

Nikki's silent tears ran down her face. Georgie stretched her arms out and Nikki fell into them and the sobs came, great racking anguished sobs, as Georgie held her tight and stroked her hair, gently kissed the top of her head.

'Please help me,' Nikki whispered.

Gillian took one look as she walked in, coughed, and Georgie simply looked up at her and silently shook her head. Gillian nodded and quietly withdrew, leaving Nikki in Georgie's arms.

'I'll be there for you,' Georgie whispered.

EIGHT

At least five people had remarked on Nikki's good humour before 9.45 a.m. Marion, accustomed to Nikki's mood swings, had a private bet with herself that the mood would have disappeared before 11 a.m. The first to remark upon it had been Steve. Nikki had actually been singing in the shower as he got dressed for work.

She had belted out a couple of tunes in the car, oblivious to the fact that three people who saw her were convinced she was having a seizure at the wheel.

She actually hummed as she bounced into work. Even a curt memo about her inflated expenses could not dampen her. A poorly executed visual put under her nose by a junior member of the design team was dismissed with a highly constructive critique and sensible suggestions, rather than the usual tirade of expletives about his biological lineage or ability to draw a straight line.

Nikki Jones had found an ally. A friend. A fully paid-up member of the sisterhood. A key to the gateway for the start of her new life. She and Georgie had talked for hours. For so long that Gillian had had to raid her freezer for an impromptu late supper. It was the longest period that Gillian had ever endured without talking – apart from when she slept. She had nothing to contribute to the conversation, which had consisted of Georgie outlining where to go, how to go about it and what sort of women Nikki should definitely avoid. Gillian was also very worried that the conversation might swing towards slightly more graphic instructions for Nikki, in which case she would have had to disappear to the village pub.

Georgie had hugely enjoyed herself. Her initial reservations about having to take the 'married bint' under her wing had magically been forgotten. It helped that Nikki was drop-dead gorgeous. It was also rapidly clear to her that Nikki didn't have a clue. She had had, Georgie now knew, infrequent encounters with women, although the experiences as far as she was concerned had been more than pleasurable. Georgie's explanations about butch, femme, lipstick lesbians, how to drink bottled beer and give coded signals out on the scene, bottoms, tops, fetishes, intrigued Nikki and embarrassed the hell out of Auntie Gillian.

In fact Georgie had to patiently explain certain expressions several times for Auntie Gillian, who still looked somewhat bemused at the end of it. Even highlighting that there were several gay publications with contact ads, and gay details of friendly venues, resorts and hotels had come as news to Nikki. Georgie went through the list of popular lesbian icons in film and music for Nikki's benefit and promised to scour her flat for back issues of lesbian mags.

Hearing that there were specialist bookshops, mail-order videos and visual training manuals, and dedicated lesbian sex shops had sent Nikki off on a tangent about where the hell she would store such stuff without Steve finding it. She would have to buy a combination-lock suitcase to keep in her car, she decided. When Georgie started to reel off some of the popular Brighton, Birmingham, London and Manchester venues, Nikki asked Gillian for pen and paper.

'You don't need to write it down. Come with me. I'll show you the best places to go,' said Georgie. 'There's two places in this godforsaken town we can go to for a start.'

'That's a bit too close for comfort for me,' said Nikki.

'What, in case one of your straight friends, or one of your clients, sees you walking out of the door with some dyke on your arm?' Georgie sneered. 'What's to say you won't see a colleague or a client in there? You haven't even started to develop a talent for spotting a dyke, have you? You never spotted it with me. You didn't have a bloody clue. Stick with me and I'll look after you. There will be quite a few dykes interested in a fine piece of fresh meat, even if you are a little bit too lipstick girly, girly. They all know me quite well: you'll find the gay scene is very insular and cliquey. If you're with me they'll leave you alone, unless you tell me otherwise.'

They had arranged to meet later that week. Georgie refused to meet her in a straight pub so they had compromised with a Burger King car park.

'Don't get me wrong,' Georgie had explained. 'I don't have any objections to straight people, it's just that I never feel comfortable; I never feel I can be myself in a straight place. I've missed out on loads of parties that way, but then quite a few of my straight friends wouldn't be seen dead in a gay bar either. I mean, can you imagine Auntie Gillian in one?'

'She'd be too busy trying to tell all the men that what they needed was a real woman!' Nikki had spluttered.

Now, as Nikki hummed and bounced through her Monday, she had something to look forward to. She had liked Georgie's sense of humour and she felt confident that Georgie would genuinely look after her and steer her through potential pitfalls. The girl was undoubtedly experienced and Nikki was now glad that Gillian had persuaded the two of them to talk. My God, she had had no idea that there was so much out there.

'So many women, so little time . . .' She had said it aloud before she realised it. Marion had come into the office just as she said it. The two looked at each other.

'One of Steve's little pet phrases. He said it yesterday morning when he was giving me a bollocking for being drunk on Saturday. You know, his usual once-a-month attempt at asserting his authority and reminding me there are plenty of other women out there just dying to get their hands on him. Do you know who was at the party on Saturday? That freelance, you know, Georgie What's-her-name.'

'Rivers. What was she doing there?'

'Turns out she's Gillian's goddaughter. Tiny world, eh? Anyway, we had a bit of a ruckus about that last job, then we got drunk together and had a right old laugh. Water under the bridge, eh, Marion? She's a bit of a giggle actually; in fact, she's great. Turns out we have a lot in common. In fact we're going out for a drink on Wednesday, patch up our differences properly. Life's too short to bear grudges, don't you think?'

Marion was still stunned by the frantic gabble and benevolence in Nikki's voice to take in too much. Nikki had barely paused for breath. Marion registered something about grudges and made a mental note to remind Nikki about The List in her top drawer.

The List had been compiled after one of Nikki's therapy sessions as part of her IBS treatment. Stress counselling, coupled with cognitive therapy, had occupied Nikki for some time. As usual she had thrown herself into a new challenge with great abandon, buying up a whole section of books from the local bookshop on self-help, anger management and how to channel aggression in a positive manner. Marion had not understood a word of it but had nodded sagely in the right places as Nikki had droned on about the Power of Positive Thinking. As usual the focus had dramatically switched after six months to something else – Marion couldn't remember what – but The List had remained. On The List were as many people as possible who had slighted, insulted, upset or irritated Nikki Jones. It was a long list.

She had spent hours drawing it up, putting down descriptions of people if she hadn't remembered, or known, their names. Next to the names was a summary of the emotions they had made her feel at the time. It was supposedly therapeutic, reducing a negative emotion engendered by another person into cold black and white. That emotion was then channelled on to the paper to remain there and fade with time. All Marion knew was that the top five people on The List were still a constant source of irritation or anger for Nikki, who had plotted many supposedly foolproof ways of killing them over the years. Steve, naturally, was top of The List, but her boss, Alistair, was a close second. Her father was third, and for some reason a boy who had jumped on her arm at junior school was fourth. When it came to grudges, Marion thought, Nikki had the memory of an elephant.

'Well –' Marion had spotted her chance to speak '– it's nice that you've made up with her. Am I to assume then that you will use her again? It's just that I haven't got round yet to filling in a contact card for her in the freelance box.'

'Yeah, yeah, whatever. I'm sure there will be something coming up we can give her. You'd better tell accounts to ignore that fifty-quid invoice I got you to send her. She'll probably think that's just small minded and petty of me and I don't want to fall out with her again, do I?'

Marion had ignored Nikki's magnanimous instruction about the invoice, anyway, because she thought it had been small minded and petty. She also knew that such instructions, issued in a blaze of temper, were probably just hot air anyway and would have been forgotten in a matter of moments.

Marion lost her private bet. Big time. Nikki's humour lasted way beyond 11 a.m. that Monday. Nikki was still in a great mood when she left work on the Wednesday evening. At home, Steve Jones was on the verge of a nervous breakdown: nearly three whole days now without an outburst of temper. He felt like a cartoon he had once seen of an unusually repulsive cat startled by a gesture of affection. He was wary of spoiling the mood by demanding sex. Probably pushing his luck with that one. She didn't even bite when he complained that the pizza crust was burnt to a crisp.

As she drove to the Burger King, dressed in jeans and flat boots as instructed, Nikki's stomach began to flutter with anxiety. Georgie was already there, waving as Nikki reversed the car into the space next to her. Georgie smiled to herself. She had been right: it was a flash car and the personal plate was probably a bit over the top. She opened Nikki's passenger door to be aurally assaulted by Robert Palmer at such a loud level the bass line was distorted.

'Bit eighties, isn't it?' shouted Georgie.

'Yeah, right, and if you start going on about my age I'll put my fucking Motown compilation on,' Nikki yelled back. She turned the stereo off. 'My car, or yours?'

Georgie scanned the vehicle – a good thirty grand's worth. Probably not a good idea to park it near the gay bar she wanted to go to. It would probably get nicked or vandalised. For some reason that she could never fathom, gay venues were always close to the rough parts of town. It usually meant running the gauntlet of the queer bashers late on a Saturday night, particularly in Manchester, where the straights had taken time to cotton on that the gay village had extended licensing.

That's OK, you fucking bigots, drink beer in our places and then beat the shit out of us. Do we do it to you?

She was explaining this to Nikki as they drove off in Georgie's old Granada.

'I was up in Manchester one year at the Mardi Gras, this big festival they have on August Bank Holiday weekend. It was a Saturday. We were all having a great time in the sun, pavement cafés, live music, beer tents, the works. This straight couple wandered in to the village by accident and decided to have a beer. How they didn't notice they were surrounded by queers I don't know, but I had my arm round my girlfriend and I was nibbling her ear, you know, feeling a bit horny, and the woman started making some smartarse comments about it. I gave her a right talking to, said that when we were on her patch we behaved ourselves, but this was our place and if she didn't like it she shouldn't be there anyway.

'Then another Saturday I'd gone up with some mates and a few yobs decided to pick on the fairies and pansies. There were vans full of coppers around but they weren't bothered. Then round the corner came a load of the S&M guys in leather, the ones who work out and pump iron, and they laid into the straights something chronic. It was only then that the coppers got involved, but most of them were laughing so hard they couldn't arrest anyone.'

'S&M? I thought it was M&S.'

'Yeah, right, beat me, beat me and give some vouchers for new knickers afterwards . . .'

Georgie almost folded double over the steering wheel she was laughing so hard. She was still giggling as they parked. Nikki refrained, with considerable difficulty, from commenting on Georgie's parking skills. Three attempts at reversing into a space large enough for an Australian road train resulted in the car being left at an acute angle, wheel turned outward into oncoming traffic and with enough space between car and pavement to allow for a coach trip to the kerb.

The manoeuvre gave Nikki enough time to compose herself. She realised she was very nervous. What was she walking into? What if she didn't like the scene when she finally hit it? What if it made her realise she was straight after all? What if it made her feel she didn't belong? Where the fuck would she belong then? Georgie had noted Nikki's abrupt change of mood. She linked arms with the older woman and virtually frogmarched her through the door.

'Don't worry, babe,' she said, 'my first time was horrible, too.'

The bar was quiet in terms of patrons but the blaring, pounding music and flashing lights were an almost physical assault on every nerve ending in Nikki's body. The bass line was so deep that she could feel her heart palpitating.

'Is it always this loud?' she yelled.

'What?'

'The music. Is it always this loud?'

'What? Beer?'

Nikki just nodded, her spirits sinking. Georgie must have spent years in places like this to not be bothered by the noise, to not now be suffering terminal deafness. Perhaps she was just too old for this sort of stuff. It didn't seem to have any melody, just a mindless thump, thump, thump. It all sounded the same. Gloomily, she realised she was thinking the same things that her mother had shouted at her when she played her Glam Slam LPs too loudly as a teenager. She not only played them loudly but she played them repeatedly so that she could learn the words. Nine O levels and three A levels with good grades gained at one of the county's best girls' schools and, to this day, she couldn't remember a damned thing she had learnt. But two bars of any seventies song and she could recite every lyric, who the band was and probably the lead singer's name. Sorry sad bitch.

They retreated with their beers to a corner of the bar. The music forced them both to lean into each other very closely, almost shouting into the other's ear, in an attempt at conversation.

'People will think we're a couple,' Nikki complained. 'How am I supposed to look single and available?'

'Course we're not a couple. There's no chemistry between us,' said Georgie. 'Anyway, enough people know me in here. Once it starts filling up I can introduce you to people and it will soon get around that you're young, free and single. Well, free and single.'

'I'm hardly single.'

'If I were you, I would definitely avoid any mention that you're married. Take off your wedding ring. Anyone who is interested will run a mile if they think you're some middle-aged married woman who's just bi-curious. They'll be expecting you to ask your husband along for a threesome. Some of us won't even touch a woman who's been with a man. It doesn't bother me, but there are quite a few lesbians who think that a woman who's been with a man will eventually get fed up with this gay-sex lark and run off with the first guy who chats them up. You'll find there's a huge amount of insecurity around.'

A crowd of girls burst through the door, spotted Georgie immediately, and Nikki was suddenly surrounded by more lesbians in one fell swoop than she had met in a lifetime.

Shit, thought Georgie, Phillipa.

Phillipa had already elbowed two women out of the way to be in Nikki's direct eyeline. Nikki, so far, was too busy trying to keep the look of fear off her face and act casual to notice that she was being mentally stripped and fucked. Georgie angled herself between the two. Nikki was not ready to be Phillipa'd. Georgie had struggled. What chance would poor Nikki have?

Nikki realised Georgie's arm was casually draped around her shoulder. The comforting squeeze was surreptitious, but Nikki immediately began to relax.

'This is Nikki, everyone. Make her welcome! Mine's a Bud!'

shouted Georgie above the din. Everyone apart from Phillipa missed most of the sentence.

Nikki scanned the group, realising with disappointment that she didn't actually fancy any of them. Maybe someone else will come in. Perhaps I'm asking too much, too soon, she thought. The beer was slipping down nicely but she knew she would have to switch to soft drinks next time. She warily eyed one of the girls: crop haired, tattooed and with a variety of facial piercings. She had a sudden panic that if she did get drunk she might end up getting raped in the toilet. Georgie's arm was now draped round her waist, with her thumb hooked into Nikki's belt, and she felt reasonably safe. But there was no way she would go to the toilet alone. She would rather have a bladder like a barrage balloon.

More people arrived; the bar began to fill out; the music – Nikki thought it would have been impossible – was turned up. As she watched, wide-eyed, people began to dance where they stood. Guys were snogging guys; women were fondling each other. Some were virtually having sex with their clothes on as they danced. Nikki realised she was enjoying the view.

What she was not enjoying was the furtive grinding against her left hip. She was packed into a crowd of Georgie's friends now. Georgie was still standing very close and protectively, but one of the original girls had now moved next to her and was moving against her.

It's probably what happens in gay clubs, she thought. The hand squeezing her arse, however, was too much. She had briefly glanced at the girl, who had not registered with her at all as a possible lay.

'Down, Phillipa, down!' Georgie came to the rescue. The girl looked petulant, peevish almost, at the frosty glare from Georgie.

Then Nikki spotted her, tall, blonde, as a wave of people parted temporarily. The girl must have felt Nikki's eyes on her because she turned, locking eyes immediately. They both smiled at the same time. Then her friends gathered around her again and Nikki lost eye contact.

Georgie and Phillipa were close to blows, but Nikki was

oblivious to the ruckus going on behind her back. She wanted, needed, to see the blonde again. It happened again, people parting, and it was obvious the blonde had also been trying to find Nikki again through the crowds. They smiled again.

The girl raised her empty glass and gesticulated at her. Nikki presumed it meant that the girl was going to buy her a drink. She nodded but, just as she started to move forward, chaos descended on the corner where they were packed.

Georgie, fortunately for Phillipa, was not pissed. Phillipa, however, was. As Nikki took her third step towards the blonde, a crash of glass alerted her to a potential problem behind her. She turned just as Phillipa disappeared in a welter of arms as three women attempted to pull her off Georgie. One stationed herself between the two as the bouncer suddenly appeared without warning. Various epithets were voiced above the music. Torn, Nikki stood helplessly.

Phillipa was secretly restrained from behind by one friend, who was talking in her ear as the bouncer demanded to know what had happened. Phillipa shook her head and glowered at Georgie. Georgie raised her hands to the bouncer and they became engrossed in conversation. As it progressed, Phillipa, with some reluctance, was being hauled away by her friend.

Georgie briefly looked at Nikki and winked. When Nikki turned back to find the blonde she saw her deep in conversation with another woman. The blonde raised her eyes, looked straight at Nikki and shrugged her shoulders as if to say Too Late.

Grim-faced, Nikki turned back to find Georgie standing right behind her.

'What the hell was all that about?' she furiously demanded.

'Unfinished business, petty jealousy and me watching out for your interests, basically,' said Georgie casually. 'Fancy a dance?'

The bar had a downstairs dance floor. By the time they had waded through the crush, Nikki's mystery blonde had disappeared, probably somewhere on the dance floor with her new woman, Nikki thought resentfully. It was so dark and smoky down there that Nikki's eyes stung. She couldn't make out any individuals, let alone spot her blonde.

Georgie was already moving to the pounding throb of the music, dancing in front of Nikki, who somewhat self-consciously began to move herself. She recognised, with a flare of pleasure, that she had discovered the rhythm of the club music, that she could actually dance to it.

Georgie's shirt was flung off, draped untidily over the back of a bar stool; her crop top already showed signs of the sweat that was pouring down her face and neck. Nikki wanted to do the same – the sweat was now collecting between her breasts. Then Georgie moved two steps closer, put her arm tight round Nikki's back and pulled her into her. As Nikki automatically adapted to Georgie's lead, she realised that the underlying bass throb had the rhythm of sex to it. Georgie was grinding against her; she was grinding back; Georgie's thigh was between hers, her hip rubbing against Nikki's groin with a maddeningly familiar frequency. Georgie's hand was stroking her back; her other hand was – Nikki hadn't noticed until now – entwined with hers as Georgie leant back and thrust harder at her.

Now Georgie leant right back, holding Nikki's belt so she could support her back as Georgie pumped, a hand carelessly brushing one of Nikki's breasts.

Christ, is this how lesbians always dance? Nikki wondered. She let herself go to the music. It didn't seem so loud now. Georgie's body heat, her own swelling clit, the atmosphere all combined to make Nikki light-headed. Sweat was pouring down her, dripping from her face on to Georgie's shoulder. She could feel Georgie's breasts pressed against her as Georgie once again pulled her in, both arms now tight round her, hands caressing her back and shoulders and her face now nuzzling into her neck.

Georgie wanted to taste her sweat: Nikki's neck was slippery with it. Nikki was so tall that she wanted to stretch up and kiss her ear; she wanted to move her hands round to the front and feel Nikki's breasts, slip her hand down to rub Nikki's mound. Nikki's jeans were so tight that Georgie had spent most of the evening in a sexual frenzy. She knew that her combats were virtually soaked with her juices.

Nikki pulled away so suddenly that Georgie was taken by

surprise. Nikki had spotted her blonde through the gloom: the girl was wrapped round a small brunette and they were snogging furiously. By the time Georgie had gathered her thoughts, Nikki was halfway to the downstairs bar. Two beers had been ordered and paid for by the time Georgie arrived next to her.

In the dim light Georgie could see that Nikki did not look happy. She glanced over in the direction of Nikki's transfixed gaze.

Nikki didn't even taste her beer as she drank it. Georgie knew she had lost Nikki for the rest of the evening: something had pissed her off, and it was probably best that they just leave. They walked in silence to the car.

As she pulled into the Burger King car park next to Nikki's Saab, Georgie broke the silence.

'It's only your first time, remember. She'll probably be there again another night, or there will be others.'

'But that girl she was with, I don't know, I'm sure I'm better looking than her. She was going to buy me a drink and then that argument started with that friend of yours. By the time it had finished she'd picked somebody else up. She was fucking gorgeous.'

'So that's your ideal, then, is it? Tall, blonde, slim, hairdo like a cycle helmet, bit of a slapper?'

'I don't have an ideal,' said Nikki defensively. 'I just know that out of everyone there she was the only one I fancied.'

Georgie's heart lurched with crushing disappointment. 'Well, like I say, it was your first time and there's plenty of gorgeous women out there. They're in the clubs, the villages, the adverts, wherever. I'll help you get sorted one way or another. Once you get in the circle and start making friends it gets easier. People know people – you know, the networking thing. Don't make the mistake of thinking this was your only chance. Take your time. You've still got to get used to the whole thing. With friends around you it will help build your confidence. In a few weeks, trust me, you'll be marching up to a bird like that and chatting her up. For God's sake, Nikki, you didn't expect tonight to be the night you met your one and only true love, light of your life, did you?'

Nikki smiled ruefully, as they sat in the dark. 'Yes, I did. Daft, really. I was so excited about the whole thing that I let myself get carried away. I've got quite a learning curve to go through, haven't I? I should just relax with it, have some fun and frivolity first and then she'll probably just come round the corner and knock me flat on my back and I'll be ready for her. It would be too complicated right now, wouldn't it? Too many other things to sort out. I should just be a tomcat for a while.'

'Yeah, just be careful, there's a few nutters out there. Don't do anything on your own without your minder.'

'Georgie, I'd be lost without you.' Nikki didn't see Georgie's face change in the dark. 'I really must be going. When can we do this again?'

'Whenever you like. As soon as you want. You've got my numbers; my mobile is back on line again because I've paid the bill. You can ring me any time you like, you know. That's what mates are for. I've got to look out for you anyway because, if anything goes horribly wrong, I'll have Auntie Gillian to answer to.'

Nikki laughed and leant over to kiss her goodbye. Georgie remained rigid, not trusting her treacherous body if she moved, as Nikki's lips brushed her cheek.

'I'll call you tomorrow. We'll fix something up.' Nikki was already out of the car, giving a casual wave as she de-activated her car alarm.

Georgie watched in her mirror until the red lights of the Saab disappeared, and then sat quietly in the dark.

I want you, she thought.

NINE

It had been a crazy summer. Nikki sat smiling to herself at her desk one early-September afternoon. She had thrown herself into the scene with gusto, Georgie never far from her side. Georgie's main group of friends had adopted Nikki with a protective fondness. She was now an official member of Georgie's Pussy Posse. Even that flighty Phillipa had stopped gazing at her with sad cow eyes, having found herself a seventeen-year-old nymphomaniac to occupy her nights.

Weekends were now routine outings locally or to gay villages around the country. At least twice a week Nikki and Georgie spent the evening at the local bars or at Georgie's flat. There they would pore over the classified contact ads, compiling written responses to PO box numbers, or rehearsing scripts for the voicemail messages. Nikki baulked at Georgie's suggestion to place her own advert.

'Tall, slim, desperate novice requires taking in hand and mouth by gorgeous babe magnet? No? How about rich bitch requires regular servicing. Long MOT and greased nipples guaranteed? Or horny older woman, gagging for it, urgently requires long, slow, sensual shagging session with absolutely anybody?' Nikki had asked.

She was beginning to choke as she laughed with a mouthful of beer. She had never really liked beer but membership of the Posse had strict rules. Bottled beer and ear piercing were prime requirements. So Nikki had dutifully developed a taste for Budweiser – she was relieved to see that Jack Daniel's was also allowed – and had mustered the courage to have double hoop earrings in one ear. Her wedding ring was still tucked in her purse from their first night out together. Steve had not remarked on it, probably not even noticed it, and she had had her eighteenth-birthday signet ring sized to fit the little finger of her left hand.

Georgie had suggested a few other lesbian refinements but Nikki felt that they might have been too much of a giveaway. Other parts of her own body being pierced did not hold any attraction for her, although she had admired Georgie's belly-button stud on a number of occasions. She still didn't feel like a fully fledged lesbian, still had not mastered the art of spotting a fellow sister anywhere other than at a gay venue. Georgie had told her it would take some time, and plenty of practice. It was something to do with The Look, apparently a clitoris-swelling instant reaction when one woman looked at another in a certain way in a heterosexual environment. Nikki, sadly, still had not experienced The Look outside of the clubs and bars she now frequented.

Truth be known, she had not actually experienced it very much within the scene. Georgie and the Posse had gone to great lengths to lift her spirits each time she came away having failed to pull. They took turns at dirty dancing with her in the clubs, and made a point of introducing her to their other friends on a regular basis. She was also getting used to the massive amounts of flirting that went on within the group, all of whom were openly affectionate with each other. She took a little time to get used to their habit of always kissing on the lips when saying hello or goodbye, but now it came so naturally that she had to consciously remember not to do it with her straight female friends. Gillian would have slapped her face if she had done it to her.

Invariably one of the group would have an emotional crisis or a particularly emotive period and the others would rally round like mother hens or favoured aunties. There was usually an enormous amount of group hugging going on at those times.

The evenings in at a nominated flat or house – usually coinciding with the last week before payday when money was always tight for them – always found at least one of them cuddling up to Nikki. She never felt any sexual pressure from any of them, not even the one memorable night when Georgie was persuaded to get her massage oil out to give a back massage to Tracy.

Having massaged Tracy, Georgie then found a queue of willing lesbians with real or imagined aches and pains in various parts of the body. She drew the line at giving one a breast massage but Nikki threw caution to the winds and demanded a shoulder and neck massage. Georgie was firm and the tension created by a looming deadline at work had disappeared within minutes. She had made a mental note to ask Georgie for a back massage next time if the opportunity arose again.

Spending time on the scene had been an eye-opener. She did buy lesbian books, magazines and videos, all of which she kept at Georgie's flat. It was Georgie's address she used for her so far sparse PO box replies, her mobile number for the voicemail message-line responses. She had only had three in the two months, all of whom sounded dour. She had actually agreed to meet one of them, in sheer desperation, but the girl had stood her up.

Although she had not had sex – any sex – for a while, she was not once tempted to resort to Paula's escort girls. Her Posse, despite their repeated failures to secure her a date, were still providing her with a hell of a lot of fun. Their sense of humour was as extreme as her own, and she took in her stride the repeated jokes about her advanced years. As the oldest member of the Posse, she had to. Nikki was enjoying the sense of freedom she had found in the last few weeks.

Steve, Marion, her colleagues and her clients were also enjoying the benefits. She rarely lost her temper these days. Even her boss, who had coined the oft-used expression 'Never go back to a lighted Nikki', was feeling more relaxed around her. She bounced into new-business meetings with a renewed verve and vigour and had already scooped two new accounts and whisked an advertising campaign from under the noses of the agency's biggest rival.

Any excuse she had to use Georgie professionally was exploited to the full. Georgie was now working flat out on a number of copywriting projects and video scripts, and her bank balance was healthier than it had been in a long time. Nikki had given Georgie full rein with her precious contacts in other agencies and had provided fulsome praise in at least two references.

No, she thought, I'm not getting laid at the moment but no doubt I will. The discussions late into the night when the Posse gathered round Georgie's flat, when the beer had flowed and conversation turned to sex, had whetted her appetite. Just as she had done as a teenager when the fourth formers were bragging about their sexual conquests with spotty youths, so Nikki resorted to nodding furiously in agreement when various encounters were described. Invariably she had to ask Georgie afterwards what the hell the others had been talking about, just as she had done as a teenager. She had once made the mistake of asking her mother what oral sex was, having overheard a fellow fifth former brag about it in double physics.

'That,' her mother had retorted icily, with the tone that intimated the subject would be promptly closed once she had spoken, 'is what men go to prostitutes for.'

Still unenlightened, she had been married six months before Steve had suggested it. She hated doing it to him and he only did it to her on a handful of occasions before announcing that he thought it was unhygienic. Cut to the quick, Nikki had temporarily suffered from Obsessive Compulsive Disorder and had spent a fortune on soaps, perfumed body sprays and vaginal deodorants. It was a shame really, because the odd occasions he had made the token effort had provided her with the only times she had ever enjoyed Steve sexually. Still, it had been his loss. He seemed happy with the obligatory fumble, grope of her tits, quick fiddle down below and then climbing on board for a hasty bump and grind. Steve's idea of foreplay was a fifth can of lager before suggesting an early night. She had settled into the Man from Atlantis missionary-position sex life that had by now virtually dwindled away to zilch, and she couldn't actually remember which year it had been that she had last been benevolent enough to bestow a blow job on him.

She was still trying to work it out when the phone rang. Marion by now recognised Georgie immediately and always put her straight through.

'You've had a response!'

'Well, don't make it sound like I've won the Nobel Peace Prize. If it's anything like the last disaster, then I think I'll move on to dating pit ponies.'

'Male or female? That begs the question! No, straight up, this sounds interesting. Very sexy voice, very sexy. I've saved the message with her number. She sounds ideal. Bit big-headed, but then you like a challenge, don't you? Probably be a right clash of the titans when you come together. I've written it down in shorthand. Listen to this . . .'

Nikki settled into her chair. She knew that Georgie would struggle with certain outlines, she always did. Unless Georgie transcribed her shorthand notes within seconds she ended up with great tracts of dictation that she couldn't read. It had got her into trouble many times as a sprog journalist, as Nikki recalled. As usual she waited patiently while Georgie mumbled through her notes at the other end.

'Forty-four, young-looking, elegant and into designer clothes . . . gas industry . . . something about sales and marketing . . . What the fucking hell does that say . . .? Head-turner looking for someone to make her proud in a restaurant . . . worked overseas . . . long legs . . . very tall . . . loquacious, vibrant and with an arse to die for . . .'

Nikki broke the monologue: 'Sounds complete bullshit to me.'

'Well, it went on for so long that the machine cut her off and she had to ring back to carry on all the superlatives.'

'No, I don't think so. No one could be that fucking perfect, particularly if they are bragging about it. Screw it up and throw it away. We'll have another look at the ads when I come over tonight.'

'I think you should ring her back. Christ, what if she's a Cindy Crawford look-alike? I know you like them girly. I know it's older than your preferred age range but, let's face it, Nikki, you can't afford to be choosy.'

Nikki let it ride. She was used to the banter by now. She had had more insults hurled at her since July than she had had most of her working life. At least they were creative and original, which is more than could be said for the stuff Steve had thrown at her in years gone by. She had developed a fine line in retorts herself, but strictly within the confines of the Posse. A chance insult in the wrong direction could end up in a brawl, quite a few of which Nikki had observed recently.

'Well, I'll have a listen later and make my decision then. Beer in the fridge?'

'Sadly not enough. I'll go and get some if you pay for the takeaway.'

'Deal. See you at seven.'

When Nikki looked down at her scratch pad after replacing the handset – it had been weeks since the abused telephone had been slammed – she was intrigued to see a row of question marks, all underlined at least three times. I wonder what my therapist would think of that if I was still seeing her, she thought, then spotted the other doodle. It simply said G. Twice. Circled.

She dismissed it as idle fidgeting with her pencil while Georgie had prattled on. Georgie had thrown herself into the Mission to Get Nikki Laid with as much abandon as her godmother attacked projects. While there was clearly no chance of Georgie having genetic inheritance from Gillian, she had adopted one or two rather endearing copycat traits over the years. She, like Gillian, was a terrier with a bone if set a task.

Nikki smiled as she thought of Gillian, her oldest, dearest friend, and once again mentally thanked her for bringing her together with Georgie – and for rescuing the situation that Sunday. It could all have been so drastically, sadly, different. Many times, and with continued great embellishment, both Nikki and Georgie had regaled the Posse with the saga of how they had met and what Gillian's role had been. As both could do perfect imitations of her, the story was always a popular one.

She turned up at Georgie's flat bang on time. Nikki was the sort of person who would turn up for a flight three hours early. Unlike Gillian, Nikki lived in fear of being late – for anything. Georgie had just climbed out of the shower when the bell rang. Wrapped in a towel, she flung open the door.

'You go and listen to the message while I dry my hair. I won't be long,' she called out as Nikki went into the small kitchen to raid the fridge for beer.

Here we go again, Nikki thought despondently. Another loser, probably, must be something about the type of people who put contact ads in. Can't meet anyone any other way, I suppose. But what does that say about me? I scour the bloody things week in, week out, can't pull in the clubs. Christ, I used to have to pay for it. At least I got it then. Not much luck on the horizon at the moment, is there?

She pressed the PLAY button with lacklustre enthusiasm and was assailed by the sexiest, huskiest voice she had ever heard. Her enthusiasm returned tenfold as she listened to the woman's throaty, deep purr down the phone. All she could think about was that same, hauntingly horny voice in her ear, whispering delicious fantasies.

She played the message at least five times before Georgie reappeared.

'Told you the voice was worth listening to, didn't I?'

'Christ, a voice like that could give a eunuch an erection,' said Nikki dreamily.

'Ring her back. Ring her back, for God's sake. And put her on speaker phone. I want to hear everything.'

Fortified by her third beer, Nikki finally gave in to Georgie's pleading and hesitantly dialled the woman.

The phone picked up halfway through the second ring and that voice drifted into the flat. Even the word 'hello' clutched at Nikki's clit. Georgie stifled a moan with a cushion.

'Hi, it's Nikki. You left a message for me?'

112

'I did, darling. I thought your letter was interesting, humorous. It's a shame you didn't send a photograph. I'd love to put a face to you.'

Georgie began to giggle, resisting the urge to shout, 'I'd love to put my face on you.'

Nikki refused to look at Georgie: the voice had mesmerised her.

The woman – Elizabeth – talked about herself for quite a while. Nikki didn't register the minutes ticking by. She registered, however, the height – nearly six foot; a faint South African twang to the accent; that the woman had long, curly brunette hair, brown eyes, flawless skin, endless legs; that she enjoyed fine wine and food; that she ran a successful sales consultancy within the energy industry and travelled a great deal; that she had been married and divorced, and both her children were now teenagers.

'So your children live with you, then?' Nikki asked.

'No, darling, sadly they don't. I left them when I realised what I was. It took some years but we have developed a relationship of sorts since. They accept the way I am now and are trying to understand why I had to go.'

'That must have been a difficult decision as a mother. Are they happy with their father?'

'Leaving children behind is always difficult, darling. And basically they accept that their lives have been happier without me being there full time.'

Nikki loved the spin Elizabeth put on the word 'darling'. A slight alarm bell was ringing in the back of her head but she ignored it. She had to hear more of this voice.

'So, from my letter,' she began, 'what particularly appealed to make you ring me?'

'I have an idea that you're a feisty young thing. I do like blondes, particularly tall ones. With my height I can hardly take up with a tiny little dot, can I? I do like to wear heels, you see. I tend to tower over everyone. I do attract an awful lot of looks when I have my gladrags on. I would love to be able to walk into places with an equally beautiful woman on my arm.'

Nikki might have been ignoring the slight alarm bell in her

mind but Georgie's was by now working overtime. An entire fire brigade could have been mustered by her bells. She by this point had gone well beyond the allure of the voice and was beginning to pull faces at Nikki. Nikki ignored her.

'Are you beautiful?' Elizabeth demanded.

Georgie was furiously shaking her head, trying to get Nikki to notice her.

'I've been told I'm attractive –' Nikki was coy '– bit of a resemblance to Sharon Stone, but probably at night with the lights very low and a copious amount of alcohol.'

'There's an interesting proposition.' Elizabeth's voice sounded thick with desire.

Nikki's immediate reaction was to snatch up the receiver to take the call off the speaker phone. Georgie flounced into the kitchen for more beer.

The conversation began to flow, getting fruitier and fruitier – and Georgie became increasingly alarmed. When, full of anticipation that she was about to meet a combination of Sigourney Weaver and Diana Rigg, Nikki insisted on meeting Elizabeth, Georgie nearly exploded.

The arrangement made, Nikki replaced the receiver and turned round with a self-satisfied smile on her face. Georgie's glare immediately wiped it off.

'What the hell is the matter with you?' asked Nikki.

'There's something not right. I can't put my finger on it, but it's not right. I'm getting very, very bad vibes about this, Nicola, very bad.'

For Georgie to use her full name it must be a genuine feeling, Nikki thought.

'Look, babe, things don't add up, do they?' Georgie continued. 'She was so fucking full of herself and if she was so fucking traffic-stopping wonderful why is she advertising under a PO box number? How can you possibly trust a woman who abandons her children like that? OK, she's got a voice that goes straight to your clitoris but you have no idea about anything else, do you? I would never trust anyone who talked about themselves like that. I'll bet you now she's nothing like she says she is and I'll stake my life on it that she's some fucking bunny-boiler who's just been released from an institution. Or something.'

'I think you're overreacting a little, don't you? I've agreed to meet her in broad daylight in a hotel lobby.'

'Yeah, and twenty quid says she will have a room booked for the rest of the day or night. For God's sake, Nicola, you sounded like you were gagging for it.'

'I am. If you must know, I enjoyed talking to her.' Nikki was now hugely defensive.

'Being talked at, more like. You should have had a few more conversations before plunging in for a meeting. I'm coming with you. I just don't like this. I don't like it at all.'

The pair sulked for a while, drinking their beer.

Georgie caved in first: 'You have to accept, babe, that I've got more experience than you have with women. Remember me telling you about the nutters out there? Women are emotional and insecure anyway. It can lead to all sorts of psychopathic behaviour, obsessions, stalking . . . Christ knows what when you add the persecution that homosexuality brings to the equation. Believe me, I've come across many of them in my time. I can spot them a mile off.

'She can only talk about herself. She was only interested in the superficial crap about having a beautiful woman to make her look good. Didn't you notice that? You are beautiful, Nikki, she'll probably cream her pants when she sees you. Just promise me you'll take me with you.'

'I'm used to monstrous egos in my job. I've got one myself. I can take her down a peg or two if needs be. If she's half of what she says she is she'll do for me. Don't stand there with your hands on your hips, Georgina.'

'You can't be that desperate.'

Nikki shrugged.

Georgie nagged her for the rest of the evening and on the phone at work until Nikki finally gave in and agreed that she could go with her the following evening, on condition they went in separate cars and Georgie remained in hers while Nikki went on reconnaissance.

Naturally early, with wobbly legs and luckily having a good-hair day, Nikki strode into the hotel foyer to be met by a vision.

As Nikki was the only tall, blonde, slim woman in the foyer with a slight resemblance to Sharon Stone, it was hard for her to be mistaken. She was spotted immediately and froze like a startled rabbit.

Her very first thought was that Elizabeth was by no means how she had described herself on the phone. She was mildly attractive but hardly as jaw-droppingly gorgeous as she had claimed. Her immense height reminded Nikki uncomfortably of old drawings of Amazonian female warriors. But, to her credit, Elizabeth carried herself with an almost regal air, reminiscent of Boudicca in full flight probably. Her dress sense was elegantly classic – just border-ing on old-fashioned – and she almost shone like an angel with a large amount of genuinely antique and presumably hugely expen-sive jewellery. Nikki dismissed her thoughts quickly, mentally berating herself for being crashingly disappointed on first look – so shallow and superficial.

'You're early. My, you are keen. I arrived early too, had to drive like a banshee because I needed a tiddle – little bit of nerves.' Elizabeth was looking at Nikki in a terribly coy fashion.

Tiddle? Does she mean piss? She probably says trump instead of fart. Christ, is this woman locked in a time warp, or what? What does she mean, by 'keen'?

Nikki, unnerved by her sinking gloom of disappointment that Elizabeth looked nothing like Sigourney Weaver, was subcon-sciously sending out some seriously negative vibes, refusing to make eye contact and desperately wondering how she could tactfully tell this upper-crust Amazon that she simply didn't fancy her.

Elizabeth coquettishly leant across, patted Nikki's rigid arm and purred, 'You're a hundred times better than I thought. Am I everything I said I'd be?'

'Well . . . you're tall,' Nikki muttered defensively.

Elizabeth wanted to eat; Nikki had no appetite. Undeterred by the other woman's almost sullen silence, totally unaware that Nikki had not felt the slightest jolt of any sexual electricity on meeting, Elizabeth settled comfortably and began to warble on about her favourite subject. Herself.

'It took me ages to sort out the right outfit for today. I wanted to look extra special for you. I even managed to book myself in for a manicure –' she spread her over-large hands for Nikki to admire '– although to be absolutely frank I was hoping that you would not be wearing jeans. I prefer my women to look far more feminine, you know. And to be honest your hair is a little short for my liking. A little bit butch, if you don't mind me saying. Is that the right word? I hardly ever get my hair cut, you know. I think it symbolises a certain sort of feminine strength, you know?'

While she droned on, comparing her own much finer points with Nikki's, Nikki remained speechless with indignation, at the succession of mildly insulting observations oozing from the woman's heavily lipsticked mouth. The woman was completely in love with herself. Irritated by the ongoing onslaught of critical comments about her hair, make-up, dress sense, and unable to bring herself to respond in kind, Nikki began to seethe in peevish silence. This is terrible; don't know how the hell I'm going to get out of here, she thought viciously.

Her salvation, as usual, was Georgie.

Georgie had sat in her car, as agreed, for fifteen minutes, frantic with worry. Nikki had not reappeared. She had sworn to come out and update Georgie with progress – if any – after half an hour and come up with a plausible reason for Georgie accompanying her back into the hotel. Georgie couldn't wait half an hour. She had visions of Nikki being hauled into a lift and systematically raped for three days. She marched into the lobby, saw the back of the mystery woman's head and recognised an abject look of turmoil and misery on Nikki's face.

'Nikki! How are you? This is a surprise!' She bowled up to the pair of them, theatrically waving and turning in one fluid movement to face Elizabeth. 'And you must be . . .?'

Through gritted teeth, Elizabeth almost snarled her name at the dyke interloper. Nikki was still struck dumb.

'Why don't we all have a drink, get to know each other?'

Georgie was the personification of cheerful graciousness. Nikki was still incapable of coherent speech. Elizabeth's irritation was palpable but, anxious to coerce Nikki into further discussion – in fact any conversation at all – she waved her hand in gracious agreement.

Christ, thought Georgie, she's more royal than the Queen Mother.

Nikki was rapidly propelled by her elbow towards the bar area, Elizabeth close behind them like a galleon in full sail.

Nikki's first proper sentence since meeting Elizabeth was to agree to a large Jack Daniel's. Elizabeth raised perfectly coiffeured eyebrows in distaste as she sat, rigidly straight-backed, on the edge of the chair.

'A little early for the strong stuff, isn't is, my dear? I believe in the sun-over-the-yard-arm theory myself. My darling mother always used to tell me that spirits have a nasty habit of returning to haunt your skin as you grow older. That is why I'm always being complemented on looking so much younger than I actually am.' She bestowed a smile upon them both.

'Not met many other lesbians before now?' was Georgie's opening gambit, hoping, correctly as it transpired, that Elizabeth would probably feel uncomfortable with the subject matter being so out in the open.

'I rely upon the advertisements, I must say, particularly with letters and photographs. One has to be careful, mixing with such people. It allows you to at least have some fashion of screening undesirable entities.'

'What, like aliens?' Nikki snarled.

Shocked that it appeared the blonde actually could speak after all, Elizabeth appeared to have had a major sense of humour failure. Georgie's Jack Daniel's disappeared up her nose as she sank into her glass to stop herself giggling. Elizabeth stared at Georgie with contempt for such adolescent behaviour.

'For some reason I do feel that I am not being taken seriously here.' Elizabeth drew herself and her rather matronly bosom up to a magnificent height. She reminded Nikki of her old headmistress.

She gently placed her glass of orange juice on the table, rose for what seemed to Nikki an inordinately long time, and gathered her tasselled shawl around her shoulders.

'I can see that there appears to have been a somewhat monstrous error of judgement here. I do have another appointment to go to later this afternoon. It seems pointless to me to carry on with this little charade. Good day,' Elizabeth announced imperiously, turning on her heels with furious indignation and departing.

'See? Told you! She's hardly a bunny boiler but, my God, she looked like she would be at home in some stately pile, issuing orders to servants. Christ, you'd have probably ended up as some under parlour maid, scraping out the firegrates every day and having to take off her boots after her early-morning canter.' Georgie was almost gleeful.

'Will you for fuck's sake shut up?'

'Another drink? A little sweetener? Or is it nearly time for a visit from the little hormone fairy? Babe, I know you're in shock . . .'

'I've got post-traumatic stress disorder.'

'But let's face it, babe, this is going to be an absolute doozy of a tale by the time we've finished with it. This is going to be a classic of a nightmare date from hell, beats even Auntie Gillian's encounter with a member of the upper crust. Perhaps we could get those two together instead, and they can talk about each other's people's land and have bedroom activity of a horizontal nature. She's not gay. She's probably just wanting to act out some fantasy about sex with her nanny or one of the maids in a pinny.'

'All I know is that from now I'm celibate. I'm not going to respond to any more fucking ads. I want to see the goods before I sample them. There will be some bird in a club, a bar, I'll meet through work and wham, bam, thank you very kindly ma'am. If you get any more messages on your goddamned machine don't you fucking dare tell me about them. Screen every response in future. I know we both think I like a challenge but that was serious big-time taking the fucking tiddle.'

'Tiddle?'

'Yeah, tiddle. She said having a tiddle, instead of taking a piss, having a slash, a pee or a whizz.'

'No one says tiddle. Even the Royal Family wouldn't say tiddle. Let's face it, if she had looked like Jodie Foster and said tiddle, you would have been turned off. It's hardly a cast-iron indication of totally uninhibited sex, is it?'

It was at that point that Nikki finally made eye contact with Georgie and started to laugh. They both laughed until they were crying.

'It could only happen to me. I should have sussed something on the phone, shouldn't I? But no, I fall for it because every night my cunt's been chasing me round the bed screaming, "Feed me, feed me." Can you believe she had actually suggested that if we did hit it off today we should spend the weekend in bed? If I ever, ever, respond to an ad again can you make sure I ask the right questions and ask for photos, a family tree or something?'

'Think we'll leave the ads alone, babe. Let's get the Pussy Posse Dating Agency open for business again. I know the girls are begging for a night out and a couple of them have friends you haven't met yet.'

Georgie was anxious that Nikki didn't descend into despondency again. First proper date and look what happens. She would be better off in a crowd, where they could all look after her if something went wrong. If she did end up attracted to someone whom her friends knew, at least there was a chance to avoid any schizophrenic maniacs.

'It's all very well, Georgie, this mission of yours, but you've hardly been at it yourself for a while, have you?'

'Patience, dear girl. I'm concentrating all my energies on you for the time being. I'm having a great time, a few beers, a good laugh, terrific company. I'm not looking for anything else at the moment. Going without sex has never really bothered me much. Mind you, having said that, I've never really gone for long without it. Anyway, if all else fails, I still haven't found anyone who can wank me better than I can.'

That set Nikki off on another fit of the giggles.

'I'm getting fed up of taking my hand out to dinner and the movies. The left hand complains too much – you never take me anywhere . . .'

Nikki was helpless.

'I'm lying on it to make it go numb then it feels like someone else is doing it . . .'

Nikki was almost howling, holding her aching stomach. People were looking at them.

'But it means I always end up sleeping on the damp patch.'

Georgie waited, grinning, until Nikki's giggles abated. Nikki wiped her eyes. Her mascara had run but she didn't care.

'You can always cheer me up, Georgie, even over something disastrous like this.'

'If it's any consolation, at least you haven't reached the stage I have. People ring me up when they're depressed and suicidal because something far worse has usually happened to me the day before. I provide a community service for when the Samaritans are engaged. I once got so depressed I thought I was suicidal and rang a psychiatrist from the *Yellow Pages* who couldn't see me for a fortnight. I told her I'd be dead by then and she asked what I thought my biggest problem was. I said, "I can't fucking get on with people," and slammed the phone down. I felt much better after that.'

That set Nikki off again. She was laughing so hard that she draped her arm round Georgie's shoulder for support. Georgie's arm went round her waist.

'Georgie, you're absolutely priceless, you really are,' she finally managed to splutter. 'Life with you is never dull. I don't think I've ever met anyone like you. I wish I'd met you years ago.

You've already made such a difference to my life, you wouldn't know. I haven't laughed so much, and so hard, ever. I have never felt so free, so comfortable to be just myself rather than this front I've had to put up all these years.'

Georgie's emotions were in turmoil. She was in a straight environment, her arm round a woman who had clearly not recognised how she felt about her, who was saying things that Georgie desperately wished could have been said in a different context. She swallowed the words she wanted to say and instead slipped back once more into her mode of best friend and protector.

'What front?'

'Depends who I'm with. It's normally hard-faced business-woman wielding the power and kicking ass in a man's world, making money all the time for some other fucker to enjoy; or it could be devoted, dutiful wife being paraded around like some rugby-club pennant, saying all the right things in all the right places at all the right times. Successful, conventional, hungry and aggressive middle-aged marketing floozy, got it all, with the ability to flirt and bat her eyelids at the right time, although probably getting a bit long in the tooth for it, going back to a large house with utility room, en suite and fitted wardrobes to sit in absolute silence with a complete fucking stranger.'

Georgie had no idea what to say.

'It's OK,' Nikki continued. 'Now and again I look at my life and wonder how it could have been different, better. I know I have an awful lot that other people only aspire to. I'm healthy, I look OK, I dress well, I earn a very good wage and I can afford to spoil myself. The facade of being ruthless and aggressive protects me. It hides the real me from people who could and probably would hurt me, take advantage of me because of what they see. They would want me for the wrong reasons. Steve wanted me so that he could progress in the bank as a respectable, solid and sound individual with a respectable, intelligent escort. My boss wanted me so that I could charm his clients and win lots of new business to boost his bank account. I give out the impression of being independent, smart, sassy, take it all on the chin and still come out of the corner fighting. I'm a challenge to most people but sometimes, especially in the dark, I just want to give in, give up and scream that I'm a pussycat, not a tiger. I'm tired of bouncing back time after time and in fifteen, God forbid, twenty years' time realising that I've done it all for everyone else, not for me.'

'That's quite a speech. Quite an admission. There's nothing, absolutely nothing to stop you doing it all for yourself now.'

'Divorce, money, risks.'

'Surely it's only practicalities, economies of scale? Finances can be worked out in a civilised fashion. From what you've said about your marriage, surely Steve would be happier on his own? You could go out on your own in marketing, set up a consultancy and pinch a few clients. All it would take is serviced offices, a phone line and you're up and running. I know you're well known and well respected in this town for the job you do, even if you do frighten the hell out of people. I know of at least one customer-services manager who hides in the toilet when she sees your car pull into the car park.

'You know what you want to achieve; you know damn well you're capable of it. You know where you want to go in life, and sorting it out may be difficult, even painful, at times. But you've got people around you now who understand you, who care for you. We are all here for you. Auntie Gillian will help you on the business side, you know she will. Marion is very important to you, too. I'm sure she would help you if you needed her to. Steve can't make you stay. He can't force you to continue a marriage of convenience like this. You'd end up killing each other as you got older and grumpier. Just thank God you don't have kids to think about. Just walk away, start again, do it, focus on what is more important to you.

'Like you say, you have more than many people have to help facilitate it. Sacrifice a little on the divorce settlement so that Steve's macho ego is massaged, start laying plans now. And just don't worry about finding a relationship: that will happen when the time is right. Just because you're now feeling comfortable with being gay doesn't mean to say that you have to let it dominate your life. Take it one step at a time, carefully think it all out, don't leave yourself exposed or vulnerable, and I'll bet by this time next year you'll be able to see it all coming together.'

Nikki sat in silence during the speech.

'Food for thought,' she said quietly, and squeezed Georgie's hand.

I'll be there for you, Georgie thought. I'll wait. It will be worth it, I know.

TEN

Georgie was staring listlessly at her screen. The words did not want to come this morning. She did. Badly.

She had tossed and turned fitfully all night, enjoying only a light sleep, constantly waking on the hour and staring gloomily at the clock. Her head was full of Nikki. Every time she tried to think of something else, someone else, Nikki intruded. Nikki laughing. Nikki crying. Nikki dancing with her, holding her hand, hugging her. Nikki close, bending so that she could hear Georgie above the din of the music, her ear tantalisingly close; Nikki sleeping naked on her settee – curled in a protective ball – her bare legs outside the quilt as usual; Nikki in a flap about her outfit for the evening, running around the bedroom in her bra and jeans and resorting to having to ask to borrow a stretch top. Georgie had still not washed that top: it still smelt of Nikki's perfume, Nikki's body. Nikki had never been aware of the morning when Georgie had crept into the lounge to watch her sleep. Nikki looked like an angel when she was asleep, Georgie thought, a hungover angel half-buried in a quilt. The morning Nikki had moved in her sleep on to her back, her leg stretched, the quilt moved and Georgie had a brief glimpse of paradise – those breasts, fine and round and thoroughly kissable; the soft, fine, blonde, neatly trimmed pubes so eminently lickable. Fighting hard to control the desire that swamped her, Georgie had held her breath as she gently moved the quilt back over Nikki.

Nikki's long fingers entwined in hers whenever they danced. She wanted to be stroked by those fingers; she wanted those fingers pulling her hair as she licked and sucked Nikki to climax. She wanted those fingers deep inside her, moving and probing.

Most of all, she wanted Nikki's lips on hers, Nikki's tongue in her mouth, Nikki's lips and tongue teasing and playing with her sex. Georgie had never wanted anyone so much, so achingly much, had never thought about anyone virtually every waking moment, fantasised so many times.

She had walked into Nikki's office the other afternoon with some work. Nikki had walked round the desk to greet her, gently brushing lips against lips. As Georgie's hand had naturally fallen to Nikki's hip as they kissed, she felt the suspender belt. Nikki's skirt was acceptably short, her long legs encased in shiny, sheer black Lycra stockings, her heels accentuating the shapely, slim calves and ankles. Georgie was finding it very difficult to concentrate as Nikki perched on the corner of her desk and crossed her legs. She could hear the brush of the stockings against each other and all she could think about was the creamy, pale skin of Nikki's thighs above the lacy stocking tops. Nikki was talking, oblivious to Georgie's discomfort.

Georgie's mind was racing with visions of Nikki lounging on her bed in those heels, sheer stockings and suspender belt, a tiny thong just covering her pubes, her breasts straining against a black satin bra.

God, she has no idea what she does to me. Thinking about her sends me crazy.

Georgie still could not make the words appear on screen. Disconsolate, she put the laptop into sleep mode and ambled into the kitchen for more coffee. The phone rang. It was Nikki.

'I was just thinking about you,' said Georgie. Thinking about loving you, holding you, caressing you, kissing you. Thinking how much I need you in my life. Thinking about how I'd like to be sleeping next to you every night, for the rest of my life.

'Dirty bitch. Was I good? How are you getting on with the job?'

'Slowly,' Georgie admitted. 'For some reason, I don't feel very inspired today.'

'You sound a bit down. Are you OK?'

Yeah, I'm OK. I'm just mad for you. 'It's writer's block, that's all. It's difficult to get motivated to write scintillating prose about fax machines and office stationery.'

'Just toss it out. We're just putting the finished artwork together now. All you need is bullet points, standard You've Tried the Rest Now Try the Best type crap. Do what I do, take the money, do enough to not work up a sweat, bang it out, deliver it and move on to the next piece of shit.'

'I am an artiste. I don't bang things out –'

'Don't get all precious and prima-donna like with me. Like you said, it's fax machines and staplers. I've got something else for you when you've tossed this one out. I'll bring it over with me tomorrow night, if you like.'

'Whatever.'

They said their goodbyes.

Nikki replaced the receiver. Georgie's frame of mind was strange. She hadn't heard her like that before. She had sounded very sad, depressed almost. The last time they had spoken on the phone Georgie had been her usual cheerful, raucous, loud self. But then, she remembered, Georgie had been a little muted when she had come into the office on Monday afternoon. In fact, Nikki now thought, Georgie had actually said very little the whole half-hour she was there, seemed very fidgety and on edge.

Nikki had been recounting, with glee, the latest DIY fiasco her husband had finally got round to doing. Steve had always had trouble putting pictures up, let alone embarking on a mammoth project like putting up speaker brackets. He had positioned the brackets, drilled the holes, brick and mortar dust flying, then realised as he attempted to mount the speakers that he had not left enough clearance to the ceiling.

Three re-drillings later, and a temporary filling of the other holes, had left her lounge walls looking like a war-movie set. Nikki had busied herself elsewhere in the house, making the obligatory wife noises as he grunted and sweated, but she had not cared enough to complain about the mess. She no longer cared about anything to do with the house. She had asked herself whether she cared if she lost it and realised that she didn't. Steve could have it. It had been her pride and joy for a long time, her choice of decor and furnishings within Steve's somewhat limited ideas of interior design. Now she knew she could walk away and not think once about it.

Comparing prices in the local paper, she had a rough idea of its value and the equity within it. She only wanted a fair slice of the cash: it would be enough to start her off, a start-up investment that she knew would be matched by any business banking centre. Not Steve's. She could move into rented accommodation for a while, just until her business got off the ground. Then, when it started to move into profit, she could pay herself a bonus as deposit for a smaller place, perhaps a cottage in a village. She could shop around for antique furniture – Steve had always been a light-oak or black-ash type of man – and do each room at a time. So long as she had a bed, a microwave and freezer, a sound system and a TV, a reasonable bathroom with shower, Nikki would be happy.

Georgie had not responded much to this, Nikki now realised. It was Georgie's lecture the other day that had set Nikki's thoughts into a basic outline for an action plan with targets and timescales. She now felt she had aims to achieve, all reasonable, practical and feasible. Spare moments at work had been spent photocopying certain documents which could come in useful; Marion had without question supplied a copy of the agency's new-business contacts file. It included details of companies previously contacted by other account handlers, with contact names and numbers. Marion had sat on the phone for a whole morning chasing them all up for updated information.

Nikki now had a database for a new-business drive for her new venture. She had compiled a list of current agency clients and some of her biggest rivals' favoured clients with a view to snatching them away. She knew how much her own agency charged for projects and daily rates; she was aware roughly of what the competition charged. Undercutting them all, and with her aggressive hat on, she had no doubt that she could end up with quite a lucrative turnover.

She even had a name for her new venture. Millennium.

Idle doodles on the scratch pad had given her inspiration for logos and letterhead styles.

As Nikki sat quietly sipping her coffee, her thoughts turned back to Georgie. She had thought Georgie would be ecstatic at the progress Nikki was making for her new future. Georgie had simply stared at her, nodded in the right places but had said hardly anything, no words of encouragement, no praise. Nothing. Perhaps she had money troubles again: it didn't seem that her love life was causing difficulties.

But Georgie didn't have a love life, did she? She had put her own life on hold to try to find Nikki a perfect mate instead, hadn't she? That was a crying shame. Georgie was a great girl. She should have a partner. Georgie was such fun, so generous, sensitive and caring. Georgie had a lovely face: it didn't need make-up to accentuate her best features. When Georgie smiled or laughed, her face was a joy. You couldn't help but smile or laugh with her. She had a smashing figure, too. Georgie was wasted. She should start concentrating on herself again. Nikki was sure there was someone out there who would treat her properly. From what Georgie had said, she had had a succession of brief flings, but had never had a full-scale, long-term relationship. It couldn't be Georgie's fault. She just seemed to have attracted the wrong people or was too quick to leap into a physical thing. While Georgie was without doubt one of the most popular girls on the scene, most of the relationships she had had seemed to have been abusive to some degree or other. As a friend, Georgie was so supportive and thoughtful that Nikki knew she would bring those qualities to any relationship. As a lover, Georgie apparently had a great deal of experience. It would be a lucky girl who snared Georgie, Nikki thought.

No, Nikki determined, it was time Georgie found herself a

partner. Someone with spark to keep her on her toes, to drive through her boredom threshold. Someone with verve, panache, intelligence, warmth, humour. Good-looking; slim, probably; nice arse – Georgie had a thing about bums.

She realised with a pang that, although Georgie had frequently asked Nikki to describe her ideal woman, Nikki had never asked the question back. She realised she didn't really know what sort of woman Georgie was looking for. She had been too caught up with her own quest for the Holy Cunt that she had failed to recognise Georgie might have her own needs and desires to fulfil. She would ask her tomorrow night. No, she would ring her back now and make sure she was all right.

The phone rang with a query from a client. Then her boss rang down to pencil in a new-business-development update meeting. A designer came in with a problem. Marion asked for five minutes to discuss holidays and the chat turned into half an hour. The day fell away from her before she realised it. She remembered in the car that she had meant to ring Georgie back. She tried her from the car and got the answerphone. She left what she thought was an encouraging, lift-up-the-spirits message and raced home.

Georgie debated picking up the phone when she heard Nikki's voice, but left it instead. Nikki would know immediately from Georgie's slurred speech that she was drunk. Georgie didn't want Nikki to know that she was drunk, plastered, almost out of it, at 6.30 p.m. She was ashamed of herself. She didn't want to give the game away to Nikki. Georgie just wanted to sleep, needed to sleep, without the torment of fantasies unfulfilled. She would have sobered up, freshened up by the time Nikki came round the next night and she would be none the wiser.

Steve was in one of his difficult moods when Nikki breezed in. He had had a fraught day at the bank: one or two deals had gone sour on him, and he had taken the blame. Rather than fight his corner he had agreed with everything his boss had thrown at him, choosing to sit petulantly at his desk for half an hour afterwards, brooding and seething about all the things he would have said if he had had the balls. Now he was feeling peevish. His wife's good humour irritated him. She was always so fucking cheerful these days. She was never here: that was probably the reason for her bright moods. He preferred her miserable, grumpy, tetchy. At least he knew how to deal with that. This good humour had lasted for weeks. Perhaps she had had a bonus or a pay rise and not told him about it. Perhaps she had been going through an extremely early menopause the last five years and come through the other side. Perhaps she was having an affair, a fling with some pretty young toyboy introduced to her by The Maneater.

His scowl failed to register with Nikki. She hummed as she threw the ready meal into the microwave as the frozen vegetables cooked, and bustled about in the kitchen.

'I've had a lousy, rotten, stinking day, in case you were interested . . .' he started.

Nikki shrugged. Her back was still to him. 'Have a drink. You'll feel better. Dinner will be ready soon.'

'Couple of deals went pear-shaped; they blamed me, said it was my fault; I didn't think that was fair . . .'

Nikki knew that the whining note in Steve's voice would begin to annoy her if she didn't do her wifely duty and show some concern. 'I hope you gave them a piece of your mind. Sometimes I think they take advantage of your laid-back nature – they don't expect you to bite back. Sometimes, Steve, you do let people walk all over you.'

'What, like I have with you for twenty years?' Steve's whining had turned into a snarl.

She turned, surprised. His face was red with anger, his mouth set in a peevish thin line.

'I think that could be taken as a two-way street, Steve,' she replied calmly, although her heart was hammering. 'It's hardly been a bed of roses for me either, has it?'

'There are times, Nicola, that I truly believe you don't even know or care that I exist, when you think I'm just one of the fucking paintings on the wall, an ornament in the cabinet. You have no interest in anything I do, what I'm trying to achieve at work, where I want to go with my life. You're out all the time, sometimes overnight. You never tell me where you're going, where you've been, who you have been with. You just reappear now and again, cook a meal, watch some telly with me, or spend hours on the fucking telephone, and then whoosh, off you go again like some fucking ghost in the night.'

It was probably Steve's longest speech of the last few months, Nikki realised with a feeling of dread in the pit of her stomach. Time to take command, girl.

'And you?' she said. 'Do you stay in pining for me night after night? No, I don't think so. Where do you go off to? Out with your buddies, like I'm out with mine. You use this house as a hotel just as much as I do, only the difference is that when you come back of an evening your laundry is done, there is beer in the fridge and food in the cupboard. You're right, I'm not here more often than I am here, but the house is clean and tidy, isn't it? You're not starving, are you? You have your interests; I have mine; they don't cross over. I don't walk all over you, Steve. I don't nag you; I don't bitch at you, impose a late-night curfew, check your collars for lipstick and perfume; I just let you get on with your life, whatever that may be these days. In return I simply expect you to let me get on with mine.'

'Not much of a marriage then, is it?'

'No, Steve, it's not. Never really has been, has it? It's not even companionship, friendship. It's just what we've both settled for. I accepted some time ago that whatever it was that had brought us together in the first place had disappeared over the years and that neither of us had attempted to bring it back. Neither of us could be arsed. We are now just two grown-up people sharing a house, occasionally passing each other of an evening or weekend.'

Steve sighed. He hadn't wanted to go down this route: he'd just wanted to complain about his lot in life, have a go because someone had had a go at him. Now he realised that he had opened up that old can of worms, which was tragic when he had had so many weeks of Nikki's good humour to take advantage of. It was his own fault: he should have just let it ride. Whatever was making her happy had allowed him peace and quiet: no turbulence, no arguments, frayed tempers, double-edged retorts.

'You see it how you like. You normally do,' he said, turning to walk away, anxious to end the conversation.

'I'll tell you how I see it. I see it the same way as you do only I've probably got the guts to say it. We're strangers, poles apart, have been for years. We don't have anything in common any more, not even enough as a base for a friendship. You can't be happy with this arrangement. I know I'm not. I want to be here as much as you do, Steve, and if you had the balls you would admit it, right now.'

She was draining the vegetables as she spoke, keeping her hands busy so that Steve couldn't see how much she was shaking. In her action plan, this speech to Steve was weeks away yet – there was still some more groundwork to be done. Now she had confronted the issue and the silence hung between them as Steve glared at the back of her neck.

'Are you having an affair?' he finally blurted, waiting for the cooked sprouts to be flung in his direction. She knew he hated sprouts. Is that why she cooked them?

'Are you?' With her back still to him, Nikki waited, full of hope for an affirmative answer to make life easier.

'Of course not. I'm married. I don't suppose you would care if I was screwing for England.'

'I'm not having an affair either, although God knows I've had plenty of fucking opportunity. And it's not because I'm married: it's because I can't go through this sort of crap again.' She turned and leant against the worktop. Her eyes were dead as she took a deep breath and voiced aloud what she had not wanted to say for some time yet.

'I want us to separate, Steve.'

She had said it before she realised it. She saw the change in his face; his shoulders slump.

'You can't do that.' His voice was weak. 'I won't allow it.'

'Why? In case your family, your boss, think you've failed? For God's sake, Steve, you know this is the only way out for both of us. I know you're not going to stand there and pledge undying love, say that your world will fall apart without me. If we carry on like this, it's going to destroy both of us. We're both still young enough to come through this. We will have more of the same sort of freedom we have already. Christ, we can tell people it's amicable, civilised. I'll be your escort to your functions if that makes it easier for you. People can think we're being terribly adult and staying friends. Steve, if we stay married we will end up old, regretful, resentful and fucking more miserable with each other than we are right now. We'll discuss it, make sure we are both happy with the arrangements, so that neither of us loses out. We don't need to get lawyers involved. It should be a very straightforward, simple, clean-break settlement. Keep the house, Steve, if it means so much. Buy me out. Give me what you can afford. I'm not going to take you to the cleaners, I promise you. Let's try and hold on to what respect we still have for each other and do this like adults. Give each other a way out.'

Everything she said made sense. She was so calm, so practical. 'I'm going to have to think about this overnight, let you know my decision,' he mumbled.

'For God's sake, Steve, I'm not some little potential franchise operator looking for a Government Expansion Loan. I've thought long and hard about this. I am making all sorts of plans for my future. I need to grow, do something more with my life. I want to start again.'

Steve turned away; she heard him go into the lounge and open some bottles. He returned with drinks, and topped them up with ice and mixers from the fridge.

'I worked hard for all this,' he finally said, tetchy, after two gulps of Scotch. 'Why should I let you take any of it away from me?'

'Steve, *we* worked hard for all this, and you can still have this, Steve, and be a hell of a lot happier. You know you can afford to buy me out and take out a larger mortgage to pay for it. We could even sell this and both get smaller places. There's only two of us, for God's sake. I know you wouldn't be able to cope with cleaning a house this size.'

'I'll get an au pair, a housekeeper, a nineteen-year-old Swedish blonde with large tits and long legs – make her dress up in just a pinny with a feather duster and bend over to pick things up a lot.'

Nikki, with a jolt, saw a flash of the young Steve Jones: he had a mischievous smile on his face. He had actually been relieved about separating, she realised. It was what he wanted too. Once he had recognised that she wasn't going to screw him for money, his last bastion of defence for staying in this loveless sham of a marriage had gone. She knew him so well.

'Steve,' she said kindly, 'a nineteen-year-old will kill you. Go for a thirty-five-year-old, less stamina but more technique.'

'Perhaps,' he began slowly, 'perhaps this means we can start being friends instead now?'

'We can at least try,' said Nikki, and they both smiled with the unburdened relief.

Their good mood remained all that evening. They even swapped notes and anecdotes about the day's work events, although Nikki drew the line at cuddling him to sleep when he asked. She could just about feel the stirring of his prick against her hip. She wasn't feeling that magnanimous.

As she drove to work the next morning Nikki was full of anticipation, an eagerness to tell Georgie and Gillian her news. Georgie had been right: it was all coming together. Steve had been easier than she thought. Unless . . . it was the calm before the storm. What if he thought about it, talked it over with his buddies, started to dig his heels in, got solicitors involved, started to make it difficult for her? She had a timescale to keep to, a log of potential, dated achievements.

The only achievement to aim for that was not included in her schedule was the woman of her dreams. That would be a bonus at the moment: she had far too many other things to think about and put into place before that happened. The Pussy Posse was out tonight – at least she would be among her own kind, free to be herself, the first lieutenant of the crowd, second in command to the irrepressible Georgie.

That was a point: she would have to call Georgie and make sure she was OK, hopefully a bit brighter and game for a laugh.

★

Georgie was struggling with her hangover and an obstinate set of typing fingers. She had been so drunk the night before that she had resorted to talking out loud to try to shake some sense into herself. She vaguely recalled details, most of it comprised her being adamant that she was out of Nikki's league. That Nikki had not even thought about Georgie in any other way than being a close friend.

Nothing more. That was all it would ever be. That she should move on. That Nikki had not even looked at her sexually, had not responded to her verbal passes. They had probably been too subtle, Georgie had decided. She should have been blunt and to the point. Fancy a shag, Nikki? Yeah, that would go down like a lead whatsit, wouldn't it, you dozy mare.

A lie-in and several black coffees, plus twice the recommended doseage of Nurofen, had cleared the headache. She had, however, still to tackle the sluggishness which was now affecting her. The thought that she was seeing Nikki that night was a mild incentive.

Georgie had seemed a little lacklustre on the phone, Nikki decided later, on her way to the bar. But she hadn't seemed so sad and down. It was probably just a blip. Georgie was normally so full of zest that when she was down it was very noticeable.

When she got to the bar she noticed that Georgie was not drinking beer but an alarmingly copious amount of Coke with lots of ice. Georgie's eyes were still slightly bloodshot, and Nikki knew that whatever had caused yesterday's sadness had probably been compounded by several glasses too many of JD. She was about to take Georgie aside to talk to her when Tracy tapped her on the shoulder.

'Nikki, this is my friend Ann,' she said as Nikki turned and looked into the deepest brown eyes she had ever seen. 'She's staying with me for a few days.'

Ann was Nikki's height, with long dark hair. She was slightly overweight but when she smiled Nikki's heart missed a beat. My God, she thought, she's giving me That Look. It does go straight to your clitoris. Georgie was right.

'Ann's heard a lot about you,' said Tracy, 'I told you on Saturday she was coming up.'

As neither girl had spoken yet, just smiled, their eyes locked, Tracy assumed that she had won the internal bet. Any member of the Pussy Posse who was successful in getting Nikki laid was set to win the kitty now sitting at a magnificent £50.

Georgie had been distracted by Phillipa, who was waffling on about her adventures with a frozen Mars bar. She ascertained that it had melted at an inappropriate moment and that Phillipa had had to go fishing for a recalcitrant half of a king-size chocolate, caramel and fudge combination.

'What really pissed her off,' Phillipa was giggling, 'was the idea that it would be asborbed straight into her bloodstream and she would wake up half a stone heavier. We should have left it in the freezer for longer. At least we didn't try a Topic. I couldn't have got the peanuts out . . .'

While the rest of the Posse fell about in hysterical disbelief, Georgie had noticed the girl with Nikki. The two were engrossed in conversation, standing a little way back from the group. Their body language to each other was inviting, flirting, provocative. Inwardly, Georgie sagged. When Ann turned towards Nikki, her hand resting on Nikki's arm to catch something she had just said, Georgie's stomach turned over. She debated the wisdom of topping her Coke up with something stronger, remembered her nausea of that morning and decided to go home early instead, feigning the onset of a bad period.

Nikki barely acknowledged Georgie as she left the bar: she was too absorbed.

Ann, a police officer, had spent some time in the army and her infectious humour about her life in the barracks was hugely entertaining.

'For four years I was like a kid in a toy shop, constantly dodging officers, who considered homosexual sex either a hanging offence or a reason to secure rapid promotion by exposing it. I had four years of endless, limitless acres of minge and arse and tit. Sharing showers and getting a headache and cuntache every time because I was spoilt for choice. Shagging in the back of four-tonners while on exercise – drop those keks, do it and out again. I was always being brought in front of the commanding officer. But they couldn't catch me. One night I went down one particular corridor and went down on three different ladies in different rooms and none of them found out about the others. I never got past the dizzy heights of private. I was always in trouble, answering back, a right smartarse. The powers that be wanted me. So did a sergeant. It was while she was having me that a spot check was carried out. I could hear the boots in the corridor outside, slamming of doors. I dashed to the window – stark bollock naked – and fell outside literally into the arms of a grinning SM. They'd got me.

'I had just two weeks to go of my four years, and the paperwork involved would have tied them, and me, up for six months. So they let me off with a dishonourable discharge and I at least got a good reference for future use. Not like one of my mates who also got caught, but within the timescale for punishment. Her "reference" simply said, "She was a soldier." It's all a load of bollocks: even some of the senior officers were at it with each other. Put people of the same sex in a close environment like that and they're bound to shag each other, aren't they? Never did any harm, did it? I joined up to be surrounded by women. That was the whole intention.

'A friend of mine became a prison officer so she would end up in an all-female prison with five hundred other dykes. Well, most aren't dykes when they go in. Booked in at ten; somebody's bitch by twelve. You have to be bloody careful, though.'

Nikki was entranced, captured. Ann was so matter of fact about her experiences, which must have been considerable. She had spent her working life constantly on a knife edge of being caught, an adrenalin-inducing state of affairs that Nikki could not comprehend. Christ, she thought *she* thrived on pressure. She realised that Ann was not actually overweight, but extremely fit: a stroke of her arm had revealed hard muscle underneath. Ann would probably be very useful in any altercation. The thought of Ann's protective arm round her began to play havoc with Nikki's imagination. Ann probably had to deal with awkward prisoners all the time, was probably highly trained in self-defence, restraint and control.

Nikki stifled a groan of desire. Ann, in her uniform, restraining and controlling her as she unleashed the beast of desire and passion. Wild images and fantasies ran riot in her brain.

Ann, of course, had been well primed, albeit unwittingly, by Tracy. She knew beforehand what Nikki looked like, apparently a bit of a babe; that she was generous and sensitive; that she was a novice; that she needed taking in hand. She also knew that Nikki was quite well off, probably on the verge of getting a juicy divorce settlement.

Ann had always considered she was badly paid for the jobs she had had to do. In fact, Ann was resentful about quite a few things in life. None had been her fault: she had just been too much for people to handle. That was their problem, not hers. She was more than happy with herself. Ann, of course, considered herself as close to perfection as she could possibly be. She entertained the fantasy on a regular basis of being a kept woman, having some rich bitch as a sex slave. Then Ann could spend her days working out in her own, well-equipped gym, emerging long enough to service her totally compliant, moneyed bitch and keep her happy. Servicing her well enough to get some extra treats on a regular basis. Ann had never shared these thoughts with any of her friends – too risky. They had her down as a tough cookie, well enough, but they were too soft to even contemplate treating someone like that. 'Take it and fake it while you can' was Ann's private motto. While she was one of the first to put her hand in her pocket for a round of drinks or a share of a meal, Ann kept most of her money for herself. Her friends, as a result, had the idea that Ann was a generous person. Ann actually had three or four savings accounts and had amassed a considerable amount of jewellery along the way, given by or stolen from past girlfriends.

She also had a considerable talent for spotting vulnerable women, women with secrets or insecurities that could be played upon and used to her own advantage. Ann was a classic psychopath, self-centred and with no conscience, a pathological liar, a compulsive obsessive with a wildly jealous streak.

Nikki had no idea of the turbulent waters she was about to sail into. Her friend and protector had gone. The other minders had left her alone with this fascinating woman, with her colourful past. She seemed so open, so friendly.

So horny.

ELEVEN

Nikki's mind was reeling. The memory of Ann's kisses occupied all her thoughts, as she tried desperately hard to concentrate on the way home. The two had talked for ages, with slight touches of the hands, carelessly draped arms over shoulders and round waists, then they had gone downstairs to dance. Very quickly, they had moved together, close. Ann's lips had brushed her neck and Nikki had bent only slightly to receive the first kiss. Gentle, exploratory, questioning, only very slight pressure of Ann's tongue between her lips, then she had opened her mouth wider: the kiss became stronger and deeper and their tongues explored together. Ann's strong arms had held her safely, securely, almost lovingly, then her hands had slipped to Nikki's waist, Nikki's hips, and then she had firmly squeezed her arse as they ground themselves together the whole of that seemingly never-ending snog.

They had kissed through five tracks when Ann's hand had slipped to the front of her jeans and she began to press, harder and harder, against Nikki's mound. Nikki spread her legs slightly against the insistent urging fingers and then, maddeningly, Ann moved her hand away, up towards Nikki's breast, kneading, fondling, squeezing, then stroking and caressing until Nikki put her own hand over Ann's to increase the pressure.

141

Even now Nikki was squirming against the leather seat of her Saab. She had desperately wanted Ann to sleep with her that night but Ann had suddenly pulled completely away, then held out her hand for Nikki to walk with her to the bar. With sodden jeans, she had mutely followed.

'I'll be up this way again soon,' said Ann carelessly. 'Perhaps we could meet up for a drink? Tracy has all my numbers. Give me a ring. I'll be back home tomorrow evening.'

Nikki had fought to keep the disappointment out of her voice and off her face. Now, as she remembered Ann's muscular body against hers, the intensity and passion of her kissing, she pulled the car over and sat, almost breathless, in the dark. Her hand had slipped to the crotch of her jeans and she was absent-mindedly stroking herself through the fabric.

At one point Ann had broken the kiss and breathed, 'Oh, baby,' in her ear. Nikki's hand began to move faster, harder and more urgently as she remembered the rush of pleasure that whisper had given her. She could feel that she was very, very wet; she wanted to hear that voice again; she wanted to stroke that skin, be inside her, have Ann's tongue sending her into a frenzy. She wanted to feel Ann grinding underneath her, to suck her nipples, to finger-fuck her until she exploded on her hand. Nikki was wildly aroused, but her orgasm, when it came, was muted, hampered by the denim. She sat quietly for a short while, regaining her calm, then picked up the phone.

Georgie answered after the third ring, slightly groggy with sleep.

'Georgie, I think this is The One! Did you see her? We snogged each other senseless, got really dirty on the dance floor. She wants me, I know she wants me. I don't know when I'm going to see her again but I'm going to ring her, Georgie. I've got to have her. And soon. Waiting is just going to drive me crazy.'

'I didn't get much of a chance, really, did I . . .?' the question was deliberately ambiguous and Georgie let it hang in the air.

'Oh, you didn't feel well, did you? Are you all right? God, I hope we talk tomorrow. I hope she comes back up again soon.

142

She's so fit, so strong. She's a copper, Georgie, used to be in the army. She's so funny, you know. My God, she can dance. I thought I was going to come on the dance floor. I'm going to ring Tracy tomorrow, get the low-down.'

Georgie couldn't really take any more of the drivel Nikki was talking in her excited enthusiasm.

'Yeah, well make sure you do.' She was almost dismissive in her curtness. 'Just calm down and take it slow and steady.'

'I thought you would be pleased for me,' Nikki said peevishly.

'I am. I am. I'm just worried that you go into it like a bull in a china shop. Just be careful: this girl is an unknown quantity, she's not one of our crowd.'

'Is that why you're so unenthusiastic, because you haven't had the chance to vet her properly, because it's out of your control?'

'I'm not indifferent to it all, Nikki, just cautious. I'm also very tired, it's late and I didn't sleep well last night. All I'm worried about is that you get carried away, plunge into something without thinking about it, with someone you hardly know, and it could jeopardise everything else you're trying to do at the moment. Get to know her a bit better, that's all. Doesn't she live some way away?'

'It's only an hour – probably less in this beast. And I'm hardly likely to get done for speeding any more, am I? Just think, Georgie, handcuffs, truncheons, shiny buttons on a uniform. God, it's my ultimate fantasy come true.'

Georgie stayed silent. Her own ultimate fantasy would never come true, not if this copper got her claws into Nikki. The danger with Nikki was that she was vulnerable. It would be her first proper relationship with a woman and in the wrong hands that could be lethal. All Nikki was seeing was the superficial: this bird had slotted into some sort of ideal Nikki had created in her mind. What kind of person was she? She might have someone else back home for all Nikki knew – or cared. The first woman to show Nikki any real attention and the stupid cow sounded hooked already. Why couldn't she play the field a bit longer, have some fun before realising what was right under her nose?

Georgie fought to keep the frustration and anger out of her

voice, made placating noises and begged to be left to catch up on her sleep. Nikki hung up, feeling spiteful. Then thoughts of Ann intruded again. She started the car and drove home, Georgie banished from her mind.

The following day, a Sunday, she busied herself, watching the clock tick by agonisingly slowly. She knew Steve would be out that evening, a charity darts match. The minute he left, she rang Tracy, who obligingly provided Ann's numbers. She settled herself down with a drink, curled up on the settee and dialled. Ann answered almost immediately.

'I knew you would call,' said Ann. Nikki didn't notice the arrogant tone.

'How are you? You didn't get too drunk last night?'

'I don't get drunk any more. It shows a loss of control.'

Nikki put her drink down in case Ann could hear the ice clink against glass.

'I used to drink a lot in the army,' Ann began. 'I shagged women because I was pissed and didn't care what they looked like – ten pints of cheap Naafi beer always made them look more attractive and fuckable. I never used to put on weight. I was always running it off and exercising. But one night I ended up shagging this woman – I can never remember her name but I do remember her nickname, "Grimsby Docks". She was much older than me with a face to frighten warthogs, built like a brick shithouse, and smelt. But, I was pissed, I was horny and apparently I fucked her. Apparently I was very good. It was after waking up next to her, with a stonking hangover, that I realised I had gone too far. It took me a while but I got the drinking under control. I haven't been pissed since – merry, but never pissed. I usually have just the one beer then the soft stuff when I go out.

'I've arrested so many pissheads in my time, always looking for trouble and a bit of a fight. People who drink a lot regularly are usually hiding from something. They have no pride in themselves.'

Nikki guiltily looked at her drink, fought the urge, and left it.

'That's why I enjoy working out so much. I have pride in my

body. I am in control. It releases the tension, the stress, the pressure. I love squash. Do you play?' She didn't even wait for Nikki to respond. 'That squash ball can become anyone I like, anyone who has pissed me off that day, and I can just keep slamming it against the wall for as long as I like.'

Nikki's mind was full of rampant sex. Ann taking control of her and holding her down, fingers ramming inside her; her being handcuffed to the bed and unable to move as Ann licked, sucked and teased her gushing sex; Ann peeling off that uniform; Ann in stockings . . .

'You never told me much about the force,' she said, realising there was a break in Ann's monologue.

'I've got ten years in. Came off the streets and into CID three years ago. Got made up to DS ten months ago . . .'

Ann was reeling it off like a CV in a job interview. Nikki was hugely disappointed that Ann was a plain-clothes officer. She would probably still have handcuffs, though, surely?

'And I'm moving over to drugs next summer, all things being equal. I want Regional Crime Squad eventually. I worked hard for my stripes. Never bothered looking for promotion in the army, but the police tend to be a bit more insistent about you trying to get your studies done and going for it. It was a way of making more money, you know, overtime and all that. Plus it's more on the pension when I retire.'

Nikki suddenly had an irrational fast-forward flash of the two of them growing old together. Pull yourself together, woman. She surreptitiously took a gulp of her drink, holding the mouthpiece of the receiver well away from herself. Ann was still talking.

'Look, I've got some time off due to me soon, probably take it next week, Tuesday, Thursday, something like that. Trouble is I sometimes get called to court on my days off, or some incident comes in and all leave is cancelled. It's a risk you have to take with arranging things. Gets on my tits sometimes. I hate having plans changed. Would you be around?'

'What, during the day?'

'You could come down to me. We could spend the day

together. I'll take you for a meal, whatever. I know you're married, Tracy told me. Will that cause you problems?'

'Not at all,' said Nikki smoothly. She would clear her diary for the whole week if she had to. Alistair was usually flexible about time off, because of the amount of hours his senior execs put in. 'Does it bother you that I'm married?'

'It would if I didn't know you wanted a divorce.'

'Just exactly how much has Tracy told you about me?'

'That was about it really, other than you were a stunner. She was right about that. I couldn't take my eyes off you all night, couldn't keep my hands off you.'

'And I thought you said you never lost control any more?'

'I don't. Ever.' Ann's voice was icy. 'I always know exactly what I'm doing.'

Nikki felt rebuked. Her remark had been light-hearted; Ann had been a bit sharp, hadn't she?

Ann's voice softened. 'I thought you were the most beautiful woman I had ever seen. There's just one thing wrong, though.'

'What's that?'

'Your clothes.'

Nikki was indignant. Her designer jeans had probably cost more than Ann's entire outfit. 'What was wrong with my clothes?'

'They were on,' said Ann smoothly, her voice dropping slightly. 'I would love to see you naked, feel your skin against mine, stroke you, caress you, kiss you all over. I want to be next to you, underneath you, inside you. I want to make love to you, kiss you, feel you.'

The abrupt change in Ann's attitude had wrong-footed Nikki and it took a moment for her to register what was happening. She drained her glass, not caring if Ann had heard her, and settled back into the cushions.

'Where are you now? What are you doing?' Ann's voice was mesmerising.

'Curled up, just listening.'

Ann's voice was now barely a whisper: 'I want you to be with me. We are together, in bed, right now. We are kissing; we are feeling each other's naked bodies, exploring, slowly finding out about each other and what we like . . .'

Nikki wriggled deeper into the cushions, closing her eyes, allowing Ann's voice to take over her imagination.

'I want to run my hands all over you, kiss every inch of you, slowly. I want to taste you, tease you, while you just lie back and enjoy. Can you feel me? I want to kiss your neck, your ear, run my tongue over your breasts, play with them, squeeze them, fondle them. I'm there, right there with you, next to you. I know you want me; I want you. I want to stroke your sides, your stomach. I want to feel how wet you are, slowly go inside you. I want to lick you while I'm inside you. Can you see this? Can you feel this?'

'Oh yes.' Nikki had lost herself in the fantasy.

Ann's voice had dropped again; it was deep and thick with desire. Nikki's eyes were closed, the receiver clamped so close to her ear that she felt Ann was next to her, talking to her while she stroked, fondled, caressed, nibbled.

'I want to lick you slowly, so slowly that you want more and more, you can't get enough of me licking you. It's so gentle that you are moving against me, wanting me to lick you harder, chew on you, drink from you, you want more of me inside you, you want to come; you're climbing; you're going crazy. What are you doing now?'

'Stroking myself.'

'Imagine that's my tongue, my fingers. You're spread for me, can't open your legs wide enough for me. You want me to fuck you, don't you?'

'Oh, yes, yes, I do, I want you here right now. I want you to fuck me hard, fast.'

'I'm inside you; you're riding my fingers, pushing against me, I'm holding you tight, fucking you, giving you what you want, what you need. I want you to come, ride it, baby, fuck it, come on, baby, come for me, I want to hear you come for me.'

Nikki's free hand was buried deep inside her jogging pants, her fingers rubbing her clitoris. She was gushing, slippery. She tucked the receiver under her chin; her other hand now slipped inside, pulled the hood back to increase the pressure on her clitoris. Her legs had dropped wide open; she was breathing in short gasps as the voice in her ear urged her to come, and to come and to keep on coming. Nikki's fevered mind was full of images of Ann: it was Ann's fingers now frantic against her cunt, sliding into her; it was Ann's tongue on her clit; Ann was sucking her; she could feel Ann's breasts against her thighs; she could feel Ann's head moving as the rhythm increased, faster and faster, harder and harder. She could hear how wet she was; she could imagine it was Ann's mouth making those noises; she could almost feel Ann's moans of desire vibrating against her cunt and Nikki was now climbing higher; her hips were lifting as she pushed towards her, wanting Ann deeper and deeper, and she exploded with a massive gasp, a cry of Ann's name. Then the aftershock, when the tremors started and she was trembling. Her mouth was dry. She fought hard to control her breathing, to slow her heart.

Ann was silent. She thought she had recovered it well. Nikki was now hers. 'Come down yet, baby?' she finally said. 'Can you imagine what it would be like for real?'

'Wow,' said Nikki, still fighting to breathe calmly. 'Waiting is going to drive me crazy.'

'Until next week, then. Call me tomorrow afternoon and I'll have arranged my day off.'

Nikki was slightly peeved that Ann had gone straight into her brisk mode again. She had wanted more soft words, more gentle whispers. They exchanged goodbyes and Nikki sat staring at the phone, irked.

Nikki was still annoyed the next day. She had tried to call Georgie and the girl was constantly engaged. Then, when the phone did ring, the answerphone kicked in. She had left a message; Georgie had not called her back. Something was bugging Nikki, but she wasn't sure what it was.

She spent another day watching the clock, finally cracking at 4 p.m. and calling Ann's number. Ann wasn't in; no answerphone. Nikki tried every half-hour until she left the office with no joy. She tried twice from the car. Still no answer.

She knew she would struggle to call again that evening: Steve was having a night in. Although Ann could have got her mobile number from Tracy, she couldn't take the risk of having the phone in the house. She parked around the corner from her house and tried the number again.

This time Ann picked up.

'I've been trying you for ages,' Nikki said petulantly.

Ann knew. Her caller display had shown Nikki's repeated attempts to call. She had judged it finely, knowing once the mobile number showed that Nikki would be trying her on her way home. The third call Ann knew she would have to accept: it was probably Nikki's last chance before getting home to hubby.

'Sorry –' Ann was soothing '– I've only just got in. Look, I know it's short notice and I would have called you before but I don't have a number for you. I've got tomorrow off. Can you still make it?'

Nikki immediately accepted. She would phone in sick. They made arrangements for where to meet, and the time.

Nikki was so happy she almost bounced into the house. She tossed and turned all night, her thoughts constantly full of Ann; of making love to Ann; of the delicious pleasure awaiting her the next day.

Ann had told her to meet at the Holiday Inn, just off the motorway, as the easiest place to find. Nikki pulled into the car park, slowly driving past fleets of company cars, trying to spot Ann's silver Golf. Half an hour past the designated time, Ann drove in, flashed her lights and double parked. Nikki's irritation disappeared the second that Ann smiled at her as she walked towards the Saab. She got into the passenger seat.

'I'm sorry I'm late – couple of phone calls I had to make. I hope I didn't keep you waiting too long,' Ann said.

'It was worth the wait,' said Nikki, her displeasure at being kept waiting forgotten. Then she was in Ann's arms, kissing her. Her thoughts had been only of Ann for the last three days, but she had been unprepared for her own reaction. Ann was more good-looking than she had remembered. She kissed better than

Nikki remembered. Her hands were already exploring. It was Ann who broke the kiss.

'Shall we go somewhere for lunch?' she said casually. 'I'm actually very hungry. There's a nice country pub down the road. We'll go in yours, shall we?'

Ann was putting on her seat belt as she said it. Nikki had no choice. She started the car. A mixture of disappointment, frustration and that flare of feeling bugged had resurfaced. Ann gave her directions. They drove in silence.

Nikki, having spent nearly two days in a sexual frenzy of anticipation, picked at her food while Ann talked about her job. Every nerve ending was screaming for release. She wanted sex, not conversation. She wanted to be naked and spread, letting Ann do whatever Ann wanted.

Ann knew that Nikki was sulking. The phone sex on Sunday had left the woman gagging for more. No, Ann would take her time with this one, make her wait until she started to beg for it.

Ann, whenever she paused for breath in her monologue, would wolf some more food. Nikki finally gave up and put her cutlery down.

'Not hungry?' Ann had finally seemed to notice Nikki's lack of appetite.

'Not for food, anyway,' Nikki muttered. She looked up, made eye contact. Ann's eyes were cold, and when she smiled the smile did not reach her eyes. Nikki was suddenly uncomfortable. She felt in the presence of a predator; like a frightened gazelle cornered by a lioness. She had felt the same in business, or socially, when her harmless flirting had given a man the idea that she was sexually available. The atmosphere had always turned chilly as Nikki had had to regain control of the situation. Now, with Ann, she felt distinctly powerless. For some reason she was finding it difficult to rescue the balance. Ann was just looking at her, aloof, arrogant, in charge.

Nikki didn't like it. The day was lost; the moments she had yearned for since Sunday had not appeared. Instead she felt trapped, weak, vulnerable. She had exposed herself on Sunday. Ann had the upper hand. Nikki was angry with herself. The conversation with Georgie resurfaced in her mind – Nikki had rushed into it without thinking.

Ann reached across and stroked Nikki's hand.

'You seem tense. Are you nervous of me? You're worried, aren't you? Don't be. We can take it at whatever pace you want, whatever makes you comfortable. I just want to make you happy.'

This time she made the smile reach her eyes, made her face softer, kinder. She squeezed Nikki's hand, searched her eyes until she was sure that doubt had disappeared. Nikki began to relax. Ann was sort of on the right track. Perhaps Nikki had misjudged her. That arrogance was probably trained into her with her job. She was also probably used to being in command of a situation. Sexually, Nikki was the novice: she had to let Ann take charge – it made sense. The woman had a vast amount of experience. It was not often, at work or socially, that Nikki had to consciously step back and let someone else take over. This time, she reasoned, she had no choice if she wanted a relationship with Ann. She actually had no options if she just wanted sex, let alone a relationship. It was obvious Ann wanted her. Nikki could now see raw desire in her eyes. Ann had moved her legs under the table so that she was gripping Nikki's thighs between her own. Now Ann's other hand was also underneath the tabletop, very lightly stroking a thigh.

'I think,' said Ann carefully, 'that we should take our time. We shouldn't rush this. We have plenty of time. I don't want you to think you're just another notch on my bedpost. I respect you too much for that. I got a bit carried away on the phone the other day. I'm sorry, I shouldn't have done what I did. Let's just get to know each other a little more. First.'

It was only later, as Nikki drove home, analysing the afternoon, that she realised that Ann had actually talked very little after that. The pub was open all day. They had sat for four hours over soft drinks and coffee while Nikki told Ann all about her job, her marriage, her previous clandestine encounters.

Ann now knew that Nikki had been married for nearly twenty years to a man who had no inkling that his wife was gay. That Steve had absolutely no idea his wife had spent the last few months on the gay scene, trawling for a casual pick-up to replace the paid-for encounters she had enjoyed before.

Nikki had waxed lyrical about her plans to set up her own agency and steal her clients. She had been full of her ideas for putting her life on track in time for the turn of the century. She had told Ann of her yearning to find a soulmate to share this new life with; that she knew that woman was out there. Ann had asked only a few questions during the four hours.

'Perhaps you've already found her and you don't know it yet?' was the one question that Nikki now replayed over and over in her mind. Once again, her mind was overtaken with Ann.

She had intimated, more than once, to Ann that she could stay over – somewhere, anywhere – if Ann wanted. Ann had gently shaken her head.

'I don't think you're ready for that just yet, sweetheart. I told you, we should take it nice and slow and steady. I want our first time to be something special, with plenty of time. I can come up again this weekend, see you Saturday night. We can go out with the crowd if you like. What do you call them, the Pussy Posse? Anyway, I know that once I get you into bed you're going to fall in love with me. I don't particularly want to be named in a divorce case.'

That flash of arrogance in Ann's eyes had brought back Nikki's original discomfort. It had helped her to steel herself when she said goodbye in the car park of the hotel. Ann had confused her. She had given something, then taken it away, then given it back again, the whole day. Nikki had no doubt they would end up in bed, but she was convinced that Ann thought so highly of herself that, in her eyes, Nikki would suddenly swear undying love and devotion.

She could not get to grips with the arrogance. Ann was one of the best-looking women she had ever seen. She carried herself with a natural look-at-me swagger. It could just have been her years in the army and on the beat that gave her that walk, Nikki thought. But if Ann thought she was so fucking special that Nikki would jeopardise all her plans for a shag, then she had another think coming.

That's all Ann would be, Nikki determined, a shag. Georgie was right – as usual. Nikki should play the field, catch up for lost time. If Nikki could attract someone like Ann then she could attract all sorts of other good-looking women. No, Ann would just be the first in a long line, Nikki decided. If she didn't like it then it was tough. She would see her Saturday, snog her, dirty dance with her so they would have to be separated by credit cards and then . . . well, then Nikki would have to go home. Alone.

'If she wants to play it slow and steady, then she can. But she'll do it at my pace, not hers,' Nikki said aloud as she pulled into her drive.

So why couldn't she stop thinking about her?

TWELVE

Georgie had deliberately screened her calls. She knew Nikki had tried several times to get hold of her. Georgie could not face Nikki droning on about some other woman.

In the back of her mind she had the idea that she had blown it. But how could she have blown it if she hadn't told Nikki how she felt? Somehow she knew she should have done things differently. What had stopped her? The fear of rejection, that was what had stopped her. She had built up a strong, solid friendship and she was frightened that, if she came on strong, Nikki would reject her, and the friendship would never be the same – Nikki would never feel comfortable with her again.

What if she had tried and Nikki had not rejected her? What if Nikki felt the same? Nikki couldn't feel the same: she had never once given Georgie any inkling that she was interested in her sexually. So Georgie would be flogging a dead horse, wouldn't she?

Now Georgie had to sit back and let things take their course. She was expected to support Nikki while she launched herself at that copper, whoever the hell she was. Why couldn't Nikki just look at it as something casual, to be enjoyed, just the same way that Georgie used to look at it. Why had she gone so overboard, so quickly? It would end in tears, Georgie knew it. So would the next, and the next. Nikki was so convinced that she was going to find her ideal woman soon that she was throwing herself at the first one to respond to her.

Georgie had kept track of how the copper was behaving, thanks to Nikki's messages. Apparently they had met in the week. Nikki couldn't stop thinking about her. They had had phone sex a couple of times. The copper would be there with the crowd on Saturday. Ann seemed arrogant, so Nikki was looking forward to the challenge of bringing her down a peg or two. There had been constant references to truncheons and handcuffs. Nikki had sounded like a woman obsessed and it was worrying Georgie as she got ready to go out that Saturday night.

When she arrived at the usual bar and saw Nikki alone, she worried even more. Nikki had obviously been so excited at the thought of seeing that woman that she had arrived even earlier than usual. The bar was almost empty.

'I thought you'd died,' said Nikki.

You wouldn't notice, thought Georgie. 'I've been busy,' she said instead, 'had a couple of tight deadlines to meet. So, it's going well with this Ann, then?'

'I think so. We're taking it carefully. Honestly, Georgie, we are. I'm not rushing into anything. We haven't slept together or declared any commitment. But she does make me feel special, wanted, desired. She seems very arrogant, though. I think that's her job that does that, and I quite like a challenge. Still, one day at a time, eh?'

Georgie didn't respond immediately. She slowly sipped her beer, scrutinised Nikki very carefully, and while she gathered her thoughts she lit a cigarette.

'Nikki, I think we need to talk . . .' she began, then Nikki was off the bar stool, her attention captured by Ann and Tracy walking in. Ann and Nikki embraced, and Georgie fell apart inside.

Ann surveyed Georgie coolly as Nikki made the introductions. She placed a proprietorial arm on Nikki's shoulder and pulled her closer as she recognised the challenge in Georgie's eyes. She immediately suspected that the girl didn't like her – she didn't know why – and that Georgie could be a threat. Still, she was the leader of the gang that Nikki hung around with. Perhaps that had something to do with it. Some of these lesbians were incredibly cliquey, even played Pass the Parcel with each other, swapping partners on a regular basis. Ann preferred the individual approach. Once Nikki was completely hers, Ann would isolate her from the others, remove this dependence she seemed to have on these mates. For the time being, Ann would make the effort to be a part of it all. Even the girl's body language was challenging. Georgie was standing directly facing her, legs apart, one hand on her hip, the other tightly clutching the bottle of beer. Ann's professional training kicked in and she now registered the possibility of Georgie causing her some trouble. Her arm dropped off Nikki's shoulder and she imperceptibly moved into an equally challenging stance, arms loose at her sides.

Nikki sensed the tension between the two. Georgie still had not spoken since she had introduced her to Ann. For some unfathomable reason, Georgie was looking hostile and distinctly unfriendly.

'Would you like a drink, Ann?' Nikki suggested. Without breaking her eye contact with Georgie, Ann just nodded. Nikki debated about the wisdom of leaving the two of them alone while she went to the bar.

It was Tracy who broke the moment as she spotted other friends arriving and there was the usual cacophony of yelled greetings and embraces. Ann and Georgie simultaneously relaxed their postures as various members of the Pussy Posse enveloped them in hugs and kisses. Ann moved Nikki away from the group.

'She fancies you,' she said.

'Who does?'

'Georgie. She's jealous of me because I'm with you and she wants you. That's the trouble with the scene: there's always some bastard sticking their oar in and trying to either steal you or your girlfriend. What is it about these lesbians who always think the grass is greener on the other side? They're never happy with what they've got. They want to fuck it up for everyone else.'

'Georgie wouldn't do that. She's just looking after me, that's all. She's one of my closest friends.'

'Yeah, right. She fancies you, that's all I know, and I don't like other women trying to muscle in on what's mine.'

'It's not yours yet,' Nikki flared, 'and Georgie has never even made a pass at me. So if she fancies me as much as you say, she would have tried it on, wouldn't she? I can't help your insecurities, if you think everyone is trying to steal your woman. All I know is that Georgie has always been there for me. She's helped me out of a few scrapes before now and I trust her.'

'You should put your partner first, not your friends. It should be me you trust, and I'm telling you she wants you for herself and she had better not get in my face again.'

'Just who do you think you are? I'm not your partner. You don't own me. Nobody owns me. What right have you got to start acting as though I'm some sort of possession?'

Ann suddenly realised Georgie was approaching again, alerted by Nikki's raised voice.

'Everything all right over here?' Georgie said calmly, passing Nikki her beer.

'Yeah, fucking hunky dory,' Nikki said spitefully. She gulped the beer down quickly.

'We were just agreeing to differ about something. It's sorted now. Don't worry your pretty little head about it,' said Ann.

Her patronising tone was the final straw for Georgie. 'Is it sorted, Nikki?' she said icily, not taking her eyes off Ann. 'Or do you want me to sort it for you?'

'I wouldn't advise that. You know I'm a police officer. You really don't want to make me angry with you, do you?'

'I don't give a flying fuck what you are. All I know is that you've upset Nikki about something and I don't like my friends being upset.'

'Listen, leader of the gang, back off and go and play somewhere else. Take your ball and go home.'

A large circle of space had magically appeared around the two of them as they faced off.

Nikki groaned. What the fuck had happened tonight, so quickly? They surely weren't going to have a fight over her, were they? What the hell had got into Georgie? Why did Ann rub her up the wrong way? Why did Ann dislike Georgie so much? Why did she feel so threatened and insecure? What the fucking hell could she do to put this right? All she had wanted tonight was some fun, a few laughs, a snog or two and some dirty dancing. Now, within half an hour she had ended up shouting at Ann, who was at loggerheads with her best friend, and the evening had fallen away to fuck. It would get worse if a brawl ensued.

She stepped between them.

'This is fucking silly. The pair of you just back off and leave each other alone. I don't know what it is but you two have obviously taken an instant dislike to each other and we will all have to just put up with it. Whatever it is, it's not worth fighting about and getting us all thrown out and banned for life. Ann, we'll go somewhere else. Let's all try to calm down and keep our tempers.'

'So she's upset you, got all fucking bolshie, done the big copper bit, seriously pissed me off and you're leaving with her?' Georgie was incredulous.

'Yes.' Ann's face was almost unbearably smug. 'She's leaving with me. Looks like she's made her choice, doesn't it? See you again, some time.'

Nikki was moved away so quickly, propelled by her elbow towards the door, that she had no time to say goodbye. She looked over her shoulder as they reached the door, and just before the group gathered round Georgie she saw Georgie's head shake, the anguish in her eyes, and then she couldn't see her any more.

'So, where do you want to go from here?' said Ann.

'Home.'

'What, to hubby? Don't let all that crap upset you. It's not worth it. If I had really wanted to I could have put her down – she's all hot air and bluster.'

'You really are an arrogant bastard, aren't you? I'm not sure I like it, actually.'

Ann could see Nikki slipping away from her. 'Look, baby, I'm used to this sort of stuff, either in my job or on the scene. Georgie will get used to me being around you. She's just jealous. I'm jealous. It's all new to you, I know, but all I'm trying to do is protect you, look after you. She's got some sort of hidden agenda, that's her problem. You're right, I'm feeling insecure – you obviously feel something for each other and I'm being silly because it's nothing more than friendship. It's just that, since I met you, I don't want to let you go. I don't want to lose you. I want to be with you, only you, and I probably overreacted. I'm sorry.'

She had moved closer to Nikki. Now she gathered her in her arms and held her tight. Nikki's body was still rigid with tension.

'I need to go back in there and talk to Georgie,' Nikki said stubbornly.

'Leave her be, she'll calm down in a couple of days. She has to accept that I'm a big part of your life now and, when she sees that I'm good for you, she'll come round. She may even start to like me. Next time I see her I'll apologise, I promise. What we have to focus on now is getting us back on track. I know how I feel about you, and I don't want anything to get in the way of it. Let's just go somewhere else, have a quiet drink and put this behind us.'

Ann was again moving Nikki away, her solid muscled arm tight around her shoulders. Despite Nikki's reluctance, the pressure was too strong. They walked away, but Nikki couldn't stop thinking about that last stricken look on Georgie's face.

Inside the bar, Georgie had been given a large chaser with her beer. She was still shaking with rage and indignation, an idea forming in her mind. No matter what it was that Ann had said to Nikki, Nikki had left with her. She hadn't stuck up for Georgie: she had probably been too busy thinking about getting laid.

Well, if Nikki had turned her back on Georgie, she could do the same. She would show Nikki she didn't need her, and then Nikki would come running back at some point with her tail between her legs, no doubt expecting Georgie to pick up the pieces as though nothing had happened.

'Except I won't be here,' she muttered grimly to herself.

Five chasers and beers later, she was dirty dancing and snogging with Sharon the motor mechanic, who had quickly forgiven her for never ringing her back and had made her swear she would remember the sex this time.

Nikki, meanwhile, had swallowed several soft drinks, while Ann had remained contrite and apologetic. Ann had already mentioned that she had the spare keys to Tracy's flat and that Tracy would be out with the crowd for hours yet. Nikki had allowed Ann to kiss her in the car after they drove across town to another bar but Ann could see she was still defensive and not a little disturbed by what had happened. Nikki was really making her work hard, she thought bitterly.

'Is your husband expecting you back tonight?' she asked casually.

Nikki shrugged. 'He doesn't expect anything of me any more. I can do what I like. I think I'd prefer to go home, though. I'm not really in a good mood any more.'

'Why don't we just go back to Tracy's place, open a bottle of wine and chill out and see whether your mood changes? We could just curl up and cuddle.' Ann squeezed Nikki's hand as she said it. She was relieved that Nikki returned the pressure.

Nikki finally caved in, although her mind was turbulent, churning over what had been said and done that night.

They drove in silence to Tracy's flat, but Ann was gratified that Nikki held her hand in the car. She put her arm round Nikki as they walked up the stairs; Nikki leant against her. As they walked into the darkness of the flat, Ann pulled Nikki towards her, held her tightly in the dark and began to kiss her, slowly and cautiously at first. Nikki began to respond, her hands starting to roam around Ann's tautly muscled back, as the kiss grew deeper and more urgent and tongues began to explore.

'I love the way you kiss,' Ann murmured in her ear. 'I'm so sorry, baby, that I upset you. I'm just so sorry. Let me show you how sorry I am.'

Nikki allowed herself to be led into the spare room, where Ann just stood and held her in silence.

'I want you so much,' Ann finally said as she recognised the final shred of reluctant tension disappear from Nikki's body. She began to stroke her arms, her sides, her back. The kiss was long. Nikki began to take over, pulling Ann into her, returning the strokes and caresses.

Still kissing, Ann moved Nikki backward towards the bed and, holding her strongly, laid her down. As they kissed, their hips moved together. Nikki's leg moved over Ann's and she began to pull Ann's shirt out of her jeans. Still they could not break the kiss as Ann raised herself and undid her buttons, pulled the shirt off, began to undo Nikki's belt and popped open her fly buttons.

Finally, they broke apart as Ann moved downward. Nikki raised her hips and Ann started to pull her jeans down, tugging off Nikki's boots and socks.

Ann slowly came back up, running her tongue along the inside of Nikki's calf, knee, thigh, lightly brushing against her mound, then she started to gently lick her way down Nikki's other leg. Once again she moved slowly upward, her lips barely touching Nikki's sex, and she moved her mouth up Nikki's stomach, nuzzling her hip bones, pushing up Nikki's shirt.

Nikki started to undo her shirt – she was bra-less underneath – as Ann continued to gently lick her way up her body with tantalising slowness. As Ann gratefully sank her mouth on to Nikki's breast, with light feather strokes of her fingers, Nikki began to moan. She held Ann's head, pushing her against her breast as Ann began to suck hard on her nipple. The pressure of the squeeze of Ann's hand was just hard enough to make Nikki gasp with pleasure. Now her other hand was pressing against Nikki's sex, her fingers lightly stroking, as Nikki raised her hips again.

In one fluid movement Ann had raised herself to kiss Nikki; one leg had pushed Nikki's legs open and she had her pinned down. Nikki gripped Ann's hair as she thrust her tongue deep inside Ann's mouth, her hips beginning to grind as the other woman slowly slipped inside her.

As one, then two fingers, moved inside her, Nikki arched her back and gasped. She thought the fingers would reach right up inside her, but she still wanted more. They were both moving together in rhythm, the pressure of Ann's body, her mouth on

Nikki's, dictating the speed – slow and maddeningly sensual. Nikki was awash with pleasure, as she let go to Ann's experience. Now Ann slowly withdrew and Nikki could not help the groan of disappointment.

'Not yet, baby, not yet. I want to play,' Ann whispered, and then she was between Nikki's thighs. The first touch of her tongue was delicate, experimental, almost imperceptible. Nikki shivered with anticipation as Ann raised her head, smiled almost triumphantly at her, then slowly lowered her head again.

This time Ann's mouth was fully on her, her tongue quickly darting up and down the length of her, every so often moving inside her, flicking from side to side as Nikki began to groan her name. Nikki could feel Ann's mouth sliding against her wetness; Ann had slipped her hands under her buttocks and had raised Nikki's cunt even higher against her face. Now she held Nikki tight against her, her shoulders taking the weight of Nikki's hips and thighs, as she buried her face, and rolled her tongue hard around Nikki's swollen clit. And then Ann began to suck hard.

The shock of such intense pleasure made Nikki stiffen. It was almost unbearable: part of her wanted to squirm away; part of her wanted to grind against Ann's face. She could feel herself climbing; had never experienced anything so powerful. It was beginning to take her over as she closed her eyes, but she never wanted it to stop. She wanted to stay on the crest and ride it out and take more and more pleasure and keep it coming and coming. She couldn't believe that Ann could suddenly slow. She felt her hips being lowered; she felt her body coming back down and again she whimpered with disappointment as Ann moved her face away.

'Ssh, baby, this is just the beginning,' she said, and then the tip of her tongue was flicking Nikki's engorged slit, sliding around in Nikki's wetness. Nikki could hear Ann gulp her juices, then she was again inside her, this time with three fingers, now sucking again on her.

This had never happened: no one had ever bothered enough to try like this. She had never experienced anyone enjoying her so much; wanting to give her so much pleasure. My God,

Nikki thought as she started to climb again, I've missed so fucking much.

It was her last rational thought as her mind and body gave way to what Ann was doing to her. The fingers were pounding into her in quick bursts, then Ann would slow, each time bringing her closer and closer to coming, slowing right on the edge until Nikki began to cry out for her release. Ann was sucking, licking, flicking her, drinking from her, clamping her tight as Nikki began to thrash.

All Nikki could hear and feel was Ann – Ann inside her, Ann holding her tight, Ann's moans of desire vibrating against her cunt – and then she heard herself, the long drawn-out growl from deep within her; felt herself tighten round Ann's fingers, the rush in her stomach as she began to hurtle towards orgasm, bucking and riding. She could hardly breathe – there was nothing in her world but that desperate need for headlong flight over the edge and still Ann was fucking her, harder and faster, going with her over that edge and then Nikki just exploded. It seemed to her that she would never stop coming, that she would feel this intensity for ever more – she was aware that she was crying out to God, to Jesus, to Ann, and it felt that the waves of pleasure would consume her, drown her and she would be lost.

As she lay panting, her thighs in spasm, her heart hammering wildly, she weakly raised her arms to Ann. Ann slowly, gently withdrew and moved upward so that Nikki could hold her. Nikki buried her face in Ann's neck while she tried to regain control of her breathing. She knew she had never had an orgasm so powerful, so overwhelming, before, and she knew that she would always want to go on having orgasms like that.

'For fuck's sake, what have you done to me?' she finally breathed in Ann's ear.

Ann raised herself so that she could look down at Nikki. Nikki opened her eyes and again had that disconcerting feeling of being trapped. Ann's face seemed cold; Nikki could not read her eyes. The aftershock of her orgasm rapidly disappeared and, as she looked at Ann, she had an alarming flashback – Georgie's anguished eyes. Now cold brown eyes looked down at her. It was impossible to gauge Ann's emotions. Then Ann smiled.

'It can always be like this if you want it, baby,' she said.

It was at that moment that Nikki registered the triumph in her voice and that those brown eyes were flat, dead, expressionless.

This was not what she wanted. No way.

THIRTEEN

Ann's courtship of Nikki had begun in earnest – roses arrived at her office twice that following week with ambiguous cards; her mobile phone was stacked with long, lingering and loving messages; three times she had had mysterious hang-ups, number withheld, at her home when Steve had answered the phone; a large greetings card had arrived at her house, plastered with private and confidential on the envelope. Luckily she had got to the post first that day and hidden it in her briefcase.

Now she sat at her desk and stared at the envelope. She did not want to open it. She had had an underlying current of fear all week, a sense of doom around the corner, and she knew it had something to do with Ann. Nikki was in a turmoil. She had left Tracy's flat that night with unfinished business. The atmosphere had been cordial, but a little uncomfortable, and she had made a vague promise to call Ann later in the week with a view to seeing her for a drink. She still hadn't called. It was now Friday.

It would be nothing more, Nikki determined, if she even did meet her for a drink. There were two things preying on her mind – how had Ann got hold of her home phone number, and her home and office addresses? And where the hell was Georgie? Her stomach was constantly knotted with anxiety. She knew she had to tackle the issue but was at a loss as to how. Keeping her restless at night was the recurring image of Ann turning up at work – or, even worse, at home. Ann had obviously got the information through her job – she must have done – or she had interrogated the Pussy Posse. But then none of them knew her home number, just her mobile, and only Georgie knew exactly where she worked. Thinking through the problem was giving her a headache.

The sex had been undeniably good, better than anything she had ever enjoyed before. She had feigned tiredness to excuse herself from returning the favour to Ann, who had simply shrugged.

Nikki took a deep breath and opened the envelope. The card print declared, 'You are Very Special.' The handwritten message was: 'I Miss You, I Want You. A.'

Nikki ripped the card into four pieces and tossed it into the bin. She reached for the phone. Georgie was still on answerphone, probably ignoring her, probably still pissed off. She had phoned one or two of the girls, who all said Georgie had been plastered on Sunday and had left the bar with Sharon but otherwise they had not heard from her either.

How the hell did I get into this? How do I get out of it? I've lost my best friend and I'm now being stalked by an arrogant, obsessive nutter. She has information that could cripple me if it comes out now, before I'm ready. On the other hand she has probably abused her position as a copper. All I have to do is ring her like I promised, just tell her we need to cool it and I'm not ready for an intense relationship. Thanks for the shag, it was brilliant, I shouldn't have done it, but let's leave it there, shall we? That wouldn't be too difficult, would it? Would it? By the way, don't you dare contact me at home or work again or I'll get you disciplined, thrown off the force. Great.

Where was Georgie? Nikki had spoken several times to Gillian, asked her to ring Georgie's mum to see if she knew anything. Even that had drawn a blank. Georgie hadn't spoken to her mother in weeks.

Nearly a week now without her, and she had hated upsetting her. That too was unfinished business. She had never seen Georgie look so wounded. She needed to apologise, make it better, and Georgie had disappeared off the face of the earth.

She suddenly remembered that Georgie had been finalising a project for a business contact she had provided. No matter how angry she might be with Nikki, Georgie still had work to do and wouldn't avoid clients. She rifled through her time manager and found the number.

'Hi, Phil, Nikki Jones at BFCP. I put you in touch with a freelance copywriter, Georgie Rivers, remember? She's doing something for you at the moment, isn't she? Yes, that's right, it's just that I've got an urgent job on at the moment for her and I can't seem to get hold of her. It's a while since I used her. I wondered if possibly she'd changed her number, moved or –'

'She's gone away,' Phil interrupted. 'Marched into my office on Monday afternoon, a week earlier than the deadline, gave me my stuff and said she wouldn't be available for a few weeks. Said she hoped it was OK but she wouldn't be able to do any rewrites if they were needed. If I had any queries or problems I should call her mobile up until Tuesday morning. And that was it, really.'

'Did she say where she was going?'

'All I know is that she said her mobile would be switched off after Tuesday because she hadn't got the international service on it. I presume she's gone abroad, probably on holiday.'

After they exchanged some business trivia, Nikki hung up and put her head in her hands. Georgie was gone – God knows where, or for how long. Nikki suddenly felt very cornered, isolated and alone with her problems.

Her schedule was light for the rest of the day as she scanned her time manager. It could all wait until Monday. She rang Gillian.

'Free for lunch? Friday girly jaunt?' She tried to keep her voice buoyant. Gillian knew her too well.

'For you I'll clear my diary. Make it a late lunch to give me time to do what I was going to do this afternoon and I'll come and pick you up at the office. I gather something has happened? Is it going to be a Don't Fuck With Us Girlies summit meeting?'

'Something like that. I just need to discuss it with someone, see

167

if I can sort it out. Georgie, by the way, has fucked off on holiday without telling anyone where she's going or for how long. Could be weeks. You might want to let her mother know.'

Gillian arrived in time to get to the pub for last meal orders, but Nikki by that time was only interested in alcohol. She recited her tale of woe to Gillian. It took three rounds, by which time she was slightly pissed.

'The first thing that needs to happen is that you contact this weirdo and get her off your back. She probably got your address through a PNC check on your vehicle, and of course you're not ex-directory at home, are you? How she got your work number and address I have no idea, unless of course she followed you there one morning. Strikes me she's playing a very dangerous game, although I suppose she would claim that you gave her the information willingly, and that you were making a complaint about her as a malicious ex-girlfriend. Remember that one idiot I made the mistake of getting involved with? Even getting the tosspot arrested for blackmail didn't deter him. He managed to sweet-talk his way out of it, didn't he? Took me a year to keep him away, until he attached himself to some other poor bitch and forgot about me. That's the problem, they're compulsive obsessives, can't believe you don't want them. They do it In the Name of Love.'

Gillian, years on, still kept the Dictaphone tapes logging the bizarre and heated conversations she had received from him. It had cost her a lot of money in legal fees to try to keep him away from her. Even now, on the odd occasion she saw him, she actually felt the same pitch of anger, fear and loathing she had felt at the time. She wouldn't wish it on her worst enemy, let alone such a dear friend.

'At least, darling,' Gillian placated, 'you've not embarked on a full-scale relationship. I was with him for six months before the cracks appeared. She surely must get the message if you tell her this early on that you made a mistake, you weren't suited, you don't like her. Tell her you're going back to your husband – that'll put her off. It was only the third time you've seen her, after all.'

'That's all very practical and logical but there's something about her. I don't think she'll give up that easily. She's obviously gone to a lot of trouble already. I should have gone with Georgie's gut instincts. She didn't like her at all: they nearly came to blows. Ann thinks Georgie fancies me. Georgie now thinks I took Ann's side – I just wanted to get them away from each other. I know I should have just taken Ann away and then gone back to talk to Georgie, and now I can't. I miss her, Gillian, and she's buggered off angry with me.'

'Does Georgie fancy you?'

'If she does, she's never made it obvious to me. We're very close. I don't deny that.'

'Do you fancy her?'

'Georgie is a wonderful girl, lovely. I feel an awful lot for her – she's made such a difference to me in such a short space of time. I feel like my arm's been chopped off without her here to talk to. I'm so gutted that I made her angry. I wouldn't hurt her for the world.'

'So Ann just misunderstood the situation, then? I remember that tosspot tried to keep me away from my male friends. He felt very insecure that I was going to run off with one of them. Didn't matter what I said to reassure him, he felt he should be the focal point in my life. Bollocks to that – I've got lots of other things I enjoy too much to put on hold while he obsessed about me. A relationship should be about sharing. You both should have your own interests, space and friends.'

Nikki didn't hear a word of it: she had retreated into her own thoughts.

'I think,' Gillian said firmly, 'that you should ring this nutter this afternoon. Do it now, make it plain that you are not to be trifled with. People like that are control freaks, bullies, only interested in having power. They like to think they can tame people like us because it feeds their own pathetic, fragile egos. That's why she hides behind her uniform. The ultimate position of power, isn't it, being a police officer? The only way to deal with a bully is to challenge them back, show them you are stronger than they thought you were. Call her bluff.'

'And what do I do about Georgie?'

'Nothing you can do right now, is there? You could write a letter to her for when she gets back. If she has gone on holiday then she'll have time to think herself. Knowing Georgie, if she's anything like her mother she'll seethe and smart for a while then something will pop up to distract her and she'll forget all about it. After all, you said you were very close. You always seemed very close when I saw you together. Friends will always forgive. May take some time, but friends stay friends.'

Nikki was not so sure. The letter idea was good: at least she could put her thoughts down without Georgie having a chance to challenge them. She could say exactly what she felt. Gillian was right about Ann: she should nip it in the bud now before it got out of hand, before the bitch could do anything to threaten her plans. She had six months, max, then Millennium would be launched. At least three clients were lined up for when their contracts came up for renewal; the paperwork for the limited company had been drawn up with her and Gillian as equal partners; and her business plan was shaping up nicely. The first tentative steps towards a legal separation and agreement for the house had been made with Steve. Why had she told Ann so much about her plans to start the new century with a bang? She should have kept her mouth shut: although Ann couldn't prove anything, she could make life extremely awkward. The last thing Nikki wanted right now was to embark on further webs of deceit.

'What I would add is, remember we women are devious, can hold grudges for years, will always carefully plot revenge. You can always spot the next move from a man – they can only do one thing at once and they usually telegraph it a mile off. Just make sure your back is covered, that's all,' said Gillian.

'Perhaps I should have just let Georgie beat her up,' said Nikki despondently.

'Cerebral, darling, that's the approach. Think it through and plan every avenue carefully. Then, if all else fails, let Georgie break her legs.'

Finally Nikki smiled. Somehow she knew that she could salvage her friendship with Georgie, once Georgie had cooled off.

Georgie probably would do it if Nikki needed her to do it. That was Georgie for you. She just wished she knew where Georgie was. She needed her.

Georgie was on a beach, Walkman at an almost unbearably loud volume, as Sharon massaged lotion into her aching back. The second thing she had done on that Monday morning – Sharon had proved too horny to resist – was to scroll through late offers on Teletext. Three phone calls later and the two of them were booked to fly out the following afternoon to St Lucia, all inclusive, for three weeks. The first call was to her credit-card company to increase her limit; the second was to Sharon's employer to arrange one week paid, two weeks' unpaid leave; the third was to book the holiday.

She had tied up the loose ends for work, hurriedly packed, helped Sharon gather her stuff together, and the holiday had begun. Now, as the sun beat down on her back and Sharon's hands roamed her body, she could begin to relax. The flight had seemed endless; there was an argument over the standard of accommodation; the hotel staff had looked bemused at her request for a room with a double bed, not twin beds; and she had already got so drunk that she had been sick.

Now, on her third full day, she and Sharon had developed a routine. Despite hangover, straight out for early-morning sun, into the bar for happy hour and food when the sun was at its strongest, back to the room for a shag and a siesta, out for the weaker late-afternoon sun then hit the bars for happy hour again.

'This is fucking paradise, mate,' said Sharon.

The two of them had caused various comments already, by holding hands around the complex, and Georgie knew there were at least five guys who had to lie face down on their loungers when she or Sharon were applying suntan lotion to the other. She and Sharon had probably improved the sex lives of all the heteros around the pool, particularly as Sharon looked so fucking magnificent in a thong bikini and seemed to have developed a deep tan within hours of arriving. We're probably indulging everyone's secret fantasy, Georgie thought, smiling to herself.

171

If Nikki were here, they'd really be creaming themselves because I wouldn't be able to keep my hands off her. I'd be fucking her on the lounger or up against the palm tree in front of all the kids in the pool. I'd be throwing her on the sand, snogging her under the stars in the deep black sky with just the sound of the cicadas.

Georgie moaned; Sharon thought it was a moan of desire. She was massaging the lotion into the tops of the backs of Georgie's thighs. She slowed the motion, made it deeper, harder, her thumbs surreptitiously slipping closer to Georgie's sex, her hands beginning to filter through the edges of Georgie's bikini pants. The guy on the next lounger coughed and turned away, wondering where his sunglasses were so he could watch them without being observed by his wife.

Sharon now moved so that she was partly shielding what she was doing. Her hands ran the lotion up Georgie's sides. Her fingers slipped inside Georgie's top and she began to squeeze and fondle her breasts. Her sweat dripped on to Georgie's back, mixed with the creamy white lotion. Her hands were sliding back down towards Georgie's buttocks, her hips, the tops of her thighs.

Georgie sensed that Sharon was getting close to doing something that would probably get them both thrown out of the resort, if not deported off the island. She closed her legs, crossing them at the ankles. Disappointed, Sharon took the hint and moved away, and then Georgie heard the splash as Sharon threw herself into the pool. One way of cooling off, Georgie thought.

Sharon was OK, a fairly decent shag if not a little bit too energetic, probably due to her youth. She was a very enthusiastic and lively pupil. They didn't have an awful lot in common but then conversation was not why Georgie had offered to pay for her ticket. Sharon was a diversion, a distraction, and Georgie sensed that Sharon, as young as she was, was under no illusions. She never complained when Georgie drifted off into a world of her own, sometimes for hours. Sharon never even asked any questions. She just patiently waited for Georgie to break her reverie, and then would brightly suggest a bar, or a shag.

That's all she is, Georgie thought bitterly, something to keep me occupied, perhaps something to help me get Nikki out of my system. I'm not using her; she accepts the situation. She's got a Caribbean holiday out of it and the drinks are free. I don't need to feel guilty. I was not the one who took sides; I wasn't the one ignoring all the signals. I did give Nikki signals, I know I did. All right, maybe not very strong signals. Nikki had said certain things that Georgie could have picked up and run with, taken a risk with.

Georgie had taken on too well the role of best lesbian buddy, gay mentor, leader of the gang, minder. That's all Nikki wanted her for: she couldn't possibly feel anything else. Georgie hadn't really shown her anything else, had she? All this time, all the way through that glorious summer of fun with the Pussy Posse, Nikki had no idea of Georgie's strong feeling for her.

What would happen when she returned? What had already happened? Had Nikki thrown in the towel, left Steve, moved in with that copper? They'd probably slept together, declared mad, passionate love for each other, sworn to grow old, grey and toothless together, swapped rings.

That would mean Georgie would probably never see Nikki again. Once friends embarked on relationships and became couples they seemed to disappear off the scene. There was no way Ann would ever countenance Nikki retaining any sort of relationship with Georgie after that fiasco on Sunday.

The thought of never seeing Nikki again, with so much left unsaid, crippled her. A silent tear rolled down her cheek, dripped on to her towel.

'Oh, Nikki,' she groaned aloud, just as Sharon appeared with drinks from the bar.

Sharon heard but said nothing.

'Here you go, mate, Sex on the Beach for you, Tropical Tequila Tornado for me. Barbecue for lunch today, home-made burgers with loads of garlic, and there's a shopping trip to Castries planned for this afternoon and a calypso night tonight. What do you think?'

I think that the next twelve days are going to be the longest of my life. Without Nikki I'm dying a little each day. With her I come alive, without her I'm nothing. That's what I think.

'Yeah, great, sounds wicked,' said Georgie.

She was withdrawn for the rest of the day. It was as they walked along the beach hand in hand that evening that Sharon finally broke.

'So who is this Nikki, then?' She tried to keep the venom out of her voice.

'A mate of mine. We had an argument that Sunday over a woman I don't think is suitable for her. I was so pissed off that I had to get away. You probably didn't see her – it was all over and done with by the time you came in. Tall, good-looking blonde?'

'You were on your own when I got there. I was just so surprised to see you after so long. It had been a few weeks. You should have rung me before. It was good, though, in the end. It's worked out well. I'm glad you brought me here. I've only ever been to Spain before, and no one has ever done nothing as nice as paid for a holiday for me.' Sharon squeezed her hand.

'Why don't we go and see if there's anyone at the pool?' she said, and Georgie grinned.

She had suggested it twice already but they had both ended up so pissed every night that they had barely managed to get back to their rooms before passing out.

The pool area was deserted, the security lights off, just the moonlight reflecting off the water, a faint warm breeze rippling the leaves of the palm trees.

Sharon leant back against the palm tree at Georgie's insistent snog. As they kissed, Georgie tried hard to dismiss the image she had had earlier of Nikki leaning against a tree, legs apart, as Georgie, on her knees, drove her wild in the dark with her tongue and fingers.

Instead it was Sharon squirming against her and, although very pleasant indeed, it was the imagery of Nikki naked and spread that captivated Georgie's mind behind her closed eyes. In Georgie's now vivid and somewhat fevered, alcohol-fuelled imagination, it was Nikki she was leading to the edge of the pool; Nikki who was peeling off her shorts and diving into the welcoming water.

She leapt into the pool herself, gasping at the shock of the cold water and coming up for air.

Nikki waited for her in the shallow end, leaning against the cool tiles, her arms spread on the edge of the pool, her T-shirt clinging, nipples erect. Georgie lazily swam towards her, dived under the surface and came up with her hands either side of Nikki's hips. They moved straight into the kiss, Georgie leaning into her, the water streaming down their faces, and Georgie parted Nikki's legs under the water with her own. Her hand was already down there, rubbing and kneading, and Nikki began to grind against it. Georgie broke the kiss, moving to lick the pool water off her neck, nuzzling harder, sucking and lightly chewing on her earlobe, at the nape of her neck.

The fingers of her other hand were pulling and tugging on a nipple, not too hard to be painful – the groans of pleasure and the whisper of her name in her ear told her the pressure was just right. She could feel Nikki's cunt begin to gush against her hand, warm, slippery and mixing with the cool water, and she gently teased the clitoris. As Nikki raised her hips towards her she moved inside with two fingers, began to slowly fuck, biting slightly harder on Nikki's neck, feeling their wet T-shirts riding up together as the pool water rippled around them, as she increased the pace and the rhythm. Then, as the urgency in Nikki's hips rose, she started to kiss her again, tongue probing deep, sucking on her tongue. She knew Nikki was wet and wide enough to take three fingers, and slipped deeper into her.

Nikki broke the kiss to gasp as Georgie pinned her back against the tiles, filling her up, riding her hard and fast. Georgie was close to coming herself, imagining Nikki grinding away underneath her, making the water slap lusciously against her back. She could almost smell Nikki's perfume; it was Nikki's cunt closing tight and spasming round her fingers; it was Nikki biting on her shoulder and then the dream was shattered.

'Fuckin' hell, mate, this is lush,' Sharon almost shouted right in her ear.

Desire disappeared immediately. Sharon actually winced as Georgie pulled straight out.

'We can't do this.' Georgie was well aware that Sharon hadn't come, had probably just been on the verge. 'We'll get arrested or something. Sorry, I can't do this. Let's get out and dressed before somebody comes.'

'Well, I didn't.' Sharon's justifiable complaint was delivered petulantly.

'Come on, quick, before someone sees us.' And Georgie was climbing the steps, retrieving her shorts. 'We've got loads of time for you to come, just not here, not now.'

She knew that Sharon would be within her rights to sulk, but the duty free in the room would soon sort that out.

All she had to do was sort herself out, get that bloody woman out of her head. Her heart. Her blood. Her soul. That's all she had to do.

FOURTEEN

Another day without Georgie dawned for Nikki. It had now been two weeks and no postcard, nothing, no word from anyone in the crowd about where she was, who she was with, when she would be back. If she would be back.

I must have monumentally pissed her off, Nikki thought, her stomach churning with a fresh anxiety attack, a sharp stabbing pain under her ribs. Her Irritable Bowel Syndrome had returned with a vengeance. So had her mood swings, her temper. She had avoided the Pussy Posse, staying in every night, even Saturdays.

Every time the phone rang at home, at work, she jumped guiltily, racked with fear. She ran to the front door every morning at the first sound of the postman, almost ripping envelopes out of his hand.

Nagging at the back of her mind every waking moment was the worry that, despite her conversation with Ann, this was the calm before the storm.

It had been a week ago. Emboldened by Gillian's persistent persuasion, she had sat in the car, Gillian beside her, and called Ann from her mobile on hands-free, a rehearsed script in her head. The plan of attack was to let her down gently, offer to stay friends, rather than antagonise the woman. At least that was the idea. She was hoping for an answerphone at the other end.

Ann had picked up on the first ring, wrong-footing her straight away. Nikki stumbled and stammered her way through the hellos and social trivia.

'When am I going to see you again? I'm desperate for you. I miss you so much, baby. Do you miss me? I've missed your voice, your face.' Ann's voice had been soft, gentle, almost mesmeric.

'I . . . er . . . wanted to say thank you for all the flowers. They're lovely . . . You know, there's no need to send me flowers . . . cards . . .' Nikki could see Gillian's encouraging gestures from the corner of her eye. 'I've been busy at work this week . . . I've not rung before . . . er . . . I just really wanted to tell you . . . er . . . How have you been?'

'Falling in love with you.'

Shit. Bollocks. Oh Christ. What now? She had looked in mute appeal to Gillian, who shrugged, curled her lip in contempt, and then again nodded in encouragement.

'Yes, well, er . . . that's what I wanted to talk to you about. I think this is probably going a bit too fast, too soon, for me . . .'

Silence.

'You know, I've got a lot going on at the moment and I don't really want any more complications. I don't think I'm really ready for any of this intense, deep stuff . . .' She tailed off helplessly. Gillian slumped, shaking her head.

'Complications? Stuff?'

'You know, stuff. I think I'd really prefer it if we could just stay friends, at least while I get my life on track. I'm sorry, Ann –' she took a deep breath '– but I really don't feel as strongly as you do. I'm sure we can be good friends. Can't we at least try?'

'Try to be friends? Well, if you have to try then that doesn't say a lot, does it?' Ann's voice was beginning to rise in indignation.

Nikki and Gillian both winced, waiting for the outburst. The crash of the phone as Ann slammed it down reverberated around the car through the speakers. Nikki imagined the car was rocking on its axles.

'Well, that went down like a lead balloon, didn't it?' said Nikki.

She had heard nothing since; had no mysterious hang-ups, no cards, no messages on her mobile from Ann. Tracy, however, had left five messages the following week – increasingly more demanding and strident – asking her to call. Nikki knew Ann was using Tracy as a mediator, had probably given Tracy some horribly one-sided story of deep, unrequited love; how Nikki had led her on and promised her the earth then dumped her like a hot potato. It was probably all round the Pussy Posse by now, what a bitch she was. No, she reasoned, they would probably be a little more objective than that. Partners come and go; friends stay friends. It was one of the unwritten laws – some girls were passed around the scene like after-dinner mints.

Ann would get over it. Nikki surely couldn't be the great love of her life. They hardly knew each other. But Ann was so arrogant that being dumped was probably a huge dent in her pride, a real sideswipe for her massive ego. Why did she have to tell Nikki she had fallen in love? She couldn't possibly have done. It was all emotional bollocks as far as Nikki could see. Falling in love to Nikki would be like sudden impact, losing your breath, not being able to eat, being consumed by the other person, totally, madly, utterly and completely falling into that other person. Reaching inside and sharing hearts.

She was broken from her reverie by Steve's whining about his inability to find a pair of clean socks.

God, is this still what it is all about?

'Top drawer, at the back, as usual, all nicely paired up like your mother taught me to do, as you were incapable of finding matching socks every morning as a child. I'm surprised she doesn't expect me to still be dressing you as well,' she hissed, getting out of bed.

Steve sighed. He had had a few months of respite, while she had done whatever she had found so absorbing. But she had been home every evening for the last fortnight, hanging around the house at the weekend like a spare part, her face stern and set. The old Nikki was back, snappy, short-tempered, spiteful. He said nothing, but rummaged in the back of the drawer, found a pair of socks that did not match his suit but would do. Keeping his head down was probably the best policy short-term. If he aggravated her she might change her mind about the settlement proposal, start increasing her demands, inflating the lawyer's bills even further. Whatever it was that pissed her off, he was convinced it wasn't him. He did know, however, that he was getting the fall-out and, as irritating as that was, at least the settlement was still heavily weighted in his favour once finalised. He took a deep breath and willed himself to keep his mouth shut. They both dressed, ate breakfast and departed for work in silence.

The postcard was on top of her mail on her desk. A Caribbean sunset with a half-naked dollybird on a sun lounger. She turned it over and immediately recognised Georgie's scrawl: her heart lifted.

Weather here, wish you were beautiful. We're back on 23rd, get girls together. You're forgiven.
Georgie xxx

The first word to really register was 'we'. The second was the date – two days away. The third was 'forgiven'. Thank God. Who was she with? At least she hadn't disappeared for good. She would be back in just two days. Hopefully the letter she had sent her, amended after a few helpful suggestions from Gillian, would strengthen Georgie's forgiveness.

Those two days seemed to be the longest of her life. She had called a number of the girls – ignoring two more messages from Tracy – and they were all meeting on Saturday night. Her mood had brightened marginally, but as she drove to the bar her stomach was tight with fear, apprehension and anticipation. She was fervently hoping Ann and Tracy weren't there. She circled the block three times, then parked, waiting for Georgie's car to appear and the customary ten minutes of Georgie struggling to slot the Granada into a suitably large space. The cover of darkness shrouded her Saab as the silver Granada hurtled around the corner. Surprisingly, Georgie parked it first time, even if the rear wheel was on the pavement. Nikki waited as Georgie, as usual, leapt out of the car, surveyed her parking and shrugged.

Nikki was surprised at the intensity of her physical reaction to seeing Georgie after three weeks. Under the limited beam of streetlight Georgie looked fit, very tanned and relaxed. She was grinning at the other person Nikki could now see getting out of the passenger side. She couldn't quite see the other girl but, as Georgie came round the front of the vehicle, the girl automatically slotted under Georgie's outstretched arm and they went into the bar together, heads close.

Nikki's heart had leapt at seeing Georgie; now a fist had grabbed it and squeezed it tight. The anxiety attack had started: her stomach had turned over and she was almost nauseous. All the excitement at seeing Georgie again had disappeared in the second that the girl had wrapped her arm round Georgie's waist. They were clearly a couple.

With a sudden dread, Nikki remembered parts of her letter. She hoped that Georgie had not shown the letter to anyone, much less this new girlfriend. They had probably had a right good laugh about it, giggling about Nikki's grovelling apology, her admission that she had taken the wrong side that night, that Georgie had been right, how disastrously Ann had turned out – a real *Fatal Attraction* obsessive bunny-boiler – how much Nikki missed Georgie, would do anything to put it all right, how important Georgie was in her life, that she needed her.

Well, you won't know until you go in there and find out what's going on, she thought. She steeled herself, took several deep breaths to calm her pounding heart and tried to look casual.

Georgie's back was to her as she walked into the bar, but the adoring, faithful, puppydog look on her girlfriend's face was almost enough to make Nikki turn on her heel and walk straight back out. What stopped her was Georgie's half-turn, almost as if she knew Nikki was behind her. Their eyes met, and suddenly the bar faded away to black, the music seemed to disappear, and there was no one else there. Nikki was trembling; her throat was dry; she couldn't speak. Just a few feet separated them, and the gap was closing as Georgie moved towards her, her arms rising, and then Nikki was enfolded, held tight, her arms around Georgie. Nothing was said but Nikki felt safe again. Georgie's body was warm, her perfume was familiar and comforting. Nikki buried her face in Georgie's neck and the tears pricked at the corners of her eyes. She felt she couldn't get close enough; couldn't hold her tight enough; didn't want to let her go. Ever.

Her three-week, sun-and-sex-sodden sojourn had, Georgie thought, been enough to heal the wound, mend the heart that she had thought ripped out, stamped on. As the days had passed, so the time spent thinking about Nikki had dwindled from 24 hours a day to about 10. Every time she had made love to Sharon, though, she had been making love to Nikki in her mind. Once she had cried Nikki's name out loud as she reached orgasm and Sharon had not spoken to her for the best part of two days. It had cost her a vague promise and an expensive helicopter trip over the island – taking her right up to her credit-card limit – before Sharon finally, if somewhat grudgingly, forgave her. She had blamed it on the Screaming Orgasms: she had had at least ten of the sickly cocktails, all layered and presented in test tubes to drink in one gulp, the liquor mixing at the back of her throat.

As they had flown home, Georgie had been determined that, having sent the postcard forgiving her, she and Nikki would go forward as best friends, nothing more. Sharon could partly fill the gap, the yawning chasm of need, and with time Georgie would learn to love her and still have Nikki in her life. As the flight attendant had bent to refresh her drink, the girl's resemblance to Nikki was a painful stab in her heart.

Reading Nikki's letter on her return, hidden in the bathroom from Sharon's prying eyes, she had fallen apart again. She had never read anything so open, so honest, from anyone. Now, as she held Nikki and felt the two tears on her neck, the Caribbean and Sharon, the promises they had made to each other in the sunshine and the balmy dark, were forgotten. All that mattered was Nikki, and here she was, in her arms, where she was meant to be, where she was destined to be, where she belonged. Georgie could feel her own tears beginning to well.

'I've missed you so much,' Nikki murmured in her ear, at exactly the same time as Georgie said it.

They parted slightly with the shock, and looked at each other, their eyes glistening.

It was all getting too much for Sharon, who had stood seething with increasing impatience and intolerance as the embrace had gone on, and on. 'You must be Nikki,' she said with as much friendliness as a three-day-starved Rottweiler on guard duty. 'I'm Sharon.'

Nikki and Georgie finally left go of each other, but stood close, their fingers entwined behind Nikki's back.

'Yes, Sharon, this is Nikki,' said Georgie, and Sharon logged the pride in her voice.

At that moment Sharon's world shattered. The dreams for her future faded away as her jealous eyes raked Nikki from head to foot. Georgie had never been hers. She had never had a chance against this woman, had she? Sharon had tried so hard to resist her emotions during that holiday. But as each day had passed she had felt closer and closer, that Georgie was letting her in, would allow Sharon to help mend her broken heart. Georgie had insisted that Nikki was just a friend but Sharon had instinctively known better. Her gut feeling had helped her keep some of her final barriers up, but now her youth and immaturity took over. Her mouth tightened peevishly and she stormed off to the toilet.

'So . . .?' Georgie turned back to Nikki. Sharon had been instantly dismissed from her mind.

'Did you get my letter?'

'I'd forgiven you anyway. It took me a while, but I figured you would want me here to pick up the pieces. I had to get away, Nikki. I couldn't get my head round what was going on. I knew I'd probably let my temper get the best of me and then I'd lose you for good. Say the wrong thing, do the wrong thing. I just thought that running away and leaving you to it was the sensible thing to do. You had to learn the hard way, perhaps.'

'I was worried sick. I couldn't find out where you were for ages. I think I've dealt with Ann, but I'm not entirely sure yet, and if you want to say I told you so then go on. I made a complete twat of myself, because I didn't listen to you. Without you there my life just ground to a halt. I couldn't believe that you would just take off like that. I had no idea when, or if, you would be back. Whether you would want to see me again, and whether it would it be the same, or different? I've never felt so alone, so lost.'

Their fingers were still entwined as Georgie took hold of her again. They were still hugging in understanding silence as Sharon returned, took one look then stomped off to the bar. They were still together when Ann and Tracy walked in. Georgie spotted them first, and registered the look on Ann's face. Her adrenalin kicked in, and she pushed Nikki gently away.

'Oh Christ,' was all Nikki could say as Ann approached.

Ann's eyes never left Georgie. She was pumped up with a mixture of pleasure at seeing Nikki again and jealous rage. That tiresome girl was here again. She had been wrapped around Nikki, her Nikki. Ann conveniently forgot the last conversation they had had, the slamming down of her phone. All she saw now was the challenging stare, the intimidating stance of the little pipsqueak.

'I gather you've been making a bit of a nuisance of yourself,' said Georgie.

Nikki closed her eyes and groaned. She had perhaps gone into a little bit too much detail in her letter. She had a flashback to Gillian's remark about broken legs. She fervently hoped that it wouldn't be Georgie in plaster by the end of the evening. She opened her eyes and realised with fear that Ann was now glaring at her. Oh shit, perhaps it would be her in plaster.

'What have you been saying, Nikki?' Ann's question was deceptively calm.

'The truth.' Nikki bit her lip to try to quell the rising bile in her throat.

'The last I heard, you had been dumped. Been a bit too forward, had you?' Georgie's tone was unmistakeably provocative.

'Who died and put you in charge? I wasn't dumped. We agreed to stay friends, that's all – just take our time, nothing heavy.'

Nikki turned in astonishment.

'That's not quite true, is it?' Georgie deliberately dropped her voice so Ann had to strain to hear her above the music.

'Believe what you like. That's the way it is,' Ann replied.

'The way it is –' Georgie's voice was now firm '– is that I believe what Nikki has told me, not what you say, and I suggest you stay the fuck away from both of us. Neither of us wants a relationship of any sort with you. Go and be a pain in the arse to someone else, why don't you?'

'Why don't I take you outside and bounce you round like a fucking football?'

The bouncer, a huge black guy with no neck, had appeared on the fringe of the group. He was watching carefully.

'Why don't I just take a bottle of beer and shove it up your arse?' said Georgie.

The bouncer finally spoke: 'Why don't you ladies both just calm down. It's too early in the evening for me to be throwing pretty girls out on the street.'

Tracy was torn. She had allegiance to both Ann and Georgie, but Ann's recent pestering of her to try help get Nikki back in line had worn her out. Having known Georgie for longer, she knew that Georgie only threatened violence when it was absolutely justified. She had seen Georgie in action twice: once Georgie had talked a woman out of a confrontation in the toilets; once Georgie had traded punches and won. Ann, however, she had never seen like this. She stepped between them.

'Come on, he's right. It's also fucking cold out there,' Tracy said with a slightly hysterical note in her voice. She had noticed the bouncer had assumed position: his enormous shoulders were shifting under his tailored jacket; those huge hands were clenching and unclenching; he was rocking on the balls of his feet, eyes switching from one woman to the other, anticipating the next move. He had probably worked out which would go under which of his arms like a rugby ball, Tracy thought, and how many seconds it would take to carry them both out of the door.

Then there would be an extremely undignified and unpleasant, probably very loud and messy, catfight with pulled hair and punches. As both Ann and Georgie were stone-cold sober, it could go on for ages.

But it at least proved one thing, Tracy thought to herself – the same thing that had occurred quite a while ago to most of the other members of the Posse: Georgie and Nikki should really have got it together before now.

Sharon reappeared. All Nikki could do was torment herself with projections of either herself or Georgie being beaten to a pulp by Ann or Sharon. It would be a close call. One way or another, Nikki thought sadly, she would be called upon to dredge up some of the moves she had learnt at school, and would still end up going to work on Monday either scalped or with obvious markings on her face.

'Well, ladies, how is it going to be? Easy, or hard?' The bouncer now grinned, two gold teeth flashing, but his eyes were menacing.

Ann recognised his threat and sensibly decided that her career could grind to a halt if the force heard she had been fighting in the street outside a gay bar.

Nikki wanted to get out; so did Tracy.

Sharon wanted Georgie to be punished; humiliated by either Ann or the bouncer. She didn't care.

Georgie didn't give a shit.

'One day, girlie,' Ann hissed at her, 'when you're least expecting it. And you –' she turned on Nikki '– watch your back. I know where you are.'

Tracy caught the comment, and a flare of anger mixed with disgust and contempt made her grab Ann's arm and pull her backward towards the door.

Georgie had also heard the threat and was moving at the same time, but so was the bouncer. Being pulled backward affected Ann's balance. She started to stumble as Georgie reached her before the bouncer could reach Georgie. The slip gave Georgie the advantage; the red mist appeared before her eyes and she was at Ann's throat with both hands before Ann could react. Both went down in a tangle, bar stools flying, but Georgie grimly held on, Ann taking the full impact on her spine. As Georgie straddled her, one hand still at Anne's throat, the other pulled back for a full punch, the bouncer grabbed her round the chest and began to squeeze. Georgie's temper had taken her over and she was hardly aware that the breath was being squeezed out of her, that the bouncer's massive arms were also lifting her up and off. But she wouldn't leave go of Ann's throat and Ann was beginning to choke, to struggle for air.

The bouncer reached down with one arm to pull Georgie's hand away. She began to wriggle out of his other arm, her rage multiplying her strength and determination. The bouncer began to lose his grip – it seemed the woman had developed two or three more pairs of arms; it was like trying to hold on to an octopus. As he grabbed one arm, another appeared and began to rain punches. He caught a couple on the nose as her fist came back for full reach. At least she wasn't trying to strangle the other one any more. Finally his bulk took over, and he got her arms pinned to her sides behind her, as he began to rise and pull her up with him. Ann lay on the floor, coughing, as Georgie was taken off her, dragged off to the side.

He stood with her, his grip on her wrists just hard enough to warn her, his body partly shielding her, partly preventing her from moving. He hated it when the women started fighting. He had never had to hit one yet, but he had come close with this one. He and Georgie stood, breathing heavily.

Ann could hardly breathe as Tracy bent to help her up. She shrugged off the hand and began to struggle to get up. Everyone in the bar was watching in stunned silence. She locked eyes with the bouncer, who silently shook his head. She could only just see Georgie's eyes behind him, but she saw they were filled with loathing, an undiminished fire of anger. Then she saw Nikki move towards Georgie. She had lost. All round. Big time. She stood erect, adjusted her shirt, tried to muster her dignity, and walked rather shakily and unsteadily towards the door, another bouncer following to ensure that she left the vicinity. Tracy looked back once as she followed, and mouthed the word 'sorry' to Georgie.

'Give it ten minutes,' the first bouncer said quietly to Georgie and Nikki, 'then I suggest you leave.'

'Can we have a drink before we go? You can keep an eye on us,' said Nikki, flashing her eyes and warmest smile at him.

He nodded.

Nikki put her arm round Georgie, led her to the bar. The sea of people parted. Two patted Georgie on the back. They were served straight away.

The large bourbons on ice, tossed down in silence, helped both of them. Once the drinks were finished, the bouncer reappeared and gently laid a massive hand on each of their backs.

'Time to go, girls, sorry,' he said. His colleague had declared the coast was clear outside.

A quick check on Sharon, who seemed engrossed in conversation with someone, and the two were walking out into the fresh air. They stood awkwardly by Georgie's car.

Georgie finally broke the silence: 'I think you can assume we're banned. Well, at least until their cash flow begins to suffer. They'll probably let us back in again in a few weeks.'

'I don't know whether I should be grateful for what just happened, Georgie. Do you think she'll leave me alone, or will this make her worse? She's a loose cannon. She knows where I work, where I live. You humiliated her. She might decide to get her own back by turning up –'

'I think she will disappear off the face of the earth. Tracy was pissed off with her. I don't think we'll be seeing Ann in this neck of the woods again. I've hurt my hand,' she suddenly said.

Nikki took her hand, and lifted it up to the streetlight. She could see grazes on the knuckles. Georgie winced.

'Come on, I'll take you home,' said Nikki. 'We can pick your car up tomorrow.'

They stopped at an off-licence. Nikki bought a slab of beer and carried it into the flat. It was cold, so they huddled together on the sofa in front of the gas fire to try to get warm.

'You never really answered my question. Did you like my letter?' asked Nicki.

'I've never read anything so raw and honest. It must have taken a lot for you to write it, eat humble pie like that and apologise. I've read it several times. There's a couple of things in there that I'm not quite clear on, though,' Georgie said, reaching under the newspapers scattered on the coffee table.

When she brought the letter out, Nikki realised the paper was looking a little dog-eared. She suspected Georgie had read it many times.

Georgie went straight to the phrase in question. Nikki realised she knew the letter by heart.

'This bit, here, about how being away from me is like having a huge part of your life missing. And here, about how you wish you'd told me how important I was to you, how you needed me in your life. Is that just as a friend?' Georgie turned to Nikki. Her heart seemed to have stopped, waiting for the answer that could change her life.

'I used to think that,' Nikki said quietly, 'then I realised when you went away how I really felt. Being without you was physical. I ached. I couldn't stop thinking about you. My life seemed empty – nothing else seemed to matter. I couldn't concentrate on work, couldn't think straight. All I could see was your face, that hurt in your eyes the last time I saw you. The thought that I had done that tore me apart. I kept remembering all the fun times we had had, the two of us, how you helped me turn the corner, how much you make me laugh. You were always there for me. Until that night Ann said that you fancied me, I had no idea. Then I started thinking about it, some of the things you had said to me.'

'I was perhaps a little bit too subtle.' Georgie's voice was almost a whisper.

'Subtle? Why didn't you just come straight out with it?'

'I was frightened you would turn me down. You had never given me any signals that you fancied me, or saw me as anything but a friend. It could have been the biggest mistake of my life. I could have lost you completely, even as a friend. And I felt you were out of my league, that I'm just not good enough for you. So off I went, charging off to the Caribbean with Sharon, thinking I was coming back to see you living with Ann, all your plans down the drain. I thought that Ann would never let me be your

189

friend, that I would never see you again.' She was turning the beer bottle in her hand as she spoke, absently pulling at the label.

'Look at me,' Nikki said gently.

Georgie raised her head. Nikki was smiling.

'Kiss me,' said Nikki.

FIFTEEN

In that split-second Georgie knew that there was no going back: her response would determine her future; Nikki's future. It could be the future she had dreamt of, fantasised about. Nikki had had a huge, secret slice of her heart for so long now, and here she was, waiting patiently, expectantly, knowingly – silent and smiling – for Georgie to take that step. Georgie looked into Nikki's eyes. She could read the sparks of desire there. She dropped her gaze to Nikki's slightly parted lips. Within a fraction of a second she could be kissing those lips. She could feel that paradise beckoned.

Trembling with emotion, she put her beer down on the table and leant forward in one fluid movement, only placing a very slight grazing kiss on Nikki's lips, and then almost pulling away with the flash of fear that Nikki was playing with her, had no idea of how she really felt.

Nikki felt the charge between them as their lips met, briefly, tantalisingly. Then Georgie almost withdrew and Nikki's arms pulled her shaking body close. Nikki bent her head and their lips were almost, but not quite, touching as they just looked at each other.

'I've wanted you for so long,' Georgie murmured. Nikki could feel her breath against her lips as she spoke. 'Seeing you with someone else was driving me mad. I knew she wasn't right for you, knew she would treat you badly. I wanted it to be me that you were talking about. I couldn't stand it.

'That night I gave you a massage I was going crazy. Every time we've danced together I've wanted to take you to bed. I've watched you sleep. I've been in your office wanting to throw you on your desk and take you there and then. When I came in and knew you were wearing stockings I thought I'd die on the spot. Holding you, thinking that you didn't want me tore me apart every time. Every day I couldn't see you, couldn't speak to you, was torture for me. Those three weeks in the Caribbean, it was like a lifetime. I thought I could get over you. I never want to get over you. I want to be with you. I need to be with you. You're my life; why I'm here; why I breathe; why I exist. Until now, right now, I've been drifting: something has always been missing. You came into my life and bowled me over, knocked me sideways. I'd never wanted anyone so badly, never dreamt about anyone every night like this. I want to give you everything, all I have, all I am now, all I ever want to be.'

Nikki was almost speechless. She couldn't tear her face away from Georgie's. Their eyes were locked; she was mesmerised by Georgie's look of love, her voice, the outpouring of emotion. She had never felt so needed and wanted. It seemed her whole past had been rewritten and Georgie had always been there in the way she was now, in her arms, looking up at her with open trust. Why had she never seen it before? Why had it taken Georgie's drastic step of running away to make her finally realise what had been there all along, right in front of her? All that wasted time, those false starts, desperately trying to find her ideal woman, ignoring all the signals that Georgie was sending her.

The sudden rush of deep, heart-stopping emotion for the girl in her arms took her by surprise. She needed to hold her even tighter, not let her go. Not now, not now they had finally found each other.

'Kiss me again,' she whispered into Georgie's ear. 'I want you to take me, make love to me, teach me, show me how much you've wanted me.'

Georgie's kisses were gentle, soft, tentative, light butterfly wings against her lips, her lashes, her cheeks, her ears, while Georgie held her face in her hands. And then they came together, the months of desire unleashing and exploding in the first deep, probing, powerful kiss, mouths opening to exploring tongues. Both of them moaned, the need, the yearning, taking them over at the same time. Nikki leant back as Georgie came forward. She was now underneath her, hips already moving, as Georgie's hands began to stroke and caress. She began to suck on Georgie's tongue deep inside her mouth. Nikki could imagine that tongue some-where else, as Georgie lightly flicked her top lip, ran her tongue along her bottom lip, lapped at the corners of her mouth, then kissed her deeply, her caresses more insistent and urgent. The passion was driving them both. Nikki was running her hands up and down Georgie's back, scraping her T-shirt with her nails. She slid her hand inside Georgie's waistband. Georgie was squeezing her breasts, still thrusting with her tongue. Nikki needed that tongue inside her, tasting her juices.

Georgie started to pull away; Nikki went with her.

'Come with me,' Georgie whispered into her mouth, taking her hand, pulling her up, towards the bedroom.

Nikki was suddenly, irrationally, shy and nervous. 'I don't want to let you down,' she said quietly.

Georgie stood in silence, holding her hand, and immediately understood. It would have to be slow – gentle, gentle, gentle. She would have to give Nikki the time to gain her confidence. For Nikki she would wait for ever. She would fight for her, die for her, do whatever Nikki wanted her to do. Georgie was suddenly in awe of this woman standing before her, exposed and vulnerable and in the palm of her hand.

'Why don't you go and get ready for me. I'll sort the flat out,' she whispered to Nikki.

Nikki nodded, and Georgie smiled as Nikki closed the bed-room door behind her. She went into the bathroom and stripped, wrapped a bath sheet round herself, wandered around the lounge slowly, turning the lights out, turning the fire off, resisting the temptation for a cigarette, giving Nikki plenty of time. Her heart was in her mouth. She was just as nervous as Nikki, just as afraid of letting the other woman down. Her ultimate fantasy was behind that door, naked, open, wet and waiting. Georgie's hands were shaking; the anticipation was overwhelming. She took a deep breath, and opened the door.

Nikki was on top of the quilt, naked, propped up on one elbow, one leg bent at the knee, as Georgie walked in. She took one look, hungry eyes raking Nikki's body from head to toe and back again: those long, long slim thighs; full rounded breasts with erect nipples; soft, downy, damp, blonde hair between her legs; the hairs on Nikki's thighs backlit by the table lamp. Silently, fighting to control her hammering heart, she let her towel drop to her feet, standing proud as she heard Nikki's gasp of pleasure and saw her drink in every inch with equally avid eyes.

Nikki had never seen Georgie naked, not even half-clothed. She fought the urge to leap off the bed with voracious hands. Georgie had always dressed in jeans or combats with loose shirts: Nikki had never had an inkling of the actual delights awaiting underneath. Georgie had bigger breasts than she had ever realised; her body was slimmer than Nikki expected; her legs and arms were firm and well defined; her skin was flawless and smoothly tanned apart from the bikini outlines.

Now they were both smiling, savouring the thought of what was to come.

Georgie's first touch on Nikki's bare skin was electric, a languorous stroke up her side, a lazy circling of her breast, a feather-light touch of her nipple. Nikki shivered; every nerve ending seemed to be screaming inside of her. Then Georgie's tongue took over as Nikki reclined on the pillows.

Time stopped for Nikki; nothing else in the world mattered but Georgie's tongue on her skin – it was just touching the surface, very slowly, running up her side, her arm, the outside of her breast, up to her neck, as Georgie straddled her and again bent to her task. Georgie's tongue softly lapped back down again, the other side of Nikki's neck, across her shoulder, up her arm to the inside of her elbow, down her other side to her hip, a slight flick across a nipple, down between her breasts, and moving – maddeningly slow – in circles on her taut, flat stomach. Georgie's hands began to stroke as she licked, almost hovering over Nikki's breasts; then each hand was moving further down Nikki's body. Her tongue softly slid up and down one thigh as Nikki parted her legs wider.

Georgie could smell Nikki's perfume mingled with the musk of her arousal; she could see juices glistening on Nikki; she could hear Nikki moaning her name; she could taste the salt on Nikki's skin.

Every sense was at its peak; Georgie could smell, hear, feel, taste and see Nikki's desire. Her head was full of Nikki; her hands were full of Nikki; she wanted to fill her mouth with Nikki. But not yet.

Small, light kisses on the insides of her thighs, moving from one to the other, and a gentle flick of Nikki's clit in between, until Nikki started to lift her hips each time, desperately but silently willing Georgie to sink into her with lips and tongue. Still Georgie fought the urge to do what she had wanted to do for months; she could feel her own juices beginning to gush as Nikki groaned, squirmed. Nikki's hand was on her head, pushing and insistent.

Georgie lifted her head; Nikki was looking down at her, eyes half-closed, an arm flung back on the pillow. Nikki smiled and said one word.

'Please.'

Georgie lowered her head and delved, finally, with relief and longing, into her.

Nikki couldn't stop the sharp intake of breath as Georgie took all of her sex in her mouth, held it, released it, then began to lap hungrily. Nikki's senses began to swim as Georgie's experienced tongue circled her clitoris, slid the length of her and probed inside her, increasing the pressure as she licked upward, flicking the clit with the tip of the tongue, side to side then up and down. Georgie moved her hand, pulling the hood back and sucking hard, almost nipping it with her teeth, then rolling her tongue round and round.

Nikki could hear Georgie, could feel her clit throbbing, her cunt tightening. Her eyes were closed as she let the noises and the sensation fill her mind. Georgie's other hand was now pushing her thigh further back against the bed and Nikki felt she couldn't open herself any wider. She wanted to give all of herself to Georgie; this wasn't enough. She was pushing upward against Georgie's wonderful, beautiful, face and mouth; it was almost as if she wanted all of Georgie inside of herself; and to stay there.

As Nikki ground against her, fingers tightening in her hair, Georgie felt that she wanted to be like this for ever, giving pleasure, hearing her own name moaned; she needed to be inside Nikki, feeling Nikki tightening round her fingers. Instead she carried on lapping, slowly running the flat of her tongue up and down, quickly darting inside as she heard Nikki whispering, murmuring.

'Fill me up, baby, fill me up. I need you inside me. Make me come. I need to come. Jesus Christ this is heaven, this is so much pleasure.'

Georgie raised her head only slightly and Nikki could feel her hair against her thighs at the slight shake of her head.

'There's so much more to come yet,' Georgie murmured. The pleasure was just as intense for her as she moaned with desire against Nikki's sex.

Georgie could taste each flood of new juice on the end of her tongue as Nikki began to climb. Her face was beginning to slip in the wetness; she had to grip the inside of Nikki's thighs to clamp her to her mouth, tongue probing deeper, increasing the pressure on Nikki's clit with each upward stroke. Then she struck, knowing Nikki was not far away from it, sucking hard on the engorged clit, tongue flicking from side to side.

Nikki had been ready to peak for some time – the sudden intense darts of pleasure, when she thought she could not experience anything more sensuous, exciting, unreal seemed to go to the core of her soul. In her wildest dreams and fantasies she had never imagined such intensity of sexual sensation, powered by such intense emotion; had never imagined that someone would so willingly want to give her so much bliss, for so long and so unselfishly. Every single fibre of her being was focused on that one solitary part of her body. Part of her was trying to squirm up the bed away from it; the other part was pushing her towards it.

'Jesus Christ, what are you doing to me!'

On the very edge, right on the edge, just there, she was only vaguely aware of crying out Georgie's name when suddenly Georgie pulled back, slowed down, just the very tip of her tongue flitting across her clit.

Nikki let out a huge sigh of disappointment and longing.

'Baby, we have all night,' Georgie purred against her throbbing clit.

Nikki could barely conceive of the idea of this delight lasting for yet more hours to come.

Georgie was still stroking Nikki's thighs, just lightly raking her nails against the skin. She raised herself, still stroking, and moved up Nikki's body with delicate kisses. She kissed Nikki's mouth gently, then deeply, and at the first taste of her own juices on Georgie's lips – no one had ever done that to her before – Nikki went wild, responding fervently, grabbing Georgie tightly, scraping her back with her nails, Georgie squeezing her breast as they moved frantically against each other.

Georgie traced her hand down Nikki's breasts, her stomach, and found her sex, as Nikki again raised her hips to meet those insistent, practised fingers.

Georgie slid inside easily, moving with a tenderness Nikki found exquisite and divine, now slowing down the rhythm, still kissing her deeply, then sliding out again to brush Nikki's swollen clit with her thumb. Georgie pulled away from the kiss and Nikki opened her eyes.

Georgie's fingers against her lips, soaked in her wetness, took her aback, then Nikki started to lick, tentatively then feverishly as she relished the sweet, musky creaminess of herself, knowing that she was tasting what Georgie had just been tasting.

The feel of Nikki's tongue around her wet fingers, sucking and lapping, was almost too much for Georgie. She bent to kiss and lick those same fingers, their tongues touching and sliding. When Nikki couldn't taste her own come any more, she slowed, still gazing into Georgie's eyes with open trust.

'Turn over,' Georgie whispered.

Nikki turned over, intrigued.

Georgie knelt between her legs and began to kiss the back of her neck, her ears. Nikki could feel Georgie's breasts brushing her shoulderblades. Georgie's hands were caressing her back, the outside of her breasts, as she started to move down again with those feather kisses. Nikki began to dreamily move her body against Georgie's lips, fingers, body, fully relaxed now and trusting the experienced, eager, touch of the woman hovering over her.

Nikki was where she belonged, where she was destined to be. The speed at which they had fitted together had taken her breath away. It seemed bottomless, the depth of feeling she had unleashed for Georgie in such a short space of time. It had always been there. Without Georgie she had not been complete; with her, she felt that all the emptiness, hurt and damage of all those years had been undone at a stroke, that she could go forward and take on the world. Her only regret was that they had not declared their feelings before, that there had been so many missed opportunities.

And as for what Georgie was doing to her now, delving and probing deep with her tongue, unashamed . . .

Georgie had wanted this first time to be so special for both of them. Her heart had stopped when Nikki first kissed her. At that second her fantasy had come true. Now she wanted to kiss and savour every inch of Nikki – in case the dream shattered in the morning, the memories would always be there. Even her most fevered fantasy late at night, on her own in the dark, paled into insignificance against the reality of this fabulous creature lying beneath her.

And so she ran her tongue along the insides of Nikki's thighs, as Nikki spread her legs wider. She lapped Nikki's cunt and, with infinite slowness, began to move upward, cautiously waiting for Nikki's reaction as the tip of her tongue brushed what could be a forbidden place. She felt Nikki tense, then relax, a silent granting of permission.

As she now licked and probed gently, Nikki beginning to moan, Georgie slipped an arm under Nikki's hips, raising her from the bed until Nikki was on her knees.

Then Georgie was behind and covering Nikki, fingers inside her cunt, kissing her neck hard, almost biting, moving in a rapidly increasing tempo as Nikki began to push harder and faster against those insistent, persuasive, deep, fingers. They were riding it together. Georgie could feel Nikki's spasms, could hear Nikki's gasps matching her own. She could also feel her own stomach knotting, ready for its release, as she bent her head to Nikki's.

Nikki twisted, her lips on Georgie's, their moans vibrating in each other's mouth. Then Georgie pulled away again, one hand squeezing and pulling on Nikki's breast, still fucking her hard as Nikki started to let go, started to let the orgasm take over every part of her body, starting in her stomach and washing outward. Georgie could feel Nikki's come spurt into her hand as Nikki let out the final shout – a long, drawn-out 'Georgie'.

Nikki slumped and Georgie enfolded her, held her tight, while she almost sobbed into Nikki's neck and they were both murmuring 'I love you' over and over and trying to catch their breath and control trembling and shivering limbs. Georgie slowly withdrew her fingers, and gently raised them to Nikki's lips: she kissed them.

'Is it always going to be like this?' Nikki mumbled, as her thighs went into spasm.

'We've only just started, baby,' said Georgie, nuzzling Nikki's neck. 'Are you ready for the second round yet?'

Nikki began to giggle. 'Babe, I'm still up there on the ceiling,' she said.

Georgie looked at her wickedly. 'I've got strawberries and champagne in the fridge,' she said. 'I was going to have them for breakfast because I was feeling decadent from my holiday. Now I just feel horny and hungry. How about you?'

Nikki weakly raised an arm to wave her away. 'Whatever,' she said.

She was still in the same position when Georgie returned. With a sinking heart, Georgie thought Nikki had fallen asleep. But, at the pop of the cork, Nikki came back to life, raising herself so that she sat cross-legged. Georgie could hardly tear her eyes away from the view.

'Have I ever told you how horny I get on champagne?' said Nikki, smiling as Georgie's hands shook with the effort of pouring the champagne without spilling it.

Nikki took the glass with equally shaking hands; they clinked glasses and both drank greedily.

'What you need to do is put a strawberry in the champagne, and then you can eat it afterwards,' said Georgie.

'I'd rather put one somewhere else and eat it.' The devilment was plain in Nikki's voice.

The strawberry that Georgie was about to put in her mouth hovered in midair. Nikki took it from her, as their eyes locked, and leant forward to run the fruit up and down Georgie's dripping cunt. Still with their eyes locked, Nikki ran her tongue around the outside of the strawberry then took a bite. Georgie dropped her gaze to Nikki's mouth.

'Mmm, lush,' said Nikki, taking Georgie's glass. 'My turn now, I think.'

The confidence in her voice belied the tremors in her heart. The way Ann had made love to her and the mind-blowing orgasm Georgie has just given her had built her into a frenzy of apprehension. Nikki suspected she just wouldn't be good enough for this experienced lesbian lying back on the pillows, waiting patiently, it seemed, for her first move. She wanted to give so much pleasure back to Georgie, wanted to send Georgie to the peak of madness she had just climbed herself. All those couplings before Ann had been purely amateur on her behalf, just experimental. She had tasted a woman, she had finger-fucked a woman, but she had always baulked at the suggestion of toys. She knew she had never managed to make a woman come the way Ann and Georgie had done with her. Particularly Georgie, who had just taken her on a rollercoaster ride to ecstasy. She could almost still feel Georgie's tongue down there, Georgie's fingers deep inside her.

God, I'm going to be the worst shag of her life, she thought dismally.

This thought was betrayed on her face. Georgie took her hand

and squeezed it, leant forward and softly kissed her lips, the tops of her trembling shoulders.

'We have all the time in the world,' Georgie breathed into her ear with gentle encouragement, turning her head so that Nikki could kiss her.

As Georgie reclined again, taking her down with her, Nikki returned the kiss, her mounting passion beginning to rule her mind. Her hands strayed to Georgie's firm breasts, tickling and teasing the nipples until they stood proud. Her lips fell to lick them, tug at them, suck them, gently nip at them with her teeth until Georgie moaned with a mixture of pleasure and pain. Georgie's fingers were running through her hair, and Nikki realised that her head was being very gently but firmly pushed downward.

She took a deep breath to mask her anxiety, fighting to remember what Georgie, Ann, some of the other girls, had ever done to her down there. She desperately wanted to be the best for Georgie but was realistic enough to know she couldn't possibly be. Not tonight.

Georgie had bent one knee. Nikki ran her tongue along the underside of Georgie's thigh and back again, stroking with her hand, kneading the muscular flesh. The lure of Georgie's musk filled her senses and she couldn't wait any longer to taste her, drink her, gulp and swallow those glistening tendrils of come that she could now see as she bent her head and began to lap, to lick, to suck.

The moment that Nikki's tongue made contact, Georgie almost came.

The involuntary jerk of Georgie's hips made Nikki look up in surprise – Georgie was looking down at her, eyes half-closed with desire, and Nikki thought then that she had never seen anything so beautiful, so arousing.

Georgie was fighting hard to regain control of her body. Every night she had dreamt of this, that gorgeous, powerful, exciting woman between her legs, face buried in her; those long, sensitive fingers stroking her. Her mouth was dry; she licked her lips and again tasted Nikki upon them. The reality was almost too much to bear. Whatever Nikki did to her was likely to make her explode. Georgie thrilled to Nikki's touch – just being here naked with her would have been enough.

But now Nikki was getting into her stride, confidence increasing by the second as Georgie writhed against her mouth; natural ability taking over as she experimented with her tongue, listening to the sound of Georgie's breathing, what she was saying, how she moved her hips to try to increase the pressure of the tongue against her sex.

Gushing, dripping, sweet and thick as honey against her mouth, swollen under her tongue, Georgie's cunt made Nikki's senses begin to reel. Georgie slid her hand down to pull back the hood of her clit; Nikki sank further on to it and began to suck, then ran her tongue up and down Georgie's fingers either side of it.

'For fuck's sake,' breathed Georgie, 'go inside me.'

Nikki held on with her mouth, sucking hard on the clit, and pressed two then three fingers inside Georgie's cunt. Georgie gasped at the first feeling of Nikki going inside of her.

'This is sending me crazy, go for it, baby, go for it.' The command was unmistakeable.

Georgie could almost feel Nikki's smile against her as Nikki shook her head. Nikki wanted to stay down there, wanted to play, to tease, to learn. She had all of Georgie in her mouth, was gently tugging on the lips, her fingers just teasing the outside of Georgie's cunt, then her tongue was darting in above them, slippery and soaked.

Without warning she plunged deep inside Georgie, so deep and filling that Georgie arched her back. Nikki was sucking hard as she fucked her, the pace exactly matching Georgie's rolling hips. Nikki's arm was stretched upward and she was kneading a breast, pulling on a nipple, and all Georgie could do was start to cry out as the orgasm began to build and grow. Now Nikki had found her G-spot and, with each deep, fast thrust, Georgie was climbing further, almost arching off the bed, part of her desperate to come, the other part wanting this never to end.

She couldn't stop it; she couldn't control her body; all the fantasies, the yearning, the hurt, the disappointment and the fierce love and passion for Nikki flooded into her mind at the final gut-wrenching, heart-stopping spasm of her orgasm. It was so vehement, so intense, she could feel herself gush into Nikki's mouth, could hear and feel Nikki's reaction to it. Her cry as she erupted became a sob and she could not help the tears that welled behind her closed lids.

Nikki quickly moved as Georgie went to turn away from her, racking sobs shaking her shoulders. She was alongside her, holding her, turning Georgie towards her, arms tight round her as she wept. She felt the tears on her breasts.

'That was incredible,' Georgie finally whispered as the sobs subsided. Her thighs slowed their trembling; her hands stopped shaking. 'Nobody's ever made me cry before,' she added.

'Nobody's ever loved you like this before,' said Nikki quietly.

Georgie looked up, tears still shining in her eyes. Nikki bent and gently brushed her lips with her own.

'I'm here for you now, heart, mind, body and soul,' Nikki whispered.

They were still entwined when Nikki awoke. She glanced at the clock: it was very early. She felt the warm, luscious body against her, Georgie's leg draped over her, her head on Nikki's shoulder. Nikki could feel the girl's breath as she quietly slept.

In the dark, the two of them together, nothing else mattered: the world was locked safely outside. Nikki wanted to always be here, snug, secure and content. In her sleep Georgie moved her arm and found Nikki's hand, their fingers interlocked. Nikki smiled to herself, kissed the top of Georgie's head. Georgie moved again, snuggling deeper into her, and Nikki feel asleep again, still smiling.

When she awoke again, Georgie was kissing her breasts very softly, stroking her stomach, almost imperceptibly moving against her. Sleepily, Nikki began to respond, moving her own hips in reply. Georgie raised herself, fingers lightly teasing, and looked down at Nikki.

'I can't believe you're here,' she said softly.

'I love you,' said Nikki, pulling her head down, starting to kiss her, a kiss that seemed never ending. Neither wanted to pull away. Hands were stroking, exploring; bodies were slippery with sweat, their flattened breasts sliding against each other. Georgie pushed Nikki on to her back, and pulled her legs apart with her own leg. She pinned her down and then she was inside, deep inside, as Nikki gasped into her mouth. Georgie moved her other leg, her thigh sliding underneath Nikki as the other woman arched her back and pushed upward against the fingers.

The feeling started to rise again, quickly – Nikki couldn't comprehend how quickly – as Georgie plunged her tongue inside her mouth, to the same frenzied rhythm as her fingers. As Nikki began to tighten down there, Georgie broke the kiss, and so Nikki could shout out to her God, to Jesus, long drawn-out, throaty shouts, as Nikki peaked and rode it out, hips frantically jerking, but still Georgie wanted to give her more.

Still inside her, Georgie moved between her legs, nuzzling with whisper-soft licks of her tongue on Nikki's still throbbing clit. Nikki started to climb again, the delicate touch almost unbearable. She was still in the last throes of her first orgasm when she felt the second one building, a tidal wave taking over her whole body, the intensity washing through her. She was still shouting with disbelief as Georgie rubbed the flat of her tongue on her clit then darted inside of her, above the probing, urgent fingers.

Georgie was fighting hard to hold on to her: Nikki was moving urgently and frenetically against Georgie's mouth and fingers, desperate to unleash that final flood of feeling. Georgie was surrounded, absorbed, engrossed, by the taste, the feel, the smell.

She was moaning herself at the mixed sensations of her face slipping and sliding in Nikki's juices, the sound of Nikki's voice, that glorious tightening round her fingers, Nikki's legs now on her shoulders, pressing her in even deeper, thighs beginning to close, to clamp, as Nikki let it go, let it engulf her.

As she did, a last warm gush of come filled Georgie's mouth, the extra sensation tipping her over the edge. She couldn't hold back the mounting tide of her own orgasm as she drove into Nikki with tongue and fingers.

They both lay in silence, Georgie's head on Nikki's stomach, their breathing beginning to slow.

'I love you too,' Georgie finally said.

And Nikki was at home.

SIXTEEN

The weeks, the months, became a blur for Nikki Jones. Her whole focus was Georgie, their life, their future together.

Steve Jones hardly saw his wife. The nights she spent at home became fewer and fewer as she apparently busied herself on conferences, seminars, new-business appointments further and further away. Each night she spent at home was a physical wrench away from Georgie. She knew now what it would be like to lose Georgie, to not be able to hold her, feel her, taste her. Like a schoolgirl she looked forward to their lunches together, their evenings and nights, the phone calls. She wanted to spend every hour of every day for the rest of her life with Georgie. The sight of the two of them together in the gay bars and clubs was a natural aphrodisiac to every lesbian in the building. They were attached at the hip, never stopped touching, never danced with anyone else. A hypnotically attractive couple, they had eyes and smiles only for each other as they performed their regular floor show – many thought they would have to be surgically separated.

And the nights. The nights were something else. Their love was so real, so physical. Nikki had never been so aroused instantly just by someone looking at her with a leisurely, wicked grin; by the knowing promise in their eyes. Georgie had brought her into a whole new dimension of delight, indulgence and wonderment at the depth of response her body could offer. Nikki revelled, excelled, flourished, in the blissful contentment of loving and being loved.

Her plans for the business were falling into place. She had had a valuation for an outright cash purchase on her beloved Saab, for emergency purposes only; she and Gillian had agreed a contract for furnished office premises; she was sneaking stationery out of the company on a daily basis. Georgie had access to independent designers who had finalised the artwork on launch advertising. Nikki's logo and letterheads were ready for the green light for printing. Nikki had a number of existing clients chafing at the bit ready for the launch of Millennium. Her cash-flow and profit-and-loss projections showed a tight first few months but she knew it would work. She knew she could actually walk away from her agency, her marriage even, and succeed overnight. Georgie's love, support, faith and trust in her were total. Georgie understood Nikki's dream and implicitly believed in her. Georgie's own fantasy had come true: she now had Nikki. With Georgie's unswerving devotion and commitment, Nikki Jones was prepared to take on the world and achieve that dream.

She was speeding to Georgie now, on a long weekend away booked from the company, ostensibly undertaking a fact-finding tour in Paris for a client conference as far as Steve was concerned. Four days together, four nights – the longest time they had ever enjoyed together.

The late-spring evening was mild as Nikki unloaded her car.

Georgie leapt down the stairs to the car park, taking a bag off her, noting that Nikki was still in work clothes. The kiss of welcome was quick and surreptitious, just two friends greeting each other.

Inside the flat she didn't even give Nikki any time. They embraced tightly, kissing feverishly until both dropped what they were holding – bags, keys – at their feet and sank into each other. Nikki had heels on: she towered above Georgie so that Georgie had to almost stretch into the lingering kiss.

'Tell me you're wearing stockings,' Georgie whispered.

Nikki just smiled down at her. Georgie's heart jumped. Nikki had always been in casual clothes during their evenings and nights, but in the office when they met Georgie had been constantly tormented by visions of Nikki in sheer, shiny, stockings underneath those short, tight skirts she wore. Once, after lunch, in the car, she had run her hand underneath Nikki's skirt and had felt the bare flesh above the lacy top, but time had been short and she had had to leave Nikki in a sexual frenzy, disappointed when Nikki arrived that night dressed in jeans. No one had ever excited Georgie like this, creating a relentless succession of stirring thrills each time she saw her, or spoke to her and Nikki dropped her voice on the phone to that throaty purr. It was the knowledge that she was taking Nikki home, to bed, from the clubs; that they would be naked and into each other within moments of reaching Georgie's flat; that Nikki had eyes for no one else; that she was all that Nikki needed, wanted. To see that desire returned, in deep blue eyes smoky with lust; in a lazy, careless lop-sided smile she had never seen before on Nikki – a smile just for her.

Georgie had always thought her own body a seething mass of erogenous zones, but Nikki could touch her absolutely anywhere, with a casual, electric shock, a brush of fingers together, a light stroke across the nape of her neck. Georgie had even let Nikki massage her feet and lick her ears, which she had never allowed anyone to do before. Every millimetre of her skin had been stroked, licked, caressed as Nikki relished her role of pupil to learn more about Georgie's body every time they made love.

She had explored every facet of Nikki's body with her own tongue and fingers. Whenever Nikki was away from her, Georgie could picture her with startling clarity: the mole on the side of her left breast, the small freckles on her arms, the faint scars on her knees from childhood accidents, the vaccination mark on her arm, the blemish on her face from a bout of chickenpox when she was six. When Nikki was on the phone to her, Georgie could envisage her tucked into it, holding the receiver closely against her lips as if to make herself closer. Georgie knew this woman inside out, how she felt, why she felt, her moods, her triumphs, her memories, her despairs and fears from years gone by.

As they held each other, Georgie murmured in her ear, 'I want you now, so badly. I've wanted you all day. I've been wishing the hours away. We aren't just a couple, we just simply are. Don't you feel it?'

Nikki wordlessly led her into the bedroom. 'Baby,' she said slowly, 'I think I'm ready now.'

Georgie knew instinctively what she meant. They had talked about it, at first jokingly and then more seriously, but Georgie had not pushed it, had not wanted to rush it. They had both satisfied, satiated each other with mouths and hands, but there was still so much more to come – but only when and if Nikki wanted to, when she felt able to push the boundaries back to the ultimate. Until that time Georgie would wait patiently. She was crucially aware that the moment might not ever come when Nikki's final barrier crashed, crumbled, fell away.

The moment was now – it was here – and now it was Georgie who was nervous, shy. She sent Nikki into the bathroom, under instructions not to come out until told. Her hands were shaking. The harness seemed to be at its most recalcitrant, slipping in the sweat from her fingers as she tried to tighten the straps. Finally it was in place, snug against her, an extension of her, beckoning proudly, gleaming and slick with the baby oil she was unhurriedly, almost lovingly, applying. She was so intent on the task that she was unaware that Nikki had silently opened the door to the en-suite bathroom and was standing, watching, breath held at the back of her throat at the sight of Georgie.

Steve, fully erect, well endowed and ready, even in his trim youth, in those first early months of lust and passion, had never struck her as powerfully and erotically as this vision of Georgie, one hand at the bottom of the dildo, holding it straight and steady while her other hand stroked and rubbed – she was almost masturbating it, fingers lightly teasing the already glistening shaft, a lazy, tender thumb circling the oil into the tip.

Nikki still had not breathed. When Georgie had first suggested the toy Nikki had refused – the whole thing had seemed too close to heterosexual sex, a parody of substitution. She had thought it would look ridiculous, completely out of place, that she would break out in giggles and ruin the moment.

Now, as she hungrily watched Georgie's hands massaging the oil into the strap-on, it seemed the most natural, perfect next step. It seemed to be part of Georgie. She wanted Georgie thrusting inside her; Georgie above her, behind her, mounting her and taking her, plunging so much more deeply and completely – the most absolute consummation of their love.

When Nikki finally exhaled, Georgie looked up with a start, her concentration on her task interrupted. It was Georgie's turn to hold her breath.

Nikki was silhouetted in the doorway, the light from the fading early-evening sun just enough to allow Georgie to see the heels, stockings, suspenders, the high-cut lacy thong with Nikki's fine blonde hairs just escaping at the edges, and the full, heaving breasts almost spilling out of the straining half-cup bra. The reality of the black underwear against Nikki's smooth beige skin was more intensely and instantly sexual than any vision Georgie had conjured up in her mind.

Nikki meandered to the bed and with infinite slowness straddled Georgie, her lace-covered mound pushing against the base of the shaft as she bent to kiss her. She began to move against the dildo, controlling the rhythm to a languorous up and down stroke. At each down stroke Georgie could feel Nikki's wetness against her hand. Then Nikki reached down and pulled the thong to one side.

'Take me now, right away. I want you inside me. I want you to fuck me,' she breathed against Georgie's lips, her own hand beginning to guide the strap-on, her hips rising so that she could feel the tip of the shaft nudging at her sex. Now she held it herself, rubbing her cunt against the tip and allowing only the very slightest penetration. Georgie thrust her hips upward for that first initial dive, but Nikki moved away from her, provocatively letting the shaft circle the outside of her lips.

Georgie glanced down: the view was breathtaking as the oil, mingled with Nikki's come, glinted in the soft light of the table lamp. Nikki lowered herself on to the very end of the shaft, her breasts pushing against the lace just inches from Georgie's face.

Georgie had used the toy only on a handful of occasions. Each

210

time, she had worn it but never taken it. It had been a brief and frenetic pounding away to climax. She was now conscious that Nikki was used to penetration, would have a technique, would know what she wanted. Georgie had a stabbing pang of jealousy for Steve Jones: what a lucky, lucky bastard he had been all these years with this magnificent, horny, creature riding his prick. He probably came straight away. It's sending me crazy. I just wish I could feel exactly what he felt.

Then Nikki dropped with a groan, taking the whole length of the shaft, grinding her arse against Georgie's thighs, hips bucking, and then Georgie began to push upward at each of Nikki's thrusts, the dildo going in even further, almost to the root, filling Nikki. Nikki was squeezing Georgie's breasts hard as she rode it, increasing the speed, Georgie matching her every stroke, and raising her thighs. Nikki's breasts were now full in her face to suckle as she fucked her deeply.

We really are as one now, Georgie thought, her hands gripping Nikki's hips. Nikki's breath came in hot, gasping pants in her ear; Nikki's sweat began to drip on to her face as she writhed and gyrated above her and against her.

God, it never felt like this with Steve, Nikki thought to herself: there was never the gentleness, the care, the intensity of emotion, the softness of the skin underneath me. She's letting me take the control; she's going with me.

Then Nikki was off her, breathlessly demanding to be taken from behind, on hands and knees, suppliant and eager as Georgie scrambled into position. Jesus Christ, I've unleashed a beast, thought Georgie as she savoured the sight before her. Standing at the end of the bed, she leant forward and unclasped Nikki's bra, letting Nikki's impressively heavy breasts swing free. She hooked her thumbs into Nikki's thong and pulled it down to her knees. Georgie guided the shaft cautiously, her thumb against the tip of it, feeling her way in. She held back with an effort, then made short, sharp jabs as Nikki pushed backward, greedily wanting more, the whole length of it all the way up her.

The view was magnificent: Georgie looked down to watch the shaft sliding in and out between Nikki's firm buttocks, which were pushing hard against her. She could feel Nikki's taut thighs against her own, could see the sweat, the oil, the come from both of them soaking on Nikki's pubic hair, as she finally gave way and immersed herself up to the hilt – she truly felt it was a part of her that was now far inside Nikki giving pleasure. One hand was holding Nikki's hip tightly; with the other she bent and gathered a mixture of their juices, rubbed Nikki's arsehole and gently began to move her thumb inside.

Nikki felt the additional sensation, at first with a slight twinge of discomfort, and then, as thumb and shaft moved in unison – feeling Georgie's strong thighs against the back of her own, the barest tickle of Georgie's nipples against her back, Georgie's other hand now rubbing on her clit – Nikki became engulfed by the feeling of being totally filled, by the combination of tingles and thrills all centred on her cunt, her arse.

Her thighs and locked arms began to shake and tremble. Nikki and Georgie were grinding together, quicker, harder, the harness rubbing Georgie's clit to the same fever pitch that Nikki was now beginning to rise to. And still Georgie was pounding, hammering away at her; Nikki was beating back against her, taking it deeper, gripping it tight inside on every thrust.

Georgie was trying to hold on to her orgasm, save that final release until Nikki exploded so that they could yell and shout at the very same moment. Their breathing was identical; they were joined as one; they were one, going for it as one, climbing to even higher pinnacles as one, jumping off as one; Georgie was so caught up with it she almost felt that she was coming inside Nikki, emptying herself deep within her.

As the orgasms started to subside for both of them, Nikki collapsed, with Georgie on top of her. Nikki's thighs were saturated with their mingled come and she could feel it streaming down on to the bed.

Still inside her, Georgie was holding her tightly, sucking on her neck, her shoulders. Nikki was still wrapped up in her orgasm, in the aftershock, her whole body quivering, every sense still reeling from the intensity of the sensations, the feel and touch of Georgie against her, their sweat fusing between them, cooling them both.

'Be with me always,' Georgie mumbled against her hair, 'never let me go. I can't bear being without you, even for a moment. Come to me, live with me, wake up with me every morning, go to sleep with me, be mine.'

Nikki at that point in time would have thrown away everything, every single last plan she had ever thought of, worked towards – common sense was going out of the door – all she could focus on was the woman holding her. This felt so right: she had never been so sure of anything in her life. Thinking about Georgie never failed to amaze her – it always caught her unawares just how quickly and deeply she had fallen.

Georgie had given herself with no complications, just a complete commitment, a stability and warmth she had never felt before. Georgie could calm her, soothe her, excite and arouse her. She listened without judgement. It seemed every day she fell even further. Georgie asked nothing of her but to love her in return. Georgie cherished Nikki's love, valued it, gave it back with interest; loved her unconditionally for who she really was, not who she pretended to be, the image she had fostered and nurtured for the outside world.

She was sure that Georgie would stay beside her, believing in her with an almost childlike faith, even if Nikki was jobless, carless, bankrupt and living in a tent.

From that moment when Georgie had searched her eyes before the first kiss, Nikki had been lost within her, within a maelstrom of turbulent but positive emotions. Georgie and her simple trust had taken her over, directed her, driven her, supported her, kept her secure on those long, lonely nights without her. She would never be without her again; they would never be apart. They were soulmates, lovers, friends.

'We simply are,' Nikki remembered with a grin.

That whole weekend clarified her thoughts even further. Wherever she was, there was Georgie. They shopped for food, Georgie's fingers touching hers on the handle of the trolley, Georgie standing in front of her as they searched the alcohol section for special offers, Georgie leaning into her while she fought the temptation to gather her in her arms and snog her senseless amidst a packed, 97.8 per cent heterosexual Sainsbury's.

They walked together across fields, holding hands, at first parting when someone appeared, then forgetting the rest of the world. They held hands in the cinema; they kissed when Nikki stopped the car at traffic lights – Nikki wanted to shout it from the rooftops, no longer caring if people stared or passed comment. She and Georgie had something between them that few people had. She was proud. She was confident and content: they had believed in something and now they were both living it. The hell with everyone else, this was where she was destined to be and she was damned if she would give it up, or put up any more facades.

Now Nikki was leaning against the kitchen counter, watching Georgie with fond amusement.

'It can't be that bastard difficult,' Georgie was muttering as she scanned, again, the instructions on the packet of rice. She had had the bright idea of preparing a Chinese meal, buying in the stir-fry sauce, throwing in some chopped chicken and vegetables, and making egg-fried rice from scratch. She had done this only once before, to impress a girl, and the meal had been so disgusting it had gone in the bin after one mouthful. It was only later, when pressed, that Georgie had retrieved the sauce jar to discover it had not been a stir-fry complete sauce but a concentrate. She had cooked microwaveable rice with that meal and they had had to have rice with ketchup instead. Now, because her microwave had died the previous week, she had to boil the rice the conventional way. She turned to Nikki in anguish.

'Know any delivery restaurants?' Nikki asked kindly.

Later, satiated with food, alcohol and sex, they lay in the darkness on their last night of that long, debauched weekend.

'Did you mean what you said on Thursday night, about me coming to live with you, or was it just the throes of passion?' Nikki mused aloud. She felt Georgie momentarily stiffen.

'Probably just the passion. I can't be held responsible for the things I come out with when I'm coming,' said Georgie carelessly, holding her breath. 'Anyway, why would you want to leave that big house and come to this little flat?'

'To be with you.'

'And what about Steve, your new business, all the other stuff?'

'I'll pull the start date forward. I can raise a substantial amount of cash with the car and the plate, and buy a cheap little runabout – that will tide me over till the fees start coming in. No doubt the legal arguments will start getting really messy with Steve but he can have the bloody lot as far as I'm concerned. All I care about is you, getting this company off the ground and helping to build us a life together. I've had all the flash stuff, the material things. All I need is my clothes. Now I have you, the company should give us a comfortable living, and we won't starve, then in a couple of years we can probably buy something together, perhaps a cottage in the country or something.'

'But what are you going to tell Steve?'

'That I need space. I'm hardly ever there anyway. I'll tell him I'm moving in with a friend until everything is sorted out. He's not asked me to drape his arm for some time now. We hardly even nod to each other in passing. I don't think he even knows when I'm not there. He's getting on with whatever he does in his own little limited world. In fact, he's doing what he's been doing for the last few years. Who I'm with is irrelevant. If I just came straight out with the fact that I've been gay all these years he'd probably ask to come and watch, or bring a camcorder. He's accepted there's nothing between us, hasn't been for a very long time. Telling him everything won't make any difference, apart from denting his male ego.'

'Does this mean that you do want to move in, then?'

Nikki's answer was a deep kiss. Their bodies came alight again in an instant, that initial flash of arousal leading to the touching, stroking, licking of each other with practised, knowing, sensual ease. They melded perfectly, losing themselves in each other in the darkness, senses heightened and fine-tuned to the other's needs.

They whispered, moaned, moved in unison, driven by their encompassing passion, their blind need for each other, their need to be against and inside each other. Their experienced lips, tongues, fingers were discovering again as if to enjoy for the first time.

They changed to favourite positions, smoothly and expertly with no awkward, clumsy, fumblings, but with an implicit, unspoken understanding.

Now Georgie hovered above Nikki's waiting lips, then slowly sank with an almost grateful sigh, anticipating what was to come, holding herself still to enhance the pleasure as Nikki received her, to hear that familiar light groan of contentment as Nikki tasted her again.

Nikki was stretching her tongue deep as Georgie fought the urge to move, letting that wonderfully sensitive mouth take over. Nikki's body was moving instead. Georgie glanced over her shoulder: Nikki's legs were wide open, her hands stimulating herself as she dipped deep into Georgie. Georgie watched, fascinated, as Nikki masturbated, the rhythm and pressure of her fingers on her cunt matching her tongue on Georgie's clit and lips. She could hear Nikki having to gulp her juices, Nikki's breath getting faster and heavier against her, matching Georgie's own. Georgie took a last, lingering look and gave in to her need to start pumping her hips to go with Nikki to the pinnacle.

Nikki came first, only a second or two ahead, having to swallow her cries as she burrowed in a frenzy with her tongue to take Georgie over the peak with her. Georgie was holding on desperately to the bedhead as she drove hard into Nikki's face, then she exploded.

But Nikki, now replete, carried on, her hands now pulling Georgie back down on to her. Georgie tried to raise herself to let the tremors and trembling subside but Nikki was stronger and insistent, holding her thighs down firmly, catching Georgie perfectly on the very edge of coming down from her climax. Georgie was climbing again, very quickly, more powerfully, her stomach tensing, gritting her teeth to ride through the first sharp jabs of Nikki's tongue against her still-pulsating, enlarged clitoris. Nikki was licking fast and furiously, in circles, up and down, side to side. Georgie's mind was reeling, her stomach somersaulting, her cunt tightening in ever increasing spasms; the moment of release was so close.

Then it came, so forceful and potent that Georgie's legs and arms gave way and she slumped. Only Nikki's hands, supporting her thighs, stopped her from complete collapse. Georgie leant her forehead on the bedhead.

'Not bad for a novice, then?' she vaguely heard Nikki tease.

Georgie could not speak. Her mouth was dry – she felt every drop of available liquid in her body had gushed out into Nikki's mouth seconds earlier. All that came out was a satisfied whimper. Nikki began to giggle as Georgie tried to move off her, reluctant, trembling limbs shaking so much that she had to stop and wait. Nikki shimmied out from underneath her and gently helped her to lie down, placing soft loving kisses on her shoulders, her neck, her throat, her parched lips, as Georgie rolled on to her back.

'I thought I'd taught you well. Turns out you have a few tricks of your own,' Georgie finally managed.

'I can't get enough of you,' said Nikki. 'I never want this to end.'

'Marry me, then,' said Georgie.

EPILOGUE

The end of the year, the start of the new century, was just twelve weeks away.

Nikki woke and leapt out of the bed as Georgie turned over in her sleep and groaned.

'Today's the day, babe!'

Georgie groaned again. All the champagne from the night before seemed to have gathered at the front of her head, pounding away with an insistent, painful hammering. Then the memories began to filter through the fog of stale alcohol.

Today, Monday, was the official first day of trading for Millennium, although Nikki had been in her new offices for nearly a month now, supposedly on three months' gardening leave from her old agency. Her directors had threatened to invoke her service contract, but she had charmed them round, knowing three major clients were about to decamp to Millennium. Her smart, if functional, premises were only a short drive in the Granada from Georgie's flat.

They had pooled all available resources from the moment four months previously when Nikki had arrived at her flat, suitcases in hand, a large cheque in her pocket from the Saab dealer, tears in her eyes from saying goodbye to her cherished vehicle. Georgie had agreed to work out of the new premises so that she and Nikki could share her vehicle as and when required. It also meant that they were together nearly 24 hours a day.

Steve had merely shrugged when Nikki had announced that she was moving out, to stay 'temporarily' with one of her friends. The legals had ground to a halt as Steve had disputed ownership of a handful of objects, and nitpicked on several financial points. Nikki had put the file to one side as she had concentrated on the business start-up, with the banking facilities sorted and in Gillian's name so that Steve couldn't touch it in the future.

Gillian had expressed surprise at the speed at which Georgie and Nikki had developed their relationship, but had taken great delight on many occasions in announcing that she had been responsible for bringing them together in the first place. An honorary member of the Pussy Posse, she had gamely ventured on a handful of nights out in the gay bars, but had resolutely refused to leave her seat for drink replenishment or bladder relief in case she was accosted by a shaven-headed, earring-bedecked lesbian. Instead, she enjoyed perusing the 'delicious' young gay males who frequented the place, and secretly harboured wicked fantasies about converting each and every one of them.

Ann had apparently zeroed in on, and latched on to, a wealthy, eccentric older woman close to her home. Tracy had since broken all contact with her in a fit of spiteful yet justified pique. The Posse had closed ranks around their own and Georgie and Nikki were now undisputed joint leaders of the crew.

Sharon had grudgingly rejoined the fold, and was now ensconced permanently in Phillipa's flat. Every time they deigned to leave their bed to join the girls, the dark circles under their eyes bore testimony to their sleepless nights of stamina competitions.

It had seemed like a good idea at the time to combine the timings for the two events – the launch of Millennium and their blessing ceremony – but, as Georgie weakly tried to raise her head from the pillow, a faint pang of regret slithered to the forefront of her mind.

The past weekend had been spent in a total flurry of alcohol-fuelled excitement, tension and nerves.

The Posse had been out in force on Saturday, as Nikki and Georgie had stood before the minister.

Gillian, overcome with emotion at the honour and intrigue of being asked to attend Nikki, had performed her duties with shaking hands.

She had fussed over writing her speech for weeks and, despite regularly having to speak in public as part of her profession, had worked herself into a frenzy of fear about having to stand up and deliver it to a roomful of lesbians. Gillian had also worried herself sick about what etiquette demanded as a suitable wedding present for two mature lesbians, and settled instead for a fine vintage champagne.

She had insisted Nikki wear a tailcoat so that she could bring her own out of mothballs. It had been originally purchased from a second-hand store as part of a Marlene Dietrich fancy-dress outfit.

The thought of the two of them standing tall, in elegant black, had prompted Georgie to race around the shops in a frenzy. Settling for a superbly tailored grey suit with frock coat, she had stood proud and confident beside her woman as the minister took them through the blessing ceremony and the vows they had devised themselves.

Nikki had wept silent tears throughout the whole proceedings. Georgie never let go of her hand until they exchanged the hand-made matching rings. Georgie had fought back her own tears, swaying slightly towards the end as the second double Jack Daniel's had worked its way into her system.

They had spent the previous night apart. Nikki had insisted on tradition, with Gillian and Tracy given the respective charges of making sure both reached the venue on time and sober.

Gillian, however, recognising Nikki's nerves, had opened champagne for Nikki to drink as she luxuriated in a bubble bath that morning. Georgie had needed no persuading from Tracy to dive downstairs to the bar when they arrived to calm her fluttering stomach.

The minister had worked closely with both of them to pull the ceremony together. It was a poignant moment as they exchanged the rings, fingers shaking and sweaty. Even Gillian felt the prick of salty tears.

The alcohol had flowed freely the rest of the afternoon, evening and night. Georgie had woken on Sunday morning to find several comatose bodies sprawled on her settees and carpet. She discovered someone called Sarah passed out in the bathroom and half carried her to a comfortable chair.

Hangover cures of croissants and black coffee were dispensed in seemingly never ending succession, and one by one the Posse had drifted away, leaving them finally alone in the early afternoon.

Georgie by now was smiling as she remembered the long, languorous session of lovemaking they had enjoyed to celebrate their union, interrupted only by constant top-ups of champagne as they luxuriated against the pillows.

Now Nikki was rushing frantically around the bedroom in her usual morning fashion. It never failed to make Georgie dizzy.

'First day of Millennium, then. What's in store?' she asked.

Nikki turned to her with a devilish grin. 'Actually, no.'

Nikki dived into her underwear drawer and reappeared brandishing the plane tickets. 'I thought we should have a honeymoon first . . .'

Georgie looked in stupefaction at the destination printed on the tickets. Hawaii. Two weeks.

'And it is gay-friendly . . .'

Georgie was still stunned into silence.

'Plane leaves tonight. Come on, girl, let's get ready!'

Nikki had been planning the surprise from the day after Georgie had asked her to marry her. Only Gillian knew and had been sworn to secrecy, even though at least three times on Saturday she had come close to letting the cat out of the bag after too much champagne.

Hawaii had seemed perfect – Georgie had always enjoyed her stories about the time Nikki and Gillian had travelled halfway around the world to the exotic island, even though Nikki had complained about the time in flight. 'Now I know why the Pope kisses the ground when he gets off the plane,' Nikki had joked at the time.

'I have one errand to do on the way to the airport –' Nikki was now ferreting in the bottom of the cupboard for her summer gear '– and tradition has it that we arrive in plenty of time, get slightly squiffy in the bar, stagger on the plane, get pissed, sober up and get pissed again. Can you manage that?'

Georgie just nodded dumbly.

Finally stricken into action, she packed in a flurry. Gillian arrived to drive them to the airport. They briefly detoured and stopped at Nikki's house while she shoved something through the letterbox, and then they were on their way.

Their plane was lifting off as Steve Jones walked through his front door, tired and hungry but looking forward to his first date with Sophie later that evening. He had finally plucked up the courage to ask her out and was surprised at her ready agreement. Steve My-Main-Man Jones still had it, he thought, smiling to himself.

The envelope, addressed in Nikki's telltale scrawl, caught his eye.

The business card fell out at his feet as he read the letter and documents, brow furrowed in confusion. Nikki had told him to complete, sign and send to Gillian's address the divorce papers enclosed. She had written that she wanted no claim on the property, any of the contents, or the money in their joint account, in return for a clean break. Steve should consent to the divorce, with no further counterclaims on Nikki in the future. She was going away on holiday that day, he read, and would be back in two weeks. Probably going with the Maneater to screw their way around some tropical sun-drenched paradise, he mused grimly.

Frantic to ensure that she held good to her promise, he immediately signed on the dotted line, making a mental note to send it first class the next morning.

He had nothing to complain about now. The deal was more than weighted in his favour and – what was more important – he was bound to be thrusting inside that young, long-legged and lithe little Sophie later, giving her the time of her life within a few short hours.

His prick stirring, he bent to retrieve the card.

A full-colour logo screamed out at him.

So did the words Millennium, Strategic Marketing Solutions, Nikki Rivers, Managing Director.

Puzzled at the name, he turned the card over and there was Nikki's scrawl again.

'Steve –' he struggled to read the sentence at first '– I've turned for the century.'

At a complete loss, he tucked the card in his breast pocket, and went through to the lounge for his first shot of whisky, in preparation for the conquest of Sophie.

PREVIOUSLY PUBLISHED

Published in May 1999

☐
BIG DEAL
Helen Sandler

Lane and Carol have a deal that lets them play around with other partners. But things get out of hand when Lane takes to cruising gay men, while her femme girlfriend has secretly become the mistress of an ongoing all-girl student orgy. The fine print in the deal they've agreed on means things can only get hotter. It's time for a different set of rules and forfeits.
£6.99   ISBN 0 352 33365 0

Published in June 1999

☐
RIKA'S JEWEL
Astrid Fox

Norway, 1066 AD. A group of female Viking warriors – Ingrid's Crew – have set sail to fight the Saxons in Britain, and Ingrid's young lover Rika is determined to follow them. But, urged on by dark-haired oarswoman Pia, Rika soon penetrates Ingrid's secret cult back home in Norway. The cult is spreading through the whole of Northern Europe and its devotees revel in performing erotic rites which re-enact the Nordic creation myth. In the midst of battles, sea-journeys, scarification, fire-dancing and tattooing, Rika must make a choice: will she overcome Ingrid's psychic hold, or will she succumb to the intoxicating rituals of the cult? Thrilling sword-and-sorcery in the style of Xena and Red Sonja!
£6.99   ISBN 0 352 33367 7

Published in July 1999

☐
MILLENNIUM FEVER
Julia Wood

The millennium is approaching and so is Nikki's fortieth birthday. Married for twenty years, she is tired of playing the trophy wife in a small town where she can't adequately pursue her lofty career ambitions. Nikki's sapphic adventures have been conducted in secret, but her attraction to other women is getting stronger by the day. Already feisty, her sexual energies are getting the better of her, and turning this efficient marketing executive into a tyrant with a taste for road rage! In contrast, young writer Georgie has always been out and proud. But there's one thing they have in common – in the midst of millennial fever, they both want action and satisfaction. When they meet, the combination is explosive.
£6.99   ISBN 0 352 33368 5

SAPPHIRE NEW BOOKS

Published in August 1999

☐
ALL THAT GLITTERS
Franca Nera

Marta Broderick: beautiful, successful art dealer, London lesbian. Marta inherits an art empire from the man who managed to spirit her out of East Berlin in the 1960s, Manny Schweitz. But Marta has many secrets – for starters, she's dating a married woman, Anne. Marta is also intent on completing Manny's unfinished business: recovering pieces of art stolen by the Nazis. Meanwhile, she's met the gorgeous but mysterious Judith Compton. And as her relationship with Anne develops and blossoms, Marta's dark sexual addiction to Judith – along with her quest to return the treasures to the rightful owners – is taking her to dangerous places.

£6.99   ISBN 0 352 33426 6

Published in September 1999

☐
SWEET VIOLET
Ruby Vise

Violet is young, butch and new in town, looking for a way to get over her childhood sweetheart Katherine. And there are plenty of distractions in 1980s London, as the rarefied big-city dyke scene is both sexually and politically charged – full of everything from cosmic mother-earth worshippers to sexy girls in leather.

£6.99   ISBN 0 352 33458 4

——————✂——————————————

Please send me the books I have ticked above.

Name   ....

Address   ....

                ....

                ....

              .... Post Code ....

Send to: **Cash Sales, Sapphire Books, Thames Wharf Studios, Rainville Road, London W6 9HT.**

US customers: for prices and details of how to order books for delivery by mail, call 1-800-805-1083.

Please enclose a cheque or postal order, made payable to **Virgin Publishing Ltd**, to the value of the books you have ordered plus postage and packing costs as follows:

UK and BFPO – £1.00 for the first book, 50p for each subsequent book.

Overseas (including Republic of Ireland) – £2.00 for the first book, £1.00 for each subsequent book.

We accept all major credit cards, including VISA, ACCESS/MASTER-CARD, DINERS CLUB, AMEX and SWITCH.
Please write your card number and expiry date here:

....

Please allow up to 28 days for delivery.

Signature ....

——————✂——————————————

WE NEED YOUR HELP . . .
to plan the future of Sapphire books –

Yours are the only opinions that matter. Sapphire is a new and exciting venture: the first British series of books devoted to lesbian erotic fiction written by and for women.

We're going to do our best to provide the sexiest books you can buy. And we'd like you to help in these early stages. Tell us what you want to read. There's a freepost address for your filled-in questionnaires, so you won't even need to buy a stamp.

THE SAPPHIRE QUESTIONNAIRE

SECTION ONE: ABOUT YOU

1.1 Sex (*we presume you are female, but just in case*)
     Are you?
     Female   ☐
     Male   ☐

1.2 Age
     under 21   ☐   21–30   ☐
     31–40   ☐   41–50   ☐
     51–60   ☐   over 60   ☐

1.3 At what age did you leave full-time education?
     still in education   ☐   16 or younger   ☐
     17–19   ☐   20 or older   ☐

1.4 Occupation _____

1.5 Annual household income _____

1.6 We are perfectly happy for you to remain anonymous; but if you would like us to send you a free booklist of Sapphire books, please insert your name and address

_____

_____

_____

_____

SECTION TWO: ABOUT BUYING SAPPHIRE BOOKS

2.1 Where did you get this copy of *Millennium Fever*?
  Bought at chain book shop ☐
  Bought at independent book shop ☐
  Bought at supermarket ☐
  Bought at book exchange or used book shop ☐
  I borrowed it/found it ☐
  My partner bought it ☐

2.2 How did you find out about Sapphire books?
  I saw them in a shop ☐
  I saw them advertised in a magazine ☐
  A friend told me about them ☐
  I read about them in _____ ☐
  Other _____

2.3 Please tick the following statements you agree with:
  I would be less embarrassed about buying Sapphire
  books if the cover pictures were less explicit ☐
  I think that in general the pictures on Sapphire
  books are about right ☐
  I think Sapphire cover pictures should be as
  explicit as possible ☐

2.4 Would you read a Sapphire book in a public place – on a train for instance?
  Yes ☐   No ☐

SECTION THREE: ABOUT THIS SAPPHIRE BOOK

3.1 Do you think the sex content in this book is:
  Too much ☐   About right ☐
  Not enough ☐

3.2   Do you think the writing style in this book is:
       Too unreal/escapist ☐   About right ☐
       Too down to earth ☐

3.3   Do you think the story in this book is:
       Too complicated ☐   About right ☐
       Too boring/simple ☐

3.4   Do you think the cover of this book is:
       Too explicit ☐   About right ☐
       Not explicit enough ☐

Here's a space for any other comments:

SECTION FOUR: ABOUT OTHER SAPPHIRE BOOKS

4.1   How many Sapphire books have you read?

4.2   If more than one, which one did you prefer?

    ————————————————————————

4.3   Why?

SECTION FIVE: ABOUT YOUR IDEAL EROTIC NOVEL

We want to publish the books you want to read – so this is your chance to tell
us exactly what your ideal erotic novel would be like.

5.1   Using a scale of 1 to 5 (1 = no interest at all, 5 = your ideal), please rate
the following possible settings for an erotic novel:

       Roman / Ancient World ☐
       Medieval / barbarian / sword 'n' sorcery ☐
       Renaissance / Elizabethan / Restoration ☐
       Victorian / Edwardian ☐
       1920s & 1930s ☐
       Present day ☐
       Future / Science Fiction ☐

5.2 Using the same scale of 1 to 5, please rate the following themes you may find in an erotic novel:

Bondage / fetishism	☐
Romantic love	☐
SM / corporal punishment	☐
Bisexuality	☐
Gay male sex	☐
Group sex	☐
Watersports	☐
Rent / sex for money	☐

5.3 Using the same scale of 1 to 5, please rate the following styles in which an erotic novel could be written:

Gritty realism, down to earth	☐
Set in real life but ignoring its more unpleasant aspects	☐
Escapist fantasy, but just about believable	☐
Complete escapism, totally unrealistic	☐

5.4 In a book that features power differentials or sexual initiation, would you prefer the writing to be from the viewpoint of the dominant / experienced or submissive / inexperienced characters:

Dominant / Experienced	☐
Submissive / Inexperienced	☐
Both	☐

5.5 We'd like to include characters close to your ideal lover. What characteristics would your ideal lover have? Tick as many as you want:

Dominant	☐	Cruel	☐
Slim	☐	Young	☐
Big	☐	Naïve	☐
Voluptuous	☐	Caring	☐
Extroverted	☐	Rugged	☐
Bisexual	☐	Romantic	☐
Working Class	☐	Old	☐
Introverted	☐	Intellectual	☐
Butch	☐	Professional	☐
Femme	☐	Pervy	☐
Androgynous	☐	Ordinary	☐
Submissive	☐	Muscular	☐

Anything else? _____

5.6 Is there one particular setting or subject matter that your ideal erotic novel would contain:

_____

_____

SECTION SIX: LAST WORDS

6.1 What do you like best about Sapphire books?

_____

6.2 What do you most dislike about Sapphire books?

_____

6.3 In what way, if any, would you like to change Sapphire covers?

_____

6.4 Here's a space for any other comments:

_____

_____

_____

_____

Thanks for completing this questionnaire. Now either tear it out, or photocopy it, then put it in an envelope and send it to:

> **Sapphire/Virgin Publishing**
> **FREEPOST LON3566**
> **London**
> **W6 9BR**

You don't need a stamp if you're in the UK, but you'll need one if you're posting from overseas.